BEYOND THE WASTELAND

by AD Bane

Beyond the Wasteland
Copyright © 2013 AD Bane

Published by

BANE PRINT

British Columbia, Canada
An imprint of AD Bane Publishing
Published in Canada, printed in the USA
First Printing, 2018
Second Edition

ISBN-13: 978-0-9918330-4-7
ISBN-10: 099183304X

For more information about the author, or to read other works by him, ask all your friends if they know him. Someone might.

To obtain additional copies of this book you can find it available at Amazon.com.

"It came from the east and went into the west with a rustle of the prairie grass and a cry of the rails that lasted on the wind, even until it was well beyond the next hill."

"It was a demon-train, Tucker, an evil thing if ever I saw one . . . and I intend to catch it."

For anyone whose childhood
was filled with orcs and dragons.

For those who fight the hordes
solely for the heart of the princess.

For the few who still follow the rails,
not because they must
but because they hear the call.

For the ones that persist
against demons and storms,
even though they never feel like
they're getting any closer.

A hopeful plea to the masses who've
forsaken the suit as a childish fancy.

And finally, for the elders who,
though long in the journey,
have found the coach
and call us now to come
onward to something better.

As a fellow traveller on this journey,
I pray that your hand will be steady
and your eye true
as you yearn for the way of the coach.

ACKNOWLEDGEMENTS

I would like to thank
all those whose hard work has made this book
possible. Without you, let's face it, this
eventuality would still have happened
but it wouldn't have been as good.

Thanks to Hiram Webb and Dixie Webb
for taking the time to read and comment
on the manuscript. Your notes and honesty
have made this a better book.

Thanks to everyone who gave
me help with the rear-cover blurb. It's a monster
to write, since it's gotta sell
(and obviously it's working)
and your comments were all beneficial.
Thanks again to Hiram Webb
for the final draft.

CONTENTS

~PROLOGUE~
THE DEMON-TRAIN

It came from the east and went into the west with a rustle of the prairie grass and a cry of the rails that lasted on the wind, even until it was well beyond the next hill. He stood on the platform and watched it go, watched the smoke from its single stack rising against the deepening scarlet horizon. He watched the dust drifting from the wasteless tracts of the Frontier like a memory to follow after it. He watched the last crimson flicker of its lamps in their eerie, demonic glow. A very human shudder went up his spine, and he wondered where it would go.

Demon-trains were uncommon, though not unheard-of. They were the stuff of stories, a thing told mostly in the wild fancies of children, of which their insatiable hunger for excitement didn't care if the object was real or not, only that it was exciting. And the stories certainly excited them in the most graphic ways.

Of course demon-trains were feared. And well they might be – was it not said that Amos Donary himself had ridden one west to conquer the Inlands and the Frontier? The un-creature iron-horse would forever be marked in the minds of the people as undesirable, though little understood.

Everyone from Yorkport to Hembridge knew what a demon-train looked like. It was instilled in the minds of the young with their first words, this haunting image of a thing beyond mastery and reason that would come with no expectation, bringing darkness and cold, and leave again as wistfully as it had barrelled down the rails to begin with. And so, when the train blew through the station at Dhill and ran on he knew beyond a shadow of a doubt what it was. He knew the dread that he felt. He shuddered at the shriek it made of the rails as it thundered by with the wind so suddenly gone cold. He even knew why it was that he hated it so.

But the thing that baffled his sense of reason was his inane desire to follow it.

~CHAPTER ONE~
IN THE PATH OF THE TRAIN

The train went west, a phantom, perhaps, but he followed after it, nevertheless. His boots were dusty and his feet ached. He'd stepped from one rail-tie to the next since the day's first light, and he was tired. His clothes were hot, so hot he felt sure this was what a boiled prairie chicken must feel like. The sun was the enemy, and yet it wasn't as fierce as it would've been in earlier months. Though still plenty hot for the waning year, when he'd left the station in Dhill it'd been hot enough to boil the water in his can where he left it out on a granite boulder. The only relief was the gentle breeze that tousled his hair, and he'd taken his shirt off so it could dry the sweat on his back, in spite of the possibility of chilly nights ahead without it, if he should chance to lose it on the trail. He tucked it into his belt. But the sweat still soaked his hair at the band of his hat and ran down his face, then down his neck, and then over his back, until he felt stiff and encrusted with it. He couldn't see himself, but each step brought up clouds of the dry, Frontier dust, and with the sweat on his back, he was certain he was beginning to look more like a gutty wildman with each day.

The rails ran on, as straight as an arrow out of Dhill. He kept his eyes on them and his feet moving, always to the next tie. For three days he'd persisted, until the food in his wallet was gone and his canteen was empty. Now it was a dwindling strength alone that kept him moving, for without food or water who knew how far he might go? The sun would make short work of him. He'd heard it said a man ill-equipped for the Frontier would be dead in a day or a little more, and he'd been going on for nearly that long since his water had run dry, his thumbs on his gunbelt to feel the weight, his empty canteen bumping against the iron from time to time, just to remind him that it was still there. His lips were parched, his fingers cracked, and he knew he must soon have water or else. And the rails ran on before, hardly another turn since the hills at Perth Canyon, and not a drop of water to save his soul. He'd hoped for a stream in the cut. They did say, afterall, that canyons were oft carved by moving water. But there had been none, and as he trudged again into the west he began to realize that he'd come too far now to return, much too far; if he turned back the buzzards would have the meat from his bones before the sun would set on him again.

The sun wasn't the only enemy out here, either. A pack had been on his trail from Perth. He'd seen them in the distance when he rested at the crest of a hill. They wouldn't beset him beneath the high sun, he decided, not unless they were desperate with hunger – which they might just be out here in the Frontier. They were shrewd. More like they'd wait until it was the even, or maybe after dark, before they'd close in for the kill. But just knowing that they were at his heels kept him moving ahead, another reminder that he couldn't go back now. No, the only way ahead was forward, along the rails in the path of the coach.

It was absurd, really, following a coach-train, hoping to catch it. He knew, of course, that he never would. He *couldn't*: it was moving at least four turns to his one – and that was if he was running. And it never tired. If there was a station ahead then he might gain some ground – *might*, that is, if it stopped at all. But it mayaswell be a thousand turns in the heat and the sun and the dust of the Frontier, if it was a pace.

There *was* a town just beyond the horizon. It was a sleepy little nook of a camp built in the valley between the edge of the canyon and the Sundry Hills in the west, where the coach-train would be making its final stop before it went on into the uninhabited wasteland (the True Frontier, as it was known), if it found a way (and he had little doubt now that it would). The town was called Drayton. He'd known it was there; he'd been there before. But he'd forgotten how far it was from Dhill: days on foot could be hours on horseback.

Drayton was the last lawless camp before the hills. Perhaps it had changed; things sometimes *did* change. It'd been some twenty odd years or so, back when he'd run with the Chartleton brothers out of Hembridge. Oh, those had been the glory days. The days of plenty. The days when a man never wanted for money in his pocket to spend because he always had it. And at the very height of the waning year they'd had more loot than they'd known what to do with. That was when they'd made west for Drayton camp with the law at their backs and so much *oliveshine* between the three of them that even their dreams couldn't spend it all. The heat and dust of the Frontier hadn't quelled his spirits then, so high had they been on the *furthings* they carried in tow.

But when they'd arrived in Drayton it was a different story, all together. All his memories from the camp were bad ones: of wet nights and sweltering days (it was always hot during high summer this far into the Frontier). Garette Borough had beat him down with the butt of a *blackiron* and pissed on his face. The next day Garette was gone from the camp, having made off with the contents of every strongbox in every house, including the stolen loot. Chock Brottle, the mayor (or perhaps *boss* was a more fitting term, for Chock was the only law in Drayton) had tracked the outlaw's trail three days into the hill where he'd found not more than a sun-worn boot or two and a spot of blood where the coyotes had torn the carcass apart.

It had irked him something fierce to be played for a fool like that and then not even get his comeuppance.

That was why now, with the toes of his boots on the rails toward Drayton, Jonas Arthur was a little uneasy. It was the dust on his feet and the grit in his teeth that assured him more than all else. Having just ridden into town with the Chartletons all those years ago they'd looked, if anything, like the boys from Hembridge that they were, or maybe even Dodge itself; but now he was just as dirty and slimy as any other *gun-toter* or *groolbiter*. He had the irons strapped to his sides to prove he wasn't no gutty, though, big grey shooters, six chambers each, and with enough kick to ruin even the best man's appetite. And he knew how to use them, too: Charles had said so himself. But then Charles had also been lying in a pool of his own blood with three *blacki-ron* slugs tugging at the back of his mind, so what did Charles know?

At the crown of a hill he stayed his pace to shake the dust from his boots; and as an added pardon, he chanced a glance over his shoulder. The pack was closing in on him, hungry beyond their time, no doubt, and eager for supper well before evening. And they'd have it soon enough, one way or the other.

On the other side of the hill there was a wide anthology of standing-stones, grey and dusty as chalk. Cover, or as close as he would find out here. In the shade of one he took from his holsters his irons and checked the chargeholes. Full-up, both the same. And the shots were good, he had no doubt. But he'd been careful to number

7

the pack, and his count had come up short at nine. No less, certainly. They never travelled light. No doubt fourteen or fifteen – maybe even as many as eighteen – was closer the mark. The quandary wouldn't answer itself, but supper would. He'd have to make it up as he went.

They were closer now. He knew it because he could no longer spot them when he leant out around the stone. He'd seen it before, how a pack could vanish into the dust of the Frontier only moments prior to making the kill. The only thing now was to wait.

He saw the attack before it came. His eyes were sharp, his ears keen, for a runner's must be if he doesn't wish to be shot in the back. He was hunkered in the earth when the *cani-bitch*, starved and scrawny to the bone, came upon him from around the stone to his right, its eyes alight and its fangs dripping with saliva. The hackles at its shoulders bristled as it struck, quick as a snake. But Jonas Arthur brought his gun to bear the quicker still. He shot it without mercy, without thought, and already his other gun was in hand and wheeling on the *cani's* mate, which was quick and quiet on his heels. Again he killed as willfully. And the gunshots echoed and came back to him from across the canyon.

He could see them now, startled a little, perhaps, by the thunder his guns had made; yet they wouldn't be driven afar. They lingered on the fringe, crouching in the dust and waiting for him to lower his guard, their eyes ever-watchful. And that was good fortune, as far as he was concerned. Another time, perhaps, he may have missed, or he may have shot a whelp rather than

8

the sires. And if that were the case he'd have had no choice but to spend all his lead on their worthless hides. But for now, perhaps, they'd let him be and he could save his shots for someone more deserving.

When he left the stones he now saw truly how large their number was: fourteen, counting those two he'd slain already. So the pack truly was ravenous. Likely they'd already lost some of their number since leaving the hills at Perth in search of a kill. All those that came close enough to see were little more than skin on bone – hardly good eating. Reasonable fair to keep his hand practiced, though, and as he continued on the rails his shadow told him that he might yet find the opportunity to join them to their *canis*.

The rails turned a little as they came over the last hill out of the canyon and began the wide and gradual remark that ultimately ended in a trestle over the murked and churning waters of the Drayton. Not that he minded the sun and the heat of the Frontier, but it would be a relief to be out on the trestle with the cool and violent stir of the breeze off the river in his hair. Perhaps he would even go down to those waters for a dip, Fall-willing he could find a path that wouldn't end in broken bones and shattered ambitions. And, that is, if the tail at his back had given up the suit.

The trestle didn't make him feel easy. It looked years in disrepair, and that made sense enough, because, to his knowledge, the trains hadn't even come past Hembridge for some years. It'd been a sincere surprise to him when the coach had skipped the return point and kept going. Though, when he considered it, he supposed that if the ironhorse could cross the wild churning waters below then so could he. Even so, the eerie glow of the lanterns that swung gaily from its caboose had troubled him – and still did. Something about it just wasn't right. Perhaps a demon-train could cross the river without ever touching the trestle; a gunrunner in leather, carrying shooting-irons, however, could not.

He was standing at the point now where the first few rising piers in the ground below extended perhaps three times his height to support the rails of the track. It didn't seem like a terribly long way down, but if he took another step there'd no longer be any earth or stone beneath him, just a dizzying fall into the black depths of the Drayton River; and from that adventure there could be no return.

He hesitated. He thought again of the little camp in the valley beyond, and then of the broken and rotted trestle before him. And then his thought came again to the platform just outside Dhill, the rattle of the tracks as the rail-coach went by, the dull-red glow of its lamps in the failing light, and then, as it mounted the hill, the dreadful cry of its whistle echoing back to him.

He stepped out onto the trestle.

The old timbers creaked and moaned, as very large, old houses often do on stormy nights. His weathered boots slipped on the stained wood and smooth rails. He wondered for a moment if it was not his end. He'd only ever asked that question once before in his whole entire life, in fact, when Henry Dalton, the fastest hand west of Dodge, the Kid Darkfinger himself, had stood opposite him in the dusty street, back-bent, his hands poised about his gunbelts, one eye squint, the other turned a little down, as if of a different will than its neighbour. At that moment he'd known the Kid could blow a hole right through between his eyes before his finger could so much as twitch. He'd seen it before, for, afterall, Darkfinger had been the one who'd killed the Chartleton brothers, and he'd done that with only one bullet at nothing less than fifty turns. He'd had the sun in his eyes and the shooting finger of his left hand (his better) wrapped all up in bandages from when he'd near cut if off on a broken glass dicing in Dodge. Jonas had seen it, the look in the Kid's eye, the way his hand twitched.

But Jonas had lived. They *both* had walked away from it. He didn't know how or why, but it happened. And Jonas Arthur was left with the same question as no one before him had ever asked: was he not, perhaps, even faster than Kid Darkfinger? The thought might've driven better men mad. Now he likely would never know.

As he stood on the trestle perhaps some part of him knew that he couldn't die, not here, not now. He *would* make it across, though for all the screaming voices in his head his knees still shook something fierce and through his boots the iron rails felt like someone had run grease the length of them.

From that first moment on he counted each step and thereby each tie. By the time he made it to thirty-seven, when he looked down he was staring at nothing but old, groaning timbers and black churning depths. By the time he was at fifty he could no longer hear the rush of the wind

11

or feel it on his skin: his entire body felt numb, his neck and back taut with the strain. His dirty trousers clung to his legs, his boots felt stiff and damp, and there was sweat dripping from the brim of his hat, his head was bent so low – he was terrified he might miss his footing, and the thought of plummeting to his death made his head feel hollow.

It occurred to him now that if he could've beaten this obstacle with a draw of the iron in his holsters it would've been an easy-enough task. It was iron he knew so well, and it was quite an unfortunate thing, indeed, that not all enemies could be mastered by a quick hand and a sure eye.

He was still breathing hard when he stood again on the earth and gravel next to the rails at the west end of the trestle. And now, looking back, he wondered why he had ever started across at all, why his better instincts hadn't won out. What he hadn't noticed from the other end (but now saw, now that the sun was at his back) were the three consecutive piers missing where the east end of the trestle was rooted into the earth. And still worse was the slump in the track where even the rails had begun to sag beneath their own weight.

As he stood on the edge he breathed a prayer: "Keep my hand steady and mine eye true; pull me to when I stray."

As he turned his back to the east once more and his face to the sunset he was succinctly decided that he wouldn't be going back that way – if, indeed, he went back at all.

It was not so very far to Drayton now. The camp was only just beyond the next set of Were-piers — as the rough, weather-worn rocky mounds of the Frontier are called (called, it was said, because at night as one was passing by they might appear to be a hundred savage wolves waiting in the dark; by daylight they were beautiful in a sort of *dulk*, stony fashion). He could actually see a shed or two on the far side of the valley, and a single column of grey smoke lifted lazily into the air.

He'd come by the road into Drayton at his last visit, he and the Chartletons having with them and between them more than twice their weight in the cold olive sunshine. The wagon had nearly given out on that last hill. But they'd known before ever they truly passed the borders of Drayton that they were safe from the lawmen at their backs because Drayton was a lawless town: no men-of-the-script poking irons in their faces here.

Now, however, where the edge of the camp used to be was a high wall of stakes, probably dragged up from the river before the last timber in the hills was cut. Beyond the wall, where the camp had once been an expanding, growing entity, the workmen coming from far out east to man the machines that worked the Sundry mines, it was now a vast graveyard of weathered and abandoned shacks standing gaunt and empty, a world gone so cold. Most were missing wall or roof, probably to the needs of those now *inside* the fence. Business in the mines surely had run dry in recent years, maybe even stopped all together. Many of the houses that once had

13

been home to the miners now stood forsaken; the work-houses, which had once housed hundreds of young lads for the sweat and toil of the mines now bore the sound of piano music and the smell of whiskey and roasted beef.

And sure enough, it was nearly suppertime.

He stopped on the hill looking out on Drayton to return the shirt to his sweat-soaked back and to push his guns into his bedroll: better to be an unarmed, wayward traveller coming into Drayton than an iron-toting outlaw, if he wished to survive the night. Certainly the camp was lawless, but with that came also the given nature of men to hate each other for jealousy's sake, and many were not above putting a knife in a stranger's back to relieve him of his irons, for good shooting irons were scarce on the Frontier. Who knew: there might even be a bounty waiting for him in Dodge. The *droges* sometimes came out as far as Drayton. He didn't want to risk the possibility.

Drayton (at least what he could see of it from the edge of the hillock where he stood with the dust coming up around his knees, the weeds rolling past in the wind and the sun glaring orange on the left side of his face) was a more or less typical Frontier tumbleweed town. It was old, not so old as to be of any importance but just old enough to not be of any at all. When Hembridge began to develop, being the largest city west of Dodge, every tree had been cleaned from the hills as far as Drayton. It was a feat made possible by the railroad, which once had run through the little valley, bringing on it coaches perhaps twice monthly. Now when the frontier camps needed that timber so badly it was not to be found. And so Drayton was falling into disrepair. The old cabins were all but gone, dismantled for their lumber. The new shacks that went up were only cheap, silly replicas of what the work-houses had been; many were nothing but shanties against the wall, or each other. In recent times, it seemed, Drayton had seen a scarcity of water and an abundance of wind and sun, and the result was the little town was drying up fast.

Down the hill the road wound itself, right to the edge of the camp, and there he paused again where the prairie grass ended in an overgrown firebreak that stretched away in both directions around the perimeter of what had once been a part of Drayton and now was not more than a graveyard. The weathered and tumbled shacks rose up before him like the discarded carapaces of gaunt sentries made so old and useless with time they do not yet realize the prize they guard has become worthless. It was a dead, cold, colourless sight, even with the setting sun turning to gold and crimson on the horizon. In fact, the only color in that whole ruinous camp beyond the walls were the tufts of bloodgrass that had grown up at the corners of the old cabins and between the boards in the walks – slender, dry stalks of weed as red as crimson. Bloodgrass didn't grow east of Hembridge (or even Dhill, for that matter); it grew only very sparsely in the Frontier. Jonas had only ever seen the crimson weed perhaps thrice before in his life, and not so much as a blade in Drayton before now. But he had *heard* of those who chewed the stuff. 'Twas said that it took hold, and when it had, it didn't let go. They

15

were bound, body and soul, to some demon that would keep them chewing, rotting through and through, until the day the weed finally claimed their minds and their bodies along with it. It was a sad prophecy of the end of Drayton, and perhaps the entire Frontier and their way of life.

In the failing light, with that terrible, cold yard before him, Jonas might have supposed that no one lived in the camp anymore. He certainly wouldn't have guessed anyone now lived outside the walls. But as he strode down the dusty road toward the gate he saw someone ambling toward him up what had once been a street, someone bent and doubled and leaning heavily on a stick. It was an aged fellow with few teeth behind his cracked lips and eyes that looked and looked but saw nothing. Even his hair was like the entrails of the crypt and hung about his shoulders in garlands of coarse weed.

He stopped when he saw Jonas watching him. For a moment he stood in the street, his eyes dim where the devils danced and his old, frail bones looking like they might shatter at any moment. His hand stooped momentarily toward his belt, as if he expected something to be there, and he called out in a voice like the wind through the reed-grass, "Har, father! What's it *cah-ree*? Reach for it, else Fall 'ang y'seff!" Then he turned back the way he'd come, ambling along with the support of his crook.

A strange sight. A strange thing. A strange town. Anything could happen at the edge of the Frontier.

"Traveller!" cried the gate when Jonas approached the wide doors, the ramshackle huts now creeping in close on either side as if to tender his ensnarement in their cold clutches. It was a fairly solid door, to be sure. If he'd had a coach-wagon ram, like what the Chartletons had used to get into Fort Cardac he might have had it down in an hour or so, but as just a single man against those heavy-bound timber he was useless.

"Where is the warden?" he called up. "Who keeps the door?"

"I, Sir; 'tis I to say true," said an aging chap who'd just poked his head over the wall, his bright eyes looking down from beneath the broad brim of his hat. "But the door's locked and 'twill be 'til the sun's on the left o' my face 'gain."

"Why won't it open?" Jonas called.

" 'Tis Lord Quenn's orders, Sir."

"*Quenn?*" asked Jonas. "Does Chock Brottle not still fancy himself mayor and law in Drayton camp?"

"Nay, man, not 'nemore. He's gone from hence, see, and not to come 'gain on the pains of his life as I 'eard it! But you may sit there in the road 'til the sun, *oh-she-rise!* if it please you!" The warden laughed a bright little cackle that was not so much friendly or pleasant as it was distastefully gleeful. "But I'll warrant a jack's what wants to eat you – will have its way! Or p'haps a coyote or wolf, if'n one 'appens by. Not safe outside the walls when the sun's down, no Sir it tain't!"

"I could shoot you now," Jonas called back, "and have my way, anyhow."

"No you c'ain't, not without iron and lead, leastways!" replied the warden with another of

17

his gleeful cackles. "You best turn yourself 'round now, traveller, and be on your way 'til dawn, lest my well-trained finger slip on my well-trained trigger!"

Jonas sighed. Drayton had been more welcoming at his last visit. Chock Brottle hadn't cared a single *furthing* if the gunslingers riding into town were lawmen or outlaws; all that concerned him was that they weren't up to be stirring things in his town. And, what's more, Jonas had respected the fanciful mayor. First night in the saloon he'd seen Mister Brottle drag a man perhaps twice his size through three tables, the knuckle of his nine-iron never leaving the drunks head. Then he'd thrown him out the door with little more than a heave. And as the derelict was making way from town, back toward the road with his tail tucked well between his legs, Chock discovered earlier that night he'd been the source of considerable disquiet at the Ladies House, and he'd run up out of the camp after, shooting him at fifty turns or more with his nine-iron before the man even knew he was being followed (fifty turns was a helluva shot, if the target wasn't moving; but they'd said the fellow was making as if the Purge was upon him at that very moment).

As Jonas turned back from the gate his eye caught sight of the old man sitting on the front step of what had once been a low shack. He was pulling up tufts of the bloodgrass, chewing it and spitting it out again in great, snorting hacks like tobacco. But his face was contorted in pain as the weed bit into his fingers and mouth. When he spat it was more blood than grass, yet it was only with a terrible effort that seemed to strain him nearly to the point of breaking, as if something within him would not let go, that he coughed up the weed. His hands shook as he reached for more, his eyes dead-cold, so far beyond the point at which fear takes over, like a man bound by a will not his own, both in love and a dreadful hatred.

Perhaps they were not so different, he and the old man, Jonas thought: bound to some demon.

Jonas supposed he could head back up the hill to the road, or perhaps even back along the river gorge to the tracks, and find a place to make camp for the night. He might even find shelter up off the ground in the piers under the old trestle, but the thought of sleeping in those timbers rotting away beneath him was not a pleasant one. He rather would've faced the wolves that came from the desert by night; and dawn might as well be years away if wolves came, because no matter where he was their cries would awaken him.

Still, chances were there was another way into the camp. Often low walls and deep culverts went overlooked, and if one knew to search for them they weren't difficult to find.

He made north, first along the east wall, then a little away from it, until he could hear again the thunder of the river where its gorge became shallow and quite close to the camp. There, on those hot days, the women from Drayton would make their way to the river for water. There ought to be a way down, if the Fall cared at all for his soul, and he'd have his dip, rain or shine.

There was indeed a way. A cattle path, it wound through the scrub brush and right to the water's edge. There he stood, his boots sinking in the mud, the waters of the Drayton flowing by not a turn in front of him. To be truthful, it looked sick, black and deathly cold, contagious with some malevolent invader that had taken over the river and choked its current, streaming beneath the surface like algae in long garlands. He couldn't help but imagine those tendrils taking hold of him as he dove in, dragging him down until the crushing weight of the water on his head forced the life from him. But it would have to do.

He chanced a glance over his shoulder, then shook off his boots and put them on a rock, peeled off his shirt and breeches and put them up in a bush, pushed his bedroll (guns still tucked safely inside) beneath a particularly large boulder; and lastly he drew his stout knife and clutched it in his teeth. Then he slipped into the water. It *was* deathly cold: it stole the air from his lungs and left him a moment of panic. But he stayed in and pushed past the rock that sheltered the bank from the rushing current, right out into the life-force of the river, feeling the brush of those sick streamers against his feet. Then it was just the swift, cold water moving all around, and he had to fight against it or be swept into the canyon below.

When he again scrambled past the rock and up to the bank, he was quite refreshed and even feeling a fair sight more hopeful about catching up the coach. First thing first, though: he needed to get into Drayton before night fell.

He dressed quickly and slung his bedroll, then plodded back up the path until he was standing beneath the high eastern fence. There was no way through, not even the smallest chink for a foothold. The stakes were strong and sturdy, and they plunged perhaps his height or more into the earth so as to make the camp impregnable. But every fortress has its weakness (he'd learned that at Fort Cardac), and Drayton's was to the north where the hills began to climb away and the fence was not so high.

He followed the wall in that way until he was standing on the hillocks that bordered the river as it wound its way down the canyon perhaps several thousand turns before righting and heading east, away from the Sundry Hills and toward the prairies and the Rim. And there he found it, what he'd been looking for: a high ridge of rock, the fence built right beneath it. If he jumped he could make it, he thought. And if not then he'd find himself coming up quite short on the up-turned end of the stakes – a gruesome way to die, to be sure.

But what was life if you didn't live it?

He dug his toes in and ran.

~CHAPTER TWO~
FRIENDS UNLOOKED-FOR

It wasn't as far as it had seemed. He came down on the canvas roof of a leany with a *thump* and a *creek* as the pegs came loose and the guying lines pulled out beneath his weight. He hit the ground hard, and no doubt there'd be bruises in the morning.

It was a late-summer night on the Frontier. Saloons were crowded. Fires burned until just before dawn. Whiskey and beer were brought up from the cellar by the keg. The harvest was in full tilt, and it didn't matter where you were, the harvest season always came with ample quantities of festivities. The sound of drunken laughter and the thumping of a piano could be heard, even from the northern edge of the camp; it drifted on the cool evening air like an infectious malady, belaying the human need for work and toil. No doubt it came from the saloon, perhaps the only of its kind left in Drayton where there once had been no less than five. Saloons were places where tongues wagged freely, and sometimes at both ends; and minds did little thinking. It was the most likely place in the world to meet someone who might recall his face, however many years there were in between. But what he wanted was news and perhaps something to eat and drink. The saloon it would have to be.

When he stood at the door — that door no different than so many brawly taverns in the Frontier — he paused. Dusk at his back, hearth-light and the smell of drink and roasting beef before him: it was like standing between two worlds, there in the calm of coming night with nothing but the breath of the cool breeze gone sweet with the fading summer. He could hear the far-off cry of a wolf. It was calm, peaceful, and untamed. But inside the saloon was a whole different sort of wild to the Frontier; and it was in some ways more dangerous and less forgiving than wolves and jackals and the driving dust and the high noonday heat.

When Jonas pushed open the doors, though the music didn't break and the uproar of voices went on as if he'd always been there, eyes strayed to him: one here, another there, and his presence certainly didn't go unnoticed. Familiarity was a shield; he was a stranger.

He pulled his hat down over his eyes and shouldered his bedroll.

At the bar he tipped his hat to the gimp pouring mugs, then drew himself up on a stool. "Whiskey," he said.

The glass the boy handed him was warm and the drink was bitter. He drank it anyway.

"You t'ain't from 'round 'ere, no Sir," said the gimp.

Well that certainly was true. Jonas touched the brim of his hat again and hoped it was enough.

The boy lowered his voice. "You best watch it, man, they gut you som'n quick."

Jonas tipped his hat. "Nevermind, son," he said; "just thank-you, anyhow."

He turned to the thumping of the piano. A noisy game of Squids and Scorpions was in progress between an older fellow and a clowngirl on the steps of the staging: she seemed to be squirreling his money away faster than he could produce it from his baggy trousers. A number of ruffians were dicing cards at a table not far away. Everyone else seemed to be currently involved in boisterous accompaniment with the off-key drawling of the piano or were drinking so loudly the sounds they made might have been mistaken for singing, anyhow.

"Jonas? Jonas Arthur?"

Someone sidled up next to him, a face he knew well, a face he hadn't seen in years. A face he hadn't *wanted* to see.

"Tucker," he said with ample courtesy just the same. He touched the brim of his hat again, as men were often want to do in the Rim to show such courtesy as even thieves have between one another. He was careful not to keep his hand too near his bedroll, nor too *far* from it, either. Tucker was a thief and a crook, true enough, but he was a coward, just the same, and in some ways that made him more dangerous.

"Didn't think it was you at first, Sir," said Tucker, squinting through rheumy eyes. He'd once run with the Chartletons, however briefly; that was until he'd taken a bullet through his shin. Since then he'd been the squint-eyed cripple. But he'd come with them as far as Drayton, and there he'd stayed when the rest returned east. Jonas had thought him gone for good, but in recent years Tucker's hands had acquired a shake that had hung up his guns for good, making both halves of him quite as useless as the other. Then it'd been gin and whiskey to stop the shakes, and he hadn't gone out again.

All this Jonas heard; what he didn't hear he guessed.

"It's been years, Jonas," Tucker now was saying. "Why'd you come back? Thought those Chartleton boys would be the death of you, for right-certain!"

Jonas laughed aloud, a laugh that never got to his eyes. A little laugh could save you a hasty draw and a quick shooting. He and Tucker had never been close, though there had been times when they'd had only each other. "I've always survived," he said. And that was true enough.

"Aye, too right, too right," agreed Tucker. "Hope you know there ain't no 'ard feelings going on 'twixt you and me. You know I left company to save my own skin, and I ne'er meant you no 'arm by it. Saw trouble brewin', so I did."

"None meant, none taken," replied Jonas. "I would have set down myself, had I taken the bullet."

"So why *are* you in Drayton? New raid?" asked Tucker.

"Was, but not anymore," said Jonas. "I'm on my own now. Left my runners back in Hembridge. Came on by the tracks."

"The *tracks*?" Tucker asked suspiciously. "What'd you want to do that for?"

"I'm looking for something," said Jonas off-handedly, "something that came this way perhaps a day or two ago."

"Not by the tracks it didn't," said Tucker. "No trains out this far no more. We're on the edge of the Frontier now – the *very* edge, mind. Can't go no farther even if one wants to. Hell, even Guldry and Agate Hill are deserted now, as I 'ear it."

"I *do* want to," said Jonas, "and I intend to."

"Ye're not going west into the wasteland!" exclaimed Tucker. "It's dangerous out there, Jonas. Wild animals, savages . . . and that's only if the sun don't get you! Why, I knew a feller who went out past Sundry some several years back. Gone three months, and when he'd come 'gain they found only a few dry bones and him shiny gold spurs still strapped to his peelin' boots. P'haps years 'go I might gone with ya, being up for the challenge and the venture and all. But not these days." He sighed. "Not ne'more."

"Good," said Jonas, "cause I didn't ask. Round of whiskey, I think. And then you might tell me what it is has been going on here."

"Right-o," agreed Tucker.

27

They moved from the bar to a corner of the saloon farthest from the hearth and the cheerful laughter around the piano. The sound was enough still to drown out their voices, even to the men dicing cups at the next table. A round of whiskey was served up, and Jonas asked above the clatter of dice cups, "Now Tuck, what's been going on here? What's become of Chock?"

"Oh, poor Chock up and left the day our newly appointed Lord Quenn rode into town with his poss' trailing along 'ere his dog's arse," said Tucker. "Seems old Chock knew something we didn't, for there weren't no shootin' or holla'rin: it was a gallop and a whomp out the gate with his d'puties en tow, and we ain't seen them 'ere since."

"And Quenn?" asked Jonas.

Tucker furrowed his eyebrows together until they were touching, like windrows of hay, and his mouth was a thin line; and then he let out a long sigh of dismay. "Bad comp'ny by anyone's concern," he said. "Wasn't no 'Howdy there' and 'How do you do?' It was all a-iron and hot lead spraying this way and that. I ducked into cover as quick as anything, for by this time the shakes had set in and I couldn't shoot straight to save my life. But there wasn't much fight to be had: Chock was the one for that, and being as how he'd already left, we was done for. Ever since then it's been take and no give, and many a rumour's gone 'round the camp that Quenn and his boys are doing their own little moonlight running back to Hembridge, and even as far as Dhill. But whether it's bounties or gold they're runnin' the tale don't quite seem to know."

"What reason would he have to take the camp by force?" asked Jonas.

"Who knows?" said Tucker. "No one's ever dared ask. Mayhap old Chock knew some'n more. But the irons those boys carry speak loud 'nough for me, and I've no wish for them to speak any louder, no Sir and thank-ya kindly! So I hold my peace."

"And the wall?"

Tucker's eyes widened and he frowned. "Guess it was after you and the boys left all those years gone. My memories ain't serving what it useter. But yes, yes, one day oh p'haps three years back raiders come riding east 'cross the hill, wild men, not a gun among them, but fierce and wicked, just the same. They come with blade and bolt, bigger than desert wolves, and riding horses rather greater than *were-stalkers* in tale. The first night they killed something like twelve good men and took what they wanted as they left: women over the backs of their saddles, dragged the bodies of the men they'd killed. Mighta taken a gun or two as well, I don't recall. Then perhaps three weeks later they come back and they did it all over again. Now, no man has ever called me a coward—"

"You're a coward, Tucker," Jonas interrupted.

"—but I ain't ashamed to say I hid from those fellows, for 'twas death as they meant and 'twas death that they brought." Tucker finished his story, ignoring Jonas' interlude and downing a rather large gulp of whiskey.

"Have they returned again?" asked Jonas, "and have you any idea what they were? Men, or something else?"

29

Ooo-whee! whistled Tucker. "You best be believing they've come back! P'haps ten times or more. But now that we've a wall and guns aplenty to d'fend ourselves they do begin t' learn I think that there's nothing but death f' them 'ere now. And I've not the foggiest what they might be. Men, I s'pose, but not like any man I ever seen; 'tis more like animals that they fight, and the shadows are more like something from a story. Enough to make your skin crawl!"

"This new fellow, this Lord Quenn, he still holds the wall against them?" asked Jonas.

"For the bligh' of the stars!" exclaimed Tucker. "What else'd he be doing? They're devils, I tell ya, Jonas, devils through and through! Lord Quenn knows it good as any. First time they came they made off with his dear sweet daughter. Oh, he 'unted them in the hills for near on a fortnight and lost sixteen men, as I 'eard it."

Somewhere during the conversation the pounding of the piano and the ruckus laughter that accompanied it had died down a fair notch, and Jonas was quite presently aware that the sport at the table seemed to have turned into a game of *Silent Dice*. The boys who'd been playing now were leaning in as near as they could to Jonas, but not so near as to make it too obvious that their ears were well tuned.

"But enough about me," Tucker was saying. "What we want to hear is about you, Jonas!"

"What about me?" Jonas asked, disinterestedly taking another mug of whiskey that someone offered up. His eyes were reading the tales of the *guntoters* around him.

"Well, last time you was 'ere you was with the Chartletons, true-*nuff*," said Tucker pointedly. "That is, at least, until that *groon-slavering* Borough fool made out with the load."

"I went all the way to Fort Cardac with the Chartletons," said Jonas, deftly turning the story from the unfortunate business with Borough. "All the way and into the hold to have a little sit-down with the gov'nor, too."

"You took Fort Cardac!" exclaimed Tucker in something like awe.

"Aye," agreed Jonas, realizing it was much too late to pretend he'd kept his head down. May as well let them all know who he was. "Two days it took to breach the gate, but we did it, and took it for what it's worth, at least."

"Why, you must'a 'tired something wealthy!" Tucker slapped his knee excitedly, sporting the most ridiculous grin Jonas had ever seen him wear.

"Nay, we didn't anything of the sort," answered Jonas. "The Chartletons were shot down, the both of them, gunned in Dodge City by that Kid Darkfinger. The money's his now, and I'm a poorer man for it."

At this Tucker snarled and gritted his teeth in a show of distaste. Still the same Tuck. Still the same maddeningly dim boy.

"Found a man named Charles Getworth not far outside of Hembridge who was looking for a partner," Jonas went on, for so long as he spoke of running and gunning he had them raptured, and that was good for him while he came up with an escape. "Never seen a finer shot, save the Kid. So we ran together for a time. That is until he too

31

took a bullet or two for his name. But he had a plan, see, a plan to clean out the Drenditch Express Coach on its way from Dhill to Hembridge. So me and the boys decided we'd go ahead with the plan as he saw it. Finish the job. But the Drenditch didn't show, and instead there came along the tracks a coach the likes of which I've never seen before, a great beast-of-a-thing running on wheels as black as—" Jonas was acutely aware again of the *gunboys* and *groolbiters* around him, most of whom who had leant in at this point so as not to miss a word. "It was a demon-train, Tucker, an evil thing if ever I saw one . . . and I intend to catch it," he said shortly.

"But why!" exclaimed Tucker, now positively distressed. "If you saw what you saw, and if'n it was as wicked as y'say, why would you want to follow such a damned thing, regardless of where it was going?"

Jonas said nothing at first: the words were formulating in his head. "It draws me," he said at last and with a deep sigh he had not intended, though perhaps it was just mad enough. "Like a gull to the sea, like an eagle to the heights, like a jackal to a corpse. I can't help it; I must follow it until I've found it."

That he hoped would be enough to turn them all off the idea of jumping him in the dark. Any man fool enough to follow a demon-train must be both mad and terribly dangerous.

"Aye, then you ought to have turned yourself 'round at Hembridge," said Tucker, now resigned. "As I was a-saying, ain't no trains coming out this far no more. Hembridge's the turn-round point now; and certainly ain't no trains going out past the Sundry Hills and on into the wasteland. The rails've never run far beyond Drayton, just t'the top of the hill, I thought."

"I know what I've followed," said Jonas quietly. "I know it came this way. I don't know how, but it did. And I intend to follow it into the wastelands, if I must, if that is what I must to catch it."

"Ye are mad as a fool!" said one of the listeners.

"Crazy," interjected another.

"And what will ye do if ye catch it?" asked Tucker. "Just climb up to the *injun* and ask the eng'eer if ye might ride 'long?"

"If I must," answered Jonas.

"I tell you what it is: a phantom," said a *grooler* who was leaning on the table and breathing through his rotten teeth. "Lures you out into the wasteland, then the sun finishes you, if the buzzards don't first, pickin' yer baked corpse clean ta show yer *follish* self fer trustin' to such crazy *drems*!"

"Aye," the others all agreed.

"That's as may be," agreed Tucker. "Seems a likely-enough story to me. And anyway, folks 'ave always seen strange things out in Sundry, like it or nay."

It was the end of the conversation for Jonas. He had no more interest to be called a mad or a fool than he had to drink stale ale and listen to the piano try and yodel out "Old Marty's Broad". And so he pushed his stool back into the corner and listened to the *thrum* of the music and the drunken voices of those joining chorus, while Tucker and a few of those listening who seemed

33

to be on first name basis went on about all the things that had been happening in Drayton since the fool Borough had ridden out of town with the Chartletons' gold.

The door of the saloon banged open, bottle and mug set to clinking and rattling on table and bar, even in the hands of those who held them and now were turned to see who would enter. Three runners came in, one before the last, their boots knocking on the floor with their horseman's gait. The first was brawny and with a wicked grin on his smug face, the sort of a man who as a child had amused himself by torturing stray dogs. The second, following in the footsteps of the first, was equally smug but in a piggish way; yet his eyes were those of a coward. The third, a scrawny, quick-eyed fellow with rather fine irons in his stitched-leather holsters (certainly not the black guns carried by the gunmen of the older days in the south, but very fine, just the same) didn't follow the first two but held to his own course, wherever it might lead. For a moment he paused on the doorsill, his hands hovering at his guns and his eyes wandering over the room without ever moving. He was the sort of man who wouldn't enter a duel lightly; but neither would he hesitate on the threshold of death.

"Well isn't this place just a ruckus treat tonight!" yelled the first, turning the room in his gaze, his wicked grin becoming more devious as he took in what undoubtedly looked to him rather like a roomful of strays who might let out all manner of yowls before their end. Behind him his cohort cooed in agreement. The third said nothing.

Tucker, leaning his stool against the bar and still going on about Egress Dales this, Porta Merry that, had just laughed a long and hearty cackle to which some of his friends joined in, and he said, or rather nearly yelled, having come to the climax of some story he'd been telling, "Jonas Arthur, it was! Finest shooter, finer runner. Good friend o' mine, don't ye mistake!" And with that he laid a hand on Jonas' shoulder.

Jonas, lost in the drawl of the saloon, was yanked back to reality. "Tucker, shut it, will you!" he growled, taking Tucker by the shoulder and pressing with his thumb above the cripple's collarbone until the laughter in Tucker's eyes turned to pain.

"What ye off to?" asked Tucker abashedly, re-setting his stool quick enough to nearly spill himself onto the floor.

"Who are they?" Jonas asked.

Tucker looked up at the three runners and his face fell in dismay. "Quenn's lads," he said. "Bad eggs all three, left t'rot in the sun."

Jonas set back on his stool, back into the shadows of the corner. Bad eggs. Runners. Maybe even *droges* in search of bounties, and that was enough – enough for Jonas Arthur, cer-tainly. That meant that there *was* a price on his head in Dodgeton, and the likes of Quenn and his boys, even if they weren't used to the act, would surely see him hanged in the streets of Dodge as soon as look at him, if they kept any familiarity with the Marshals' postings.

But it was far too late. The runners had al-ready turned their mirthless gazes toward the bar, and the one in the lead (the worst of the lot, likely as not) had tarried just a moment too long.

"Look, Billie. Ain't that there a straa-aanger?" asked the second (the *a* in stranger came out long and drawling).

"Believe it is," replied the first, his eyes as steady as the midday sun and just as hot.

"Better see if there's anything we might be able to do for him," said the second. "What you think, Timber?"

The third smiled a crooked grin through his broken lips. "Aye," he agreed.

Billie crossed the floor, his boots clinking, his harness jangling. Along came his second, pushing a flat-brimmed hat farther up from his dull, expressionless eyes so as not to miss a thing. And along behind came their third, Timber, his thumbs neatly tucked into his gunbelt.

Jonas' forefinger of his left hand twitched involuntarily and an itch like fire in his palm was spreading up his arm. His mind went to those heavy irons buried away in his bedroll, still just within reach.

"Hullo brownie!" yelled Billie, his eyes still hard on Jonas. "Tucker, who's yer friend? Shame you'dn't 'troduce us. We was just gonna have us some drinks and thought ye might like to join."

"Not now, Billie," said Tucker quietly; his voice shook, his lips trembled, and a vein bulged in his forehead.

Tucker's friends who had been listening quietly-enough before now drew away even more quietly. Jonas and Tucker were left alone in the corner, and every *profit* and *grooler* in the saloon was now looking at them. Even the piano had quit his thumping to watch.

"See now," said Billie's partner, "you don't have to go and be rude like that, Tuck. We just wants to have some fun, fair as fair."

"Fall-bledding rights, we do, Terry," agreed Billie.

Timber said nothing; his eyes were smouldering like a fire that will one day rekindle anew of its own accord and then it will burn all to ash.

"You go'n tell Quenn there ain't nothing to be had," said Tucker. "I gave you all I got a'ready."

Billie's face darkened, though it wasn't really anger, more like confusion, and it was mirrored in Terry's own eyes. But Timber, his eyes turned wicked and spiteful, and Jonas didn't have to look to know that his hands were already on the hilts of his guns.

There was no warning, no calm before the storm, nothing at all that might've betrayed the sweep of Jonas' left hand as he brought to bear one of his own irons (his left, always his left, the one with the talons of the eagle cut into it). He shoved it into the side of Billie's face. The world stood still. Terry, whose remark had brought about this turn, was still standing behind Billie, his face quite empty of any reasonable thought or emotion for the shock that had come over him. Jonas thumbed the hammer, smithing his own face into iron and stone that meant every bit he was ready to touch the trigger and drive the iron-lead home. And it was that more than anything else that caught Timber in a moment's pause, his hands hovering on his holsters, perhaps only a fraction of a second away from the draw. If not for the astonishment in his eyes, either he or Jonas already would be dead.

"Sorry, Mister!" squeaked Terry, all his brazen spirit gone, his face contorting in frightened panic, the very same expression Jonas imagined Tucker was sporting at his back.

"Looking for something?" growled Jonas, tightening his grip on his gun and clenching his teeth, for his voice said what his words did not. "I know what you are, you piteous little *grooler*. No, don't say another word or your worthless little soul is going to be drinking that fine whiskey behind you off the floor, after I finish off your boss here."

As his words echoed into the silence that now filled the saloon – for even the fellow at the piano was paying homage now – Jonas felt the beat of his heart quicken. It had only been a single knock, a tap, really, but he heard it, just the same. It meant a fight was brewing, and how long it seemed it had been! Wasn't it not a week ago he'd been standing face to face with the sheriff of Hembridge? Or was it two? Maybe a month. He felt rusty as an old nail. But just the same he was itching to have it done.

"What seems to be going on 'ere, Mister?" snarled a fourth runner who'd just stepped into the doorway, the soles of his boots sounding on the floor with the jangle of his belt and harness.

"Never you mind, good Sir," said Jonas quietly. "It ain't none of your business, now is it?"

"S'pose not," replied the man, twitching his nose like a rabbit and snorting aimless spit-shine. "S'pose 'tain't none of our *bissniss*. But now what kind of man would I be if I let you go splattering nice Little Whisker's brains, or fine Billie theres, for that matter?"

"A decent fellow who don't want to get shot himself," Jonas answered quick, keeping his voice even.

"Ah, but see," said the new fellow, "see now, Lord Quenn wouldn't really go for that, now would he. Oftly concerned with 'the way of things', he is. Wouldn't like it much, and you can believe that."

Quicker than anyone in the room could blink, quicker even than he could think, Jonas drew his other gun, the one with the tally in the grip, and turned the iron sights on this new fellow, this servant of Lord Quenn, without so much as turning his eye for a second. He knew his aim was true, knew it by the sound of the stranger's voice alone, knew he wouldn't miss if he pulled the trigger. "Tell me," he said through grinding teeth, "if this lord of yours wouldn't like to come in here tonight and tell me that himself. Or maybe I should go ahead and shoot this young fellow, anyhow, and let your Lord Quenn clean up the mess tomorrow. It's all the same to me, it is."

"Won't be no mess," said an entirely different voice, a much lower one, a deep, grating, gravelly voice, the kind that might stand behind a nine-iron with a cold eye that never missed. "Thing is we toss 'em out the gate just when the moon's coming up and we ne'er see nor 'ear of 'em again. And if your Sir would care to put down those great irons before I have to shoot yer dead then we might yet get ourselfs a little chat before I throw ye in the pen for the night."

39

Jonas smiled to himself. Now this hardly couldn't help but be Quenn, not so elegant, not so pert. He was a man of class, of nobility, and however dangerous a man he was, he wouldn't be taken easily or light. And he'd gotten the drop on Jonas, something no one had done, save the Kid Darkfinger himself.

Jonas lowered his guns slowly, releasing the hammers, and he let out a cold breath that left his mind feeling colder still.

"Clear out, Gents," said the voice of Quenn, and at once the gathered crowd turned away from Jonas with sorrowful looks that made him doubt for a moment, if only for a moment, if he'd been wise to lay down.

They took him from behind in iron grips, first took his guns then kicked his knees from under him. And slowly, with the heels of his boots knocking on the floor, Lord Quenn stood over him, grey pinstripes, thin-drawn lips, waxed moustache, and cold dead eyes the color of stone.

"Seems what we really wants is a killin', ain't it?"

Quenn looked around at the few who hadn't slipped out (the ones he paid, Jonas realized). But no one said a word. No one dared. Then one brave old codger said, "Yar! Hang him, Sir!", and the cry was taken up from the bar to the piano. "Hang him! Hang the stranger before dawn! Tie him up until he's dead, may the Good Lord take his head! If he wakes, he won't be fed, cause our Lord Quenn will be 'nstead! Har har!"

"Hello jilly," said Quenn amusedly. "Looks like it's gonna be a swinging. How do ye feel 'bout that?"

"I've been hanged before," Jonas said. "A frightful ordeal, to say true." And it was.

From the corner of his eye he saw Tucker slipping quietly out the side door of the saloon. *Coward*, he thought to himself.

"See, thing is," said Quenn – and then laughed, a cruel, wicked, cold laugh at the surprise that Jonas couldn't hide – "thing is Jake here saw you come into camp earlier. And I don't think there's a well-born sir 'twixt here and Dodge who don't know a fine bounty when he sees it. So I think it only natural-like that Jake knew your face at once, being of very fine stock indeed. And knowing still further there's a fine bounty over your name in Dodge, for he watches the posters closer than any of us, you understand, he said to me, 'Lord Quenn, 'twould be a terrible shame if'n we let all them pretty coins go to waste.' "

Quenn smiled a grin that showed all his perfect teeth. "You remember this?" he asked Jake.

"Aye," the runner answered. "Aye, I do. Dead or alive was what they said in Dodge – just so long as he's dead."

Quenn looked at Jonas, his smile never fading. Then, with a raise of his clenched fist, he cried, "Take him to the hanging post!" It was only as an afterthought that he said to Jake, "Drag him quick, but let me see those irons he's carrying. Them look pretty fine."

What Jonas had said about being hanged before was true enough – that is he *had* been given the noose once in Dodge City. But Charles and Engels had been with him then and they'd put their Chartleton names to good use, been out of the ropes before the doors could fall, been off the box before it toppled. They'd had the hangman and the guardsmen by the throats in the flicker of an instant. Jonas himself had only dangled by his neck for perhaps twenty suffocating seconds or so while the fray was stirring up around him.

But Jonas didn't really think he'd survive a second hanging, not without the Chartletons in the nooses next to him. And the worst part of it was that, as they dragged him to the post, he wasn't thinking of all the wrongs he'd ever done (the list being quite extensive), nor about all the happy moments he'd had (that list being much less extensive): what he was thinking about was that rail-coach riding farther and farther away with each passing moment, and if the box fell on him this time he'd never know, never under-stand.

He'd never catch it up.

Night had fallen. With it came the chirp of the crickets in the prairie grass. The moon wasn't up yet, though, and wouldn't be for some time. It was still what some called the *Grey Hour*, when the sun still rests just below the horizon, that time of day when one wants to light a lamp if one wants to see much of anything at all. Even the best eye can be tricked by the greying light. And the yard was awash in torchlight.

"I *did* promise ye a li'l chat," said Lord Quenn now stumping up to the post, a fine, sturdy piece of timber that was driven deep into the ground just in front of the saloon. "And a chat ye shall have. That's why I'll be wanting yer name – that, and so if someone comes asking I can says as I've ne'er even so much as heard of you in these parts before."

Jonas laughed cold. "I'm Jonas Arthur," he said. "And you'll be wanting to remember that name as long as you live because you're likely to hear it again before you die."

Quenn only laughed himself and held up Jonas' guns. "These are damn fine irons," he said. "Jimmy Wester of Fort Cardac by the look of them. The eagle, nobility. Very fine indeed. And fifty-two by my count in the right handle—"

"*Fifty-five,*" said Jonas. His voice was cold as his laugh, his eyes now empty: it was best to face death that way, with a brave face.

"Oh, come what may," said Quenn dismissively, shaking the earth from his spurs. "Let 'em hang."

A rope was tossed over the post, a noose tied and fitted round Jonas' neck; the other end was lashed to the pommel of a saddled horse at the hitching rail. And as the line drew tight Quenn turned away, still admiring Jonas' guns. But he stopped mid-turn, and though Jonas couldn't see what the Lord Quenn saw, he *did* see the cold shudder that went up his back. "Kid, what's yer business 'ere?"

"Come t'see a hanging." Someone shouldered their way to the front of the crowd. His face was shadowed beneath his hat and all Jonas could see were his bright eyes. "Every sir 'ere knows how I like a good hanging. Oh, but ye might not be wanting t'ang *him*." The stranger pointed a long, straight finger at Jonas; and perhaps he was going a little strange, what with the thought of dying and all, but Jonas was more than a little certain he'd seen the eyes of that person glowing, not just reflecting the torchlight but actually glowing in some unnatural way.

"He's a friend o' mine, see. Least that's what I 'ear."

"He's a wanted man, Kid," said Quenn. "He'll hang or I'll be damned."

The runner holding the horse raised his hand: the proverbial nail in the coffin. But the hand of the stranger was faster than any. "Then be damned to you!" he said from beneath his hat.

It was over almost before it had quite begun. Jonas was looking not at a masked man in the torchlight but at a younger face, steely and hard with manhood come well before its time. His eyes were wary and watchful, though that flicker of fire was still there. Most importantly, though, the Kid was holding a long- black-barreled six-shooter with a grip of bluewood painted in ebony, not to his eye so as to aim down the iron sights, but at his side, the barrel still hot and relinquishing a lazy tendril of azure smoke. His right hand hovered over the hammer, and Jonas' ears still rang with the roar of the gunshots. A *darkiron*, he thought. It couldn't help but be. Few men still carried those ancient guns, but Jonas thought he'd seen that very one before.

He didn't at first see what marks the bullets had found: no one had. The first was lodged in the throat of the horseman; the second was in the chest of the runner to his right, who'd only a moment before been grasping Jonas' shoulder with a steely grip; the third was in that of the runner to his left; the fourth and fifth were no-where to be seen, though he doubted very much that the stranger had missed; and the sixth was lodged in the wood of the hanging post only just above his head, having nearly severed the rope in two (sufficiently enough broken most of the twisted strands, at least).

"Too bad I've missed," said the Kid. "Hand up them irons and run on now, Quenn, else *yer* up to the post next."

Anger and fury and the utmost contempt were bubbling behind Quenn's complexion, like the boiling tar pits in Jemrock (Jonas had seen them only once, but it had been a horrible sight, and the stench rising from the oily-black pools in hot waves made you want to cry). But whatever he was, Quenn was no fool. Jonas' guns he let fall to the earth. "Common, boys," he grumbled to his men, those who were still on their feet. The humiliation must have been nearly killing him. "Guess we can leave the violence till dawn."

Together they all trooped back, not to the saloon, but to the town hall — or what had *once* been the town hall and now, most likely, was Quenn's own personal villa.

"Darkfinger!" exclaimed Jonas when the Kid walked grimly to the post, gun still drawn and each chamber already refilled with his black cartridges. Jonas couldn't deny it to himself now: he'd have recognized that gun and the sure hands that held it anywhere, Dodge City, Hembridge, Dhill, the Fall-be-damned wasteland itself. When you look down the barrel of a gun and see the end of the trail you don't soon forget it.

"Aye," agreed the Kid. "Mind tellin' me, Mister Arthur, why I saved yer life just now, and why ye're in Drayton camp, at all?"

45

"My business is my own for the present," replied Jonas, taking up his guns once more from the earth where Quenn had let them fall. "But I can tell true enough that you're as weary of that fool Quenn as I am. And anyway, Chock was a decent-enough man, the sort that does what's square by the law. He wouldn't have turned a man out alone to be left to the wolves or hung him up without a fair trial. And that, I think makes us friends, after a fashion."

"Too true," said Darkfinger. "Aye, Chock was a decent fella, a-sorts. But he's gone or dead now, and Lord Quenn is the regent here in Drayton, whatever may be said. To tell the truth, I'm s'prised to find that it's you in the noose tonight."

The assembled crowd was beginning to drift away now, disappointed. They'd been itching for a hanging – or even better, a gunfight – and to be denied such a pleasure had put them off their appetite.

Tucker, having come up to the two as they stood talking, now said quietly, "Might we duck away to my cabin, good fellas, and there speak of these things?"

They were agreed, and so they all three went at once to the house of Man Tucker.

~CHAPTER THREE~
UNLIKELY COMPANIONS

"Now," said Tucker when they were all sat around on stools before a low fire with mugs of hot coffee in their hands, "best not t'be gettin' any sleep t'night. Quenn may've tol'rated you this long, Kid, but now I think he'd not hesitate to send that there Jake to cut yer throat."

"What have you done to gain his favour?" asked Jonas dryly.

Darkfinger chuckled and his eyes grew bright as gold in a sluice; but it was Tucker who said, "Time or two Kid 'ere 'as stirred the ol' trouble pot. Three o' Quenn's men fell sumpin pretty. Quenn woulda 'ad the Kid gunrunning just like the rest of 'em if he'd 'ad his way, but Kid refused, plain and simple, see, and Quenn's got sumpin of respect for 'im now."

"But yer right, Tuck," Darkfinger agreed, sitting back and lighting a cigarette he'd been rolling. "Better watch the door t'night."

Tobacco smoke filled the room; Tucker poured out more coffee; the fire burned bright and threw sparks onto a well-scored hearthrug. Outside the shadows grew long as the moon rose below the horizon.

"How long have you been in camp, anyhow?" asked Jonas.

"Not more'n two years," said Darkfinger absently. "Not really nowhere else to go now."

"And the money?" asked Jonas.

"Gone, it is," answered Darkfinger coolly. "Or lost, I should say." Though no matter how they pried and coaxed he never would explain just *how* he had lost it. "The Marshal's on my trail, and forty-seven men want me dead – forty-*six* now, actually, I take it since ye've not yet reached for yer guns. So I come to Drayton with hopes of turning a new page."

"Plain and simple," said Tucker. "That's as what Drayton is, why I've stayed all these years since you left, Jonas. Ain't no law, ain't no religiosity, not even in fidelity to the Four. It's what brings the likes of us all the way out here."

The conversation strayed between them for a bit. Mostly Tucker went on about this and that, and mostly about Quenn and the runners in town who, it seemed, made even lazy old Tucker a little edgy. A time or two he even reached for his guns which weren't there.

But somehow or other, perhaps an hour later they were sitting in the night-shadows with the fire dying to coals and Jonas mentioned the train.

"*What* train?" asked Darkfinger quickly, sitting up and blowing a long trail of smoke that drifted lazily around the room.

"Would've come through perhaps two, maybe three days ago," said Jonas.

"No trains come through Drayton no more," replied Darkfinger. "Ye're mistake."

"That's what *I* said!" chimed in Tucker. "Not since all the timber was gone and them mines a-run dry. And now the trestle's gone all rotted through."

"But now that ye mention it," Darkfinger went on thoughtfully and in ignorance of Tucker, for something had just then returned to his mind, it seemed, like the sun on the daisies, something forgotten. "I *did* hear something. 'Twas p'haps four nights 'go. Sounded like a far off whistle, it did, like a train; then the ground trembled a little; then I heard that whistle again, but it was quite close, sounded like just over the hill. It had all but slipped my mind 'til ye recalled it to me just now! I went out, y'see, into the hills, and I saw it there by the light of the moon, chuggin' away to carry its load up through the little pass just south of the valley and over into the Sundry Hills."

"Did it seem a little odd to you?" asked Jonas, quelling the excitement rising within him at these words. He choked it back with coffee (man, the stuff was bitter-good!) "Did it seem like something was wrong?"

"Right's more like it!" said Darkfinger with a laugh. " 'Twas chugging and luggin' up yar hill where the old tracks are all buried now, and in the night I couldn't exactly see it, but it 'twas a strong, powerful thing – a *good* thing. Oh Fall-be-damned, I'd thought it all a dream!"

"Was no dream," said Tucker quietly now. "Couldn't've been, 'cause I dreamed it, too. Oh, the cold autumn night's a trickster, and what with the Harvest Moon coming on fast!"

"P'haps we've shared this dream," said Dark-finger.

"Couldn't be so, neither," replied Tucker, "for if we had it'd've been the same that I dreamed. Only it weren't, no how. It seemed to me neither very *bad* nor very *good* but rather something that *just was*. And a sly thing, at that. I was wary, so I was, for at any moment that devil might've taken my wallet or my gun or even my life. It seemed a thief, a burglar, if it was anything at all."

"I tell you one thing f'certain," said Darkfinger. "It came out of the east like thunder and went into the west with a whisper. Can't say as I've ever met anything in all creation that could compare with that coach. Nor have I any wish to do so again. Good or not, that thing was the only of its kind this world can bear. By the Fall, Tucker, you sure it weren't no dream?"

Tucker returned with an *I-don't-know* straight-mouthed expression that meant he'd say no more about it.

Jonas was perplexed. "Why do you say that?" he asked. "That's it's the only of its kind and all?"

" 'Cause it was wild," said Darkfinger. "Good, yes, beautiful even as it climbed the hills toward Sundry in the moonlight. But it was also as fierce and as wild and unpredictable as the savages. But in a good way, y'understand. Why is it yer wond'ring all this, anyway?" Now he turned a very curious, almost suspicious, eyebrow, and in the shadows of the little shanty he fixed Jonas with eyes that would find out the truth of it.

" 'Cause I intend to follow it," Jonas replied. "Moreoverly, I intend to catch it up."

"But what would you want to do that for!" exclaimed Darkfinger. "I did say 'twas a lovely thing; that don't mean I'd like to meet it!"

Tucker added, "When I seen it the other night can't say I didn't think once or twice about tying a bundle of sticks to the tracks ahead of it. By gum, my flint and steel were in m'hand with just the thought. *BOOHF!*—"He mimed the volatile nature of split-sticks with his fingers. "—and my mind would ease a little."

"Aye, but that was not my experience at all," said Jonas. "I stood on the platform in Little Puretill watching the red lamps of its caboose vanishing away into the dusk. There was a man sitting not far from me, a fellow I'd not noticed at first, though whether it was that I'd overlooked him or that he'd not been there to see I don't know. He arose, his luggage in hand, as if he intended to board some coach, and he said, 'If you want to follow me I'm going *that* way'."

"*Which* way?" interjected Tucker.

"West," answered Jonas without hesitation. "West was what he meant; west was where he went."

51

"But how do you know?" Tucker persisted.

"I don't; I just do," said Jonas.

"Then it's this man yer trying to find?" asked Darkfinger. Now he, too, was bemused.

"No, the coach," said Jonas.

"But the man—?" asked Tucker.

Jonas replied: "I don't know but I've a sort of a feeling, a hunch, really, that this fellow was in some way all mixed up with the train and that if I found the train I'd find him." He paused, for the memory was fresh in his mind and he was recalling each detail to ignite the fervour of his words. "He seemed the sort that could answer any question you asked him," he went on, "even the very difficult ones. I tell you that train was a very *wicked* and *powerful* thing, a thing to fear, and perhaps that's why I long for it so. But I tell you, of all the things I've done, all the killing, all the stealing, this is the only thing that makes any sense to me."

Darkfinger grunted thoughtfully. "Could be ye're a mad man, Jonas Arthur," he said. "Could be yer even a dead man. But yer no liar, whatever they say, I can see that plainly enough in your eyes."

"Tell him, Jonas," said Tucker. "Tell him about when you saw the train; tell him what 'twas the feeling it left with you."

Jonas thought for a moment. "Dread," he said at first. "It came through Little Puretill in the fading light, and at first I had to look twice and even three times to be sure I'd seen it at all. But when it was right up at the platform the planks started trembling and the ground shook. And then it was rushing by, the steam rising from its stack like dragonfire, running against the wind. And even though it was in the heat of the evening, it brought in its wake an icy breeze the likes of which I've never before felt."

Darkfinger had been sitting thoughtfully for some time, but now he spoke. "I've half a mind to go with you, Jonas," he said, staring at the fire. "I've half a mind to chase after this phantom, though, by the Fall, I'm lost to your foolery if I do."

"Thought ye didn't want to, Kid," said Tucker.

"So I don't," answered Darkfinger. "But I've just as many questions for this fellow who goes with the train as any man does." Again the Kid was silent for a moment, staring into the fire. "I've run for so long," he said then quietly; "but a man can only run so far. Not that I've been running *from* anything in particular, if y'take my meaning. It gets tiring the farther you get from home, and I've come much too far now to go back. Oh, if there was one place I could go . . . but this train, this coach, it gives me the strangest feeling. Hope, perhaps. Maybe something else. Whatever it is, it calls me something fierce, same as it does you, Jonas, but in a different way I think. I don't long to run along behind it but to turn my guns south for the Lowlands, to go back home."

Darkfinger went on in a dreamy voice, a voice that Jonas never would have believed belonged to the Fastest Hand West of Dodge if he hadn't been sitting there hearing it for himself.

Meanwhile, Tucker sat quietly in the corner by the fire. His mug had been empty for some time and the coffeepot was empty, too. He'd been getting more uncomfortable with Darkfinger's faraway talk of wonderful things, things lost. Jonas didn't miss the relief in the cripple's eyes when he said, "Well, best off to the rack, I think. I've far to go tomorrow."

"You shan't be alone," Darkfinger said, and quite abruptly, too, as if the Kid had only just made up the certainty of the thought in his mind. "I'll come with ye, Jonas Arthur. I've no more wish for this life, and I can't go home. It seems to me the only escape is with you."

Jonas grinned: he couldn't help himself. He put a hand on Darkfinger's shoulder. "My friend, whatever awaits me, I'll be glad to share it with you."

"And ye?" Darkfinger turned quite suddenly to Tucker. "Are ye coming, Mister Tucker? Or do ye even still cower in this hole ye've created for y'self?"

A nervous dread passed behind Tucker's eyes. He whimpered a little and shuffled his feet. "Why do ye task me with such things?" he cried softly. "I don't know – I *can't* know. I'm not a slinger or a runner anymore. I've hardly ever been a fair shot, let alone a good raider. I'm hardly the adventuring sort. What I need is a mug of beer! That would settle things right and proper."

"What you need is the butt of my pistol on yer head," snorted Darkfinger. "Are yer coming or not?"

Tucker gave the door a long last glance. Something inside him hadn't quite died yet, but in the end it would have driven the last nail and filled the grave in, too. "No, I'm not going," he said. "I shan't go. I can't go. Do go'n have yer adventure without me, and if ye come again to Drayton I shall quail to learn of the dangers ye've endured. And if not, then I'll live out m'days in peace knowing as I will that I chose life when I'd been offered death."

Again Darkfinger snorted but said nothing. Jonas didn't have to ask: he knew what the Kid was thinking for the same thought also was on his own mind.

Jonas and Darkfinger agreed they should leave at dawn and no later. A hard day's work would get them beyond the Drayton rim and into the out-hills, the Sundry Hills. From there they would be looking into the True Frontier. From there the world ended and the real adventure began.

Jonas lay down on the hearthrug; Darkfinger took the hammock; Tucker kept the first watch, sitting in the dark with a long-gun across his knees. But Jonas couldn't sleep. He lay awake as the Silver Judge rose low in the southern sky, watching the acrid smoke from Tucker's cigarettes twisting this way and that on the roof of the cabin, making shapes that would hold for a second then burst into aimless clouds that drifted to the window and escaped through the crack around the sash and out into the night.

~CHAPTER FOUR~
ENEMIES IN THE NIGHT

It must've been long about midnight when Jonas awoke with a start. He couldn't even recall having fallen asleep. The fire was dead, nearly to the last coal, but night hadn't completely filled the cabin. What replaced the warm glow of the fire was the equally cold moonlight streaming in through the window: the Harvest Moon was coming on fast. Tucker's long thin silhouette stood out brazen by the sill, straight and unmoving. He wasn't smoking, and his gun was in his hand.

Jonas sat up. "What is it?"

"Someone's in the street," Tucker said; "and someone else. A bunch'a people, looks like. Can't see who. All with torches and guns."

"Just now or have they been out there for awhile?" Jonas asked.

"Just now," said Tucker. "Runners I'd say from the look of 'em. Someone's gonna be *kilt*."

"Quenn's boys do you think?" asked Jonas.

"I'd say not," said Tucker. "If Quenn had called this there'd be Billie and Timber and that imp of a fella' whose name I cain't never remember."

"What about that Jake?" asked Jonas. Jake was the only one of Quenn's men he had any reservation about meeting face to face. Well, maybe Timber, too, now that he thought of it.

"—oh! There they are," Tucker exclaimed, his voice gone dry.

"Best wake Darkfinger," said Jonas, and he took position at the window to peer out into the wolf-night while Tucker shook the Kid from sleep.

"Quenn's boys ye say?" he asked, his eyes still heavy with *moon-glimmer*. "How many ye count, Jonas?"

"Fifteen, perhaps."

"Then there's 'leas' twice that."

"Quenn's got thirty guns?" asked Jonas, not just a bit skeptical. James Howard himself, arguably the greatest runner to lift gold in the west, had only had twenty guns at the height of his reign.

They three were so intent on the sight through the window that they nearly missed the gentle *creak* on the front step – nearly, but a boy with a coward's heart like Tucker listens for that sound his whole life. "*Shhhhh!!*" he hissed now. "Someone's at the door!"

Darkfinger's eyes narrowed. "Did you see Jake in the street?" he whispered.

Tucker shook his head.

The *moon-glimmer* was gone from Darkfinger's eyes now, replaced by the *fireshine* Jonas had seen just before the Kid shot Quenn's men. Now the Kid's hands dropped to his belt and he went ridged as weathered timber. Jonas was already on his feet, one of his irons in his hands. "In the corner then, Darkfinger," he said, "where the shadows are heavy. And you, Tucker, by the fire, and don't look this way – no, not a single glance, not till we've made our move."

They waited in perfect silence, hardly daring to breath. Jonas couldn't see Darkfinger next to him. He might just as well have been alone in the corner by Tucker's strung hammock. But he *could* see Tucker quite plainly squatting by the fire, the sweat standing out on his neck and cheeks. And little wonder: Tucker was accustomed to turning from a fight when it arose, not waiting while it stood on his doorsill.

The door was actually creaking open now, riding on hinges that needed the oil so desperately, as many things did on the Frontier. It swung wide and there was nothing but night behind it, a true, solid blackness that anything might have come out of just then. Anything. Even Jake Weston of Drayton camp. He was standing tall as a gunman, not skulking like a thief. His eyes were bright, his head bare, his iron loose in its holsters. But it was a long silver-steeled nicker that was the commendation of his errand. He held it with the blade down like a Dodgeton backstreet brawler.

"Hullo, Tucker," he said, for his quick eyes didn't miss Tucker's shadow hunkered by the fire.

"What's it?" said Tucker, looking up quick, as if startled; Jonas could hear the tremble in his voice. "Why do ye disturb me, Jake? And no knock or curt!"

"Wond'rin' if'n that fine lad iss around," Jake said wryly. "And the other one, the Kid, or whatever it is you people call him. Like to have a word with 'em, so I would."

" 'Fraid not," Tucker said without looking up, even for a moment, his eyes were trained hard on the fire.

Jake grunted and stepped into the doorway, his boots on the floorboards the only sound in the cabin. His eyes turned the dark — bright eyes, eyes that saw everything, saw even through the moonless shadows. Whatever Jake Weston was he was keen and clever enough to be Lord Weston of Camp Drayton. Jonas would've been a fool to not wonder which outcome the Fall would favour if Jake and Quenn came to blows, but personally he was in favour of the younger runner.

There was still one thing about Jake that brought some comfort, however: Jonas had seen men with that sort of cold moonlight in their eyes. They were men with hard hearts, men who loved only violence and the fear it brings, men with quick fingers who shot first and never asked questions. And no matter how Jake's eyes pierced the shadows Jonas knew that if he'd seen Darkfinger and himself crouched in the corner of the cabin the situation would've already turned sour.

Still, he tightened his fingers on the hafts of his guns.

"See, thing is," Jake said, turning his head to one side as if listening to voices in secret in the next room, "I don't see how's that c'be. Think yer lying to me, Tuck. But now that couldn't be. You wouldn't lie to me, would ye, ol' buddy?"

"Nope, sure as t'star wouldn't," Tucker ageed.

"Wouldn't mind if I just took a look around now, would ye?" Jake asked, his boots already sounding loud on the floor as he stepped over the threshold and across the bare boards. He didn't stop. The air seemed colder than ever and deathly silent. And now Jake was so close to Jonas and Darkfinger that Jonas could smell the cleanness of his clothes, the rawhide of his holsters, the powder in his shells, the metallic glint of his silver tooth. In that moment he was pretty sure that wherever Jake went the air was cold and dead like the coming of death that the Harvest Moon sometimes brought. But at the last a cold smirk appeared in Jake's eyes and he turned back to look at Tucker, turned his back to Jonas and Darkfinger.

The moment had come. Jonas needn't hardly even move, that's how close they were. Jake opened his mouth, the room got even colder still, and he said, "You know that Quenn'll be mighty displeased if he find ye been hiding—" But he never finished that thought, for the next thing Jake of Drayton camp knew was that he was looking down the barrel of a *darkiron*-six, and the cold, brazen thing digging in his back couldn't hardly help but be a fine iron in and of itself, not a *darkiron* (it was too light for that),

61

but perhaps a big, heavy shooter like the men in the east sometimes sold for good gold. Neither was likely to miss, even in the hands of a child.

"*Stand as you value your life*," whispered Jonas.

But Jake was cool as the iron long after a fight. "Lay down, gents," he replied stiffly, quicker than anything. "Mean nothing to you. You don't want t'be killing me."

"Ye're a mad man or a fool if yer think'n we'll lay'er down," said Darkfinger. "Or p'haps both I'd warrant."

"And what of Quenn? What's he mean?" asked Jonas. "Bullet in my head, then Tucker here up on the hanging post?"

"That's as may be." Jake scuffed the floor-board with his boot in aimless disinterest; if he was at all afraid he didn't show it in the least.

"Then why wouldn't we see to it you go back to him cold?" Jonas asked.

"Cause if'n ye do all 'em boys gon' be kickin' in this door right quick," Jake said, the grin on his face the only assurance they needed he believed every word he said. And that was enough for them, true or no.

"Then we shoot them dead, too," Jonas answered. "Won't be no trouble." And he pressed his gun deeper, his finger touching the trigger. The cool of the iron felt reassuring.

But Darkfinger put a hand on his shoulder. He didn't say it but Jonas understood: best not t'kill if'n they needn't; better still not t'shoot, if'n they could help.

"How many?" Darkfinger asked.

"Twenty in the street with guns on the door," said Jake coolly. " 'Nother two in back with a couple of 'em chattery little things Quenn's just got from down south, the guns that spit lots o' bullets quicker'n you can think."

Jonas looked at Darkfinger; Darkfinger looked at Jonas.

"But we can't just let 'im go!" cried Tucker. "He's all we got 'gainst those rats; he'd see us all dead, sure as anything!"

Jake made a nasty smile that burned in the empty spaces behind his eyes. "Sure I would," he said, gloatful.

"Tie him up, then," said Darkfinger.

"We can always cut his throat in the morning," said Jonas.

Tucker got the cords and they sat Jake down in the corner, farthest from the fire, binding his wrists, ankles, and knees, and left him sitting pretty like a trussed turkey.

Darkfinger slipped to the window and peered around the canvas blind. "I count same as you," he said, "though whether they really 'ave any of 'em southern *mashin*-guns is anyone's guess."

It was back around the fire they now crowded when once Tucker had thrown on a log or two. Jonas reasoned Quenn wouldn't let Jake go if possible, and so an attack while Jake was still inside was unlikely for risk of shooting him in the fray — that is, unless they provoked it. But Darkfinger suggested they only had perhaps a few minutes before the boys waiting outside gave it up and tried to come in themselves. Jake had been given a mission and it if it'd gone as planned it wouldn't have taken more than a few minutes. In the dark of the cabin they'd have the upward advantage for perhaps the first few shots, but in the end the closed space would turn round the same bad end for them.

Finally Darkfinger said, "I've come to it at last."

"Come to what?" asked Jonas.

"There's only one thing for it," said Darkfinger: "we've got to go out and meet 'em."

"They'll shoot us dead," said Tucker, "quick as anything."

"Then out the back," said Darkfinger. "With any luck Jake may've lied about the whole deal as they see it."

"I'm for it," agreed Jonas, if only because he grew weary of waiting and wondering. A fight rarely grew any less of a fight if it wasn't fought.

From the shadows at their backs came Jake's raspy voice. "You fool's gon' wish ye'd shot me dead," he said with a high, maniacal cackle. "Wish ye'd shot me while ye 'ad the chance, ye will!"

Tucker paled. "You shut up now, Jake! I'll cut yer throat!" He looked around the blinds again. "I ain't going," he said defiantly.

Darkfinger's eyes smirked at Tucker's back and his left hand twitched toward his holstered *darkiron*.

"Haven't you still a long-gun?" asked Jonas, "Or have you gone soft all through?"

"Aye, I've still got one," agreed Tucker.

"Then sit in here if you will and guard the prisoner," Jonas said. "Or you can sit here like gutless meat, all the same, and be damned to you."

The little cabin had no back door but the window served well enough, and the alleyway between the back wall and the fence was so dark, being sheltered from the moon hanging in the south, that when they were crouched next to the cabin wall they could hardly even see each other's faces. Still, it was apparent Jake's game had been a bluff, at least insofar as making out that they had been surrounded before *and* behind. They shook on it, just the same, and Jonas thought that chances were it was their last, and he found that a disheartening notion. Then he slipped east along the cabin wall, Darkfinger going the other way.

In the alleyway that let out into the street was a well, walled in stone and with a hand-pump sprouting up from it, its handle running a silhouette right to the wall. Jonas slipped it by, then he was into the shadow of the next cabin, then beyond that into the next, and there he turned and held to the wall until the open street was before him.

He could see the runners plain as anything now, and Darkfinger had been right: there were at least thirty, and all wore shooting irons on their hips, though some were rather more the dreadfully old and rusted guns that sometimes came from the northlands where men thought little of such ways; many might not even shoot at all.

A handful of the gun-boys were standing around in the street with long-guns on their shoulders but most were skulking in the gutters and the shadows. This wasn't an assault, this was an ambush. Then up through the midst of them came Quenn in his fine, clean, parched suit, his hat pulled down quite pert on his face and a long cigar between his teeth. "Common now!" he was yelling in his deep, raspy voice. "Don't want to resort to violence, for I am a man of resolution, so I am!"

Jonas was a man of resolution, too. He'd always been. He'd learned it quick and early on in life: the faster the end the less the trouble, and nothing brought about an end so quick as six loaded chambers.

Darkfinger must be nearly ready now, Jonas thought, for it had been some minutes there in the shadow of the cabin, and doubtless Tucker was come to the limit of his wits with apprehension.

Keep my hand steady and mine eye true; pull me to when I stray, he prayed. And he drew his guns, pulled the hammers, and stepped into the way.

None of Quenn's men saw him: they were too intent on Tucker's cabin. But Darkfinger saw him, and Jonas could see the Kid stepping from the shadows opposite himself, like some deathly reflection, some way down the street. Their shots had better be true, he thought, else they might find lead between their teeth that was neither Quenn's nor his boys'.

Jonas raised his guns and fired; Darkfinger's gunshots echoed his own. Then the entire street was alight with the flash of powder, the *crack* of the long-guns, the *whine* of the shots, and the terrible *wheezing* rattle of something Jonas had never heard before.

Back behind the wall of the cabin he checked his chambers. All empty, though whether the shots had made their marks only the Fall could know for it had happened much too fast for him to see.

Now, as he crouched in the shadows, he noticed something peculiar. Opposite him was a tent. Certainly no one lived in it for there were no lights, no chimney. No Frontier man worth his weight would live in such a thing with fall coming on apace, not with good timber to be had outside the camp and sweat aplenty to drive a stake and notch a log. But in the canvas side dozens of holes had been torn, holes Jonas hadn't seen before: bullet holes, he thought. Had Quenn's men really got off that many shots? It was a wonder he hadn't been hit!

He refilled his chambers and listed out into the street again. The air was thick with powder-smoke turned green in the light of the high moon. Quenn's men were vanished within it like the wolves of the Frontier. And with their last fading shadow Jonas heard Quenn's voice in the night like the far-off whistle of a train, "The Fall damn you, Darkfinger!"

The drifting smoke lit up with the flicker and *crack* of gunfire. Like a running demon, a boy some years younger than the Kid stumbled from the haze, face vivid white, hands trembling. Mechanically, without another thought, Jonas shot him. Later he would curse himself for it, and the cold, pale face of the child would never leave his dreams.

The powder-smoke was beginning to clear a little now, and there were bodies in the street.

67

How many? Ten? Twenty? All the bloody gun-fights Jonas had seen now seemed far away and distant. This was real, this was now, and he felt weak. What was happening to him?

Darkfinger met him in the street. His guns were empty and he wasn't bothering to reload them. "They're gone," he said. "A dozen or so, I think. Timber's with them. I tried to get him but I missed. Quenn got out, too, though that's little surprise. He was one of the first to turn away when you opened fire."

"Who *did* we get?" Jonas asked, glancing back at the bodies and feeling again that revulsion of horror, and wondering again in the same moment what it could mean.

Darkfinger shook his head, turning over first one body and then the next. "All Quenn's boys, all from Drayton. These seven fell from you, the rest are mine. I don't know their names."

"Just as well," said Jonas.

"They won't try again," said Darkfinger, "not tonight: they've lost too many. But we best be gone by morning. Quenn's a hard man – harder when spurned by humiliation, now three times by my hand, I think."

Tucker was badly shaken when they found him hunkered in the cabin. A shot or two had come his way, and the bullets were lodged deep in the back wall. But the real scare had been when he'd discovered Jake's chair empty, the ropes cuts. Why Jake hadn't made good to open Tucker's throat before he slipped out they didn't know, but Darkfinger said they could add him to the list of fine guns against them, bringing his total back up to forty-seven. That made them all the more eager to leave camp.

Before Jonas fell asleep he added seven notches to the handle of his right-hand gun. Then he paused, knife in hand, and reluctantly he added an eighth.

~CHAPTER FIVE~
TO SUNDRY

When the sun was only just rising in the east Tucker let them out by a hole in the wall of stakes somewhere just west of the gate. They took with them horses both, Darkfinger's own and Tucker's, and when all they would take (a little food, water, and some extra clothes – commodities were scarce in Drayton with the Harvest Moon coming on fast) was safely passed through the breach, Tucker gave them a last fond farewell and a feign heart-felt apology. Then he left them: doubtless he would be well on his way to Hembridge before Quenn came round again, if he still had any sense.

While the sun was still low in the east and the air cool they made what turns they could;

come midday they'd be growing weary and exhausted with the heat of the prairie.

The hills around Drayton Valley were low and gentle, mostly, covered in rough prairie grass and coarse scrub brush; and so, even though there were no roads and few pathways they made remarkable time. There was some debate about where their path should lead. Jonas wanted to make for the tracks and follow them, but Darkfinger said that was no good because the tracks turned back at the top of the hills, just south of Drayton. They should go west right away, he said, since that had been the direction of the coach. But in the end Jonas won out and they made for the hills where the rails went on no more.

Still well before High Noon they found themselves far from Drayton and well into the gently rolling hills of the steppe. A vast land of prairie grass that flowed like a sea, it spread out around them in rolling waves, broken only by the crest of the next ridge or perhaps a small stand of brushwood that grew only very low to the ground. There was no shade from the fury of the sun, and they grew very much accustomed to the passage of the grass that was at times as high as their gunbelts. It was always the dry, lifelessness of the Frontier.

They hadn't seen the tracks yet. Darkfinger said they were still some way off, that the rails came up through the hills still farther south where the mining camp was now falling to ruin. But shortly they should be coming to the abandoned excavations, or roads, or something, for the workings had spread out from the camp in its heyday like the fingers of delta rivers. And sure enough, soon they came upon a pathway running low amidst the grass which seemed for some time to lead to somewhere that was nowhere, and then to nowhere, but always *somewhere*. It ended quite abruptly in the mouth of a black cavern, a mine that began at once to drop steeply, always getting narrower, so that before the darkness became too heavy for their eyes the walls had crowded so close that one mule with packs for carrying ore would have been well-wedged. Jonas felt his skin crawl just to look into its gaping mouth. There was, however, a set of narrow rails, the like of which miners will often use to carry the weight of their ore, and a railcar lay toppled to one side, long-since rusted and disused.

But what really interested them about this curious relic was the small shack built only just around the next turn in the side of the hillock into which the mine had been delved. It was ruinous and empty, mostly, missing shingle and slat, so that they could in places see through the walls and roof. But on the door was painted in bright crimson:

Babylon march
Let there be blood in the vale
All hail His Bloody Majesty!

"What do ye s'pose it means?" asked Darkfinger.

But Jonas didn't know.

"I want t'take another look at that mine," said Darkfinger then.

73

They returned to the mouth of the cavern, and as Darkfinger stood looking in, he said, "I must go in, Jonas. I feel it. Go on if ye will, and meet me on the other side of the hill, but I must go in, just as you must follow the coach."

"I wouldn't venture in there, not with a knife to my throat," said Jonas wearily. "I am no coward, Darkfinger, but what I'm certain of is that my path doesn't lead down any hole."

"Go, then," replied Darkfinger with a mirthful smile. "Go then, Jonas. Take yer adventure and I'll take mine. I can't say why but I feel this part we must take. We will meet again, if the Fall are willing."

And so they parted ways, though they'd been in accompaniment for only one morning, and it was not a particularly tearful parting. In a day and a little more Jonas *had* begun to realize that this, his companion, was becoming his friend; but they were not *yet* friends, and so there was only a solemn farewell and they went their separate ways, he over the rise of the hill and Darkfinger the Kid down into the mine, leading his horse by the bridle.

Not far beyond the shack with the writing on the door Jonas came over a hill and found stretched out before him the mining camp, timbers weathering in the Frontier sun, the sluices now running dry to piles of detritus that might still contain fragments of *oliveshine*. The great wheel no longer creaked with the laughter of the water as it once had done. The oil drums that upon a time had brought electricity to the camp now stood on rotting gantry, maybe empty, maybe full, he couldn't tell. The only life was the stolid prairie grass tossing in the wind and the crimson blades of the bloodgrass that had found rooting even here.

The tracks came up the hill from the east. They were low in the ground with grass and weeds growing up over the rails and between the ties, but there as anything could be. He followed them through the camp, past the water tower that still stood though the timbers that held up the tank looked like they might let go at any moment and the tank too was rusting through. On the west side of the camp the rails branched into four sets and ran on parallel. Two were empty; on the third three freight cars still stood and another was toppled so that he could see into its container, and it, too, was empty; and the fourth set of rails was buried beneath a fallen warehouse that had once housed the crane that turned the steam engines around so they could continue their run back east.

A fence ran along the edge of the camp, three strands of wire that would cut open your skin if you weren't careful. But there was a low spot where a post had rotted through and fallen. A grown man might get over, if he was careful, and the task was no trouble at all for a horse when once Jonas had put his boot on the wire.

Jonas gave a last look east and stepped over the fence and into the True Frontier.

He made due west now. Perhaps he had a moment of doubt, but deep down inside he knew that the train was before and, with persistence, he would catch it.

He walked on for the rest of that day, without respite or food to eat but a little victuals he still carried in his bedroll. This he kept safe, for who knew what hard times might still be before him on his journey. It was well into the evening before the last of the low hills of the Drayton were passed and done with, and there he stood, with the sun diminishing into the west and the high, sharp hills of the Sundry scattered about before him. Beyond them the dull-red glare of the wasteland cut out his path in an eerie silhouette.

He found a large boulder lying where some godly force had placed it, and he made his bed beneath its overhanging edge. He didn't light a fire: he hadn't any food to cook, nor did he want for the heat of it. And anyway, it might've brought to him jackals and coyotes that were hungry for a feast as he was, maybe even the pack. He fell asleep with the heavy weight of one of his guns in his hand, the other near-enough, still wrapped up in his things. One eye never closed, not quite, and when the moon rose high and the prairie wolf lifted its cry to the night all sleep vanished from him and he lay awake, watching the stars shift in their eternal passage until the darkness came again. For some time he listened to the forlorn calls of they who had come along behind, content that the howls were still far and long.

Then was the greyness of dawn.

He arose quickly, saddled the horse and rode, making remarkable time toward the Sundry Hills. Within an hour and a little more the path was sharp with rocks, and the high stony hillocks and outcroppings of that borderland were all around him, sometimes in carven shapes like gaunt sentries guarding the way; the sun alight-ing their faces as it came over the horizon made them look so much the greater.

There, in the heart of that hard land, he found the mine that Darkfinger had spoken of but it was a miserable discovery. It had long-since fallen in upon itself, the mouth all sealed off. Now the prairie grass was growing in the hollow where it once had been. He might have missed it, altogether, if his horse hadn't pulled up suddenly and refused to take another step. When he dismounted he discovered there was a little opening that let in, though far too small for any man. Still, he had some hope, and so he waited by the mouth for a little while with his ear to the wind, hoping to hear Darkfinger's voice from below. But as he sat there he heard instead far away first the cry of a hawk, and then, as if to accompany it, the long, drawing whistle of a train. That could only mean one thing. And so, with his heart beating fast, he remounted again, and with one last long look at the little crack in the ground, he turned westward once more and rode for the sunset.

It took him much of that day to cross that cruel land. It was a tedious chore of picking a path through sharp rocks and spires. It went up and down, through gravelly valleys with high crags on either side, or over hills of bare stone. More than once he had to dismount and lead the horse through some very narrow way where another man might have turned back. Then, right in the middle of that stony country he fell in a creek that seemed to come from somewhere but go to nowhere. He cursed his clumsiness and dragged himself clear again, and though he had only just thrown his gear free in time to save it the wetting, his right-hand gun fell in the water and had to be fished out. He made a mental note as he went on his way that it must be properly cleaned and dried before he lay down for the night. Right now he was far too tired. He hated himself for that.

The sun was falling into the west when at last he saw the wasteland. There the True Frontier became a timeless emptiness that went on for, well, who knew how far it went? Jonas hadn't ever heard. To the horizon, at least. There the world ended. No one had gone before – or at least no one had come back. Beyond was the outlands, the source of ghoulish tales, horrors that could quell even his sturdy heart, old as it might be. The setting sun rose off the waves of dust in a rush of heat that he could feel, even as he stood on the last hill with the wind in his face – a hot wind that stung the skin with the sand it bore. Even the glare the wastelands gave was a sore to the eye and he could not look at it for long. Now there came to him a dreadful thought that he had not considered before: how was he to make it in the desert at all?

The last rock was a single, free-standing spire of limestone that had probably stood there for a thousand years, at least, carved by time and weather until it was as a needle thrust to the heavens, the last guardian of the Frontier. One day it, too, would fall; one day the outlands would overtake the inlands and then all would be desert and waste, ash and thirst. Many people knew the Frontier was shrinking.

As he rode his horse around the north side of the last spire he spied it. And what a turn it gave him! He'd sometimes seen such things in charcoal drawings but he'd never been so far east as to come to the sea where he might have seen one for himself. Even a drawing can say only half of the truth, and neither could the tales fully depict what his eyes now witnessed. But he had no doubt: it was a ship that sat there against the rock with the wind from the outlands driving sand into its cracks and flapping its ragged sails like washing hung out to dry. It was sort of sitting up on its side, the prow buried beneath the waves of sand, the aftcastle and captain's cabin rising so high that even the keel at the stern rose up out of the earth. Someone might just have sailed it there, right into the earth, and left it — *might*, that is, have magically transported it from the sea, thousands of turns to the east, might have dumped it in the desert without any water to speak of, perhaps even with nothing more than a wave of their outstretched, crooked finger. Only wicked magic could do that.

With the day declining he was fastidious about where his camp for the night might be made. Not too *near* the ship, that was for certain, because even in the declining light of evening when he still could see it quite well the sight of it set in him a discomfort to look at it. Likewise, not too far from it, either, because in the wilds it is always safest nearest anything bigger than one's self — that is if one doesn't fancy becoming a dainty mouthful for some wandering coyote or jackal. On the other hand, if raiding wolves came from the wasteland, as they sometimes did, no place he could find would be safe enough. Now, as he stood on the edge of the outlands looking out onto the vast emptiness and knowing that when the sun came again he must continue, Fall-willing or no, it occurred to him that he might never find the way of the train again. The thought terrified him. But when he closed his eyes there it was. He was watching its red lanterns coming toward him, feeling the rails and ties beneath his feet shaking as if the very guts of the Frontier were turning themselves open at its coming. He knew he should step off the tracks but he couldn't: his feet were stuck fast in place, whether from fear or some other ill intention. It was only at the very last moment as he stood in the glare of its lamps and the roar of its fury upon the deep rolling *chugga-chugga* of its steam-powered wheels barrelling down upon him that he threw himself aside and landed quite hard upon the gravel embankment, the scream of its passing so close to his head that, for a moment, what with the deafening of the rumble, he couldn't hear it at all.

He awoke in a cold sweat. His little fire, the sort of fire that a lawless man learns to build on the Frontier when he does not want to be seen was all but coal and ash, hardly enough to keep his toes warm. Each night was getting to be colder than the last, but this was the chill of dread. The stars were burning bright though, and he could faintly see the shape of the last spire and knew that beneath it was the ship, black in the night, little more than a shadow. Then, from a very far off he heard a low cry on the horizon – a whistle, almost, the sound of a train or perhaps a wolf. "Jonas," he said to himself. "What might wont, but what might be is; but 'tis fine, and you know it, Fall-willing."

He pushed his bedroll back beneath his head: somehow the nape of his neck seemed to have found a stone. He touched the butt of one iron, just for reassurance, and went to sleep again with the cry of the jackals still quite far enough not to be of any bother but close enough that a deep sleep should never quite claim him before dawn. Just as he was drifting off once more he made up his mind that with first light he would search the hold of that strange, landed vessel to see what he might find, even if it turned out to be something very unpleasant, which he deemed more likely than not. And when he had searched it he must set out west for whatever lay beyond the wasteland – or die with his eyes to the sunset.

~CHAPTER SIX~
OF PROVISIONS AND SAILING SHIPS

When he first awoke the sun was not yet up. The horizon was greying and he could see that strange shape of the ship beneath the standing-rock. But the world was still drawing shadows. In from the wasteland came a wind in draughts so cold he woke stiff, even through his shirt and jacket. He felt for his guns, heard the nicker of the horse: it was tethered on the northern side of the rock, away from the wasteland and out of sight. He turned over once so that one eye was on the shape of the ship and the standing-rock, the other was on the eastern horizon. And then he drifted off to gain what little sleep he could before sunup, though never quite allowing himself to lose complete consciousness, as all gunrunners know just how to do.

When the sun finally did come over the Sundry Hills he arose quickly and remade his bedroll. Then, with his guns in their holsters at his sides, his luggage at his back and his hat pulled well down over his face he made off across the last blades of prairie grass he would probably see in a very long time, toward the ship.

When he was still some way off he could see her timbers were badly worn by the desert wind and sand but they surely once had been very beauteous and splendid, indeed, all clustered with barnacles and bearing the oily black of the deep ocean. Her bulwarks were carved in splendidly ornate detail, and at her prow was the masthead: the figure of a highborn daughter with hair swept back from her face, her arms thrown behind with the haste of the running vessel, her head cast back and her eyes closed and peaceful – wildly peaceful, in fact, as she was drawn into some new adventure. Jonas stood for a moment just looking up at her. Even with the wear of the wind and the sand and the sun working to fade the colour from the wood he thought she was the most beautiful woman he'd ever seen.

Because the nose of the ship was thrust down into the earth at the foot of the standing-stone, just as if it had come down from out of the sky, Jonas found himself not so much looking *up at* as looking *across to* the masthead. And so lovely and distracting was the lady carven there that he didn't at first notice the guns still standing at the ready in the bow gunports. But now he did, and he'd never seen anything like them before. Not

even the great guns that adorned the walls at
Fort Cardac were of any sort of commensurate
worth or prowess. These were large-enough that
he might've crawled inside one of the barrels
himself; and each gun had not one but three barrels at the points of an equilateral triangle, and
from the chains and gears he could even now see
Jonas supposed they might once have revolved as
they fired, perhaps so as to throw thrice as fast
as a single barrel and thus also allow for the silent tubes to cool, or perhaps so as to scatter the
shells that were thrown, he didn't know which.
But how he would have liked to climb up there
below the masthead and cling to the prow of the
ship as the air was broken by the thunder of the
guns. What a sound they would make!

As he went on around the larboard side of the
ship (the side which was lower toward the
ground as she lay a little to one side on her keel)
Jonas was not terribly surprised to see now that
there were many gunports in a row along each
gundeck, maybe even as many as fifty; and he
could see now that there were three such decks.
Each gunport had the cannon drawn to (and
loaded and primed, likely as not). It made him
wonder what battle her brave crew had been
ready for, and why had they found themselves
here, instead, on the edge of the desert. And then
he wondered even more: and where had they
gone to now?

What he really wanted was to get up into one
of those gunports. That way he could get onto the
deck of the ship and have a look around. He supposed if he could reach one he might just be able
to get in around the barrels. The question then

was how to get himself up to the porthole, for they were still maybe twice his height over his head.

The planks were smooth, fitted together and filled so tightly there weren't any handholds to be found; what holds there might once have been in the barnacles that adorned her sides were now smoothed away by the desert. But there was the frayed trailing end of a rigging line hanging down where the wind had blown it. He didn't know if it would hold him: it was eaten and rotted with the gnaw of the wasteland. But it was worth a try. He tested it first with a firm tug, just to see, and it felt sturdy. Then he tried his weight, and still it held. He took a deep breath, then up he went slowly, hand over hand, catching a footing on the planking where he could, which wasn't often what with the hull mostly lilting out over his head. His hands were hard and calloused and he didn't feel the bite of the rope, even a little. Once or twice the rigging line gave a long sigh as the desert wind caught him and set him to swing, the raw cords slipping across the bulwarks as he went. But it held true. And then he was at the lowest gunport and the big black barrels of the cannon were staring him in the face. In the gloom behind it he could see nothing: the sun was coming up on the other side of the standing rock and he was all in shadow.

The gun was sitting a little to one side. It had come free of its track. Owing to this, there was just space enough that he could slide himself in along one of its barrels when once he caught hold of the porthole. It was a stretch, and he tore his trousers and bashed the knuckles on his right hand before he fell with a crash and a sharp pain in his arm on the deck beneath the gunport.

It was dusty inside; the air was thick with it so that, for a moment, it was all he could do to keep from coughing. The crash had been loud enough and he didn't wish to awaken whatever dead things or terrible monsters might still be in the hold. He supposed the wind coming in from the wasteland had filled the portholes with dust, and it, in turn, had then collected on the floor which must now be what he was laying in that felt so soft, if not a little coarse.

What he really needed was a light.

His flint and tinderbox were tucked comfortably inside of his bedroll, and he now brought them out in the light of the gunport. A strip of his threadbare shirt would have to suffice for a torch, and it caught the spark quite easily when he had doused it lightly with oil from his box. When the light flared up and it donned on him what it was that was under his feet he nearly cried out in alarm. He *did* toss the burning strip of his shirt out the porthole, for it wasn't sand or dust beneath his feet but heaps and piles of gunpowder with many more unbroken kegs standing by quite close. He cursed himself for a clumsy fool for he ought to have known the smell of it at once for what it was. Oh, what one little falling spark would have done! He sifted the powder through his fingers; he held it up to the light of the gunport. There wasn't a speck of dust to be found in it, and how this could be when just beyond the gunport was the wasteland driving dust upon its winds ever over the Frontier he couldn't begin to guess. It was as smooth and as clear as the day it must have been milled. It was finer even than his own powder which he kept rolled up with his other things for refilling empty cartridges. He'd never seen such clean flour, and so he took another strip of cloth from his shirt and rolled up as much of the fine grain as he could.

There were many – perhaps hundreds – of kegs strewn all across the deck, some broken open, some still whole and stacked one on top of the other, lashed together and to the stanchion upon wood pallets. What wasn't tied down had slid toward the larboard, until they piled upon each other against the inner hull: powder kegs, iron chests of munitions, old dusty firearms, broken lanterns, a chair or two, and even a number of rusted falchions. But Jonas wasn't really interested in any of these. What he wanted was the stairs down into the hold because that, if there was any left, was where the supplies were stored. A couple strings of dried hams or venison would go a long way; and supposing there was even some stale bread and perhaps a lump or two of cheese and a little sugar. The thought drove a hunger into his gut like a worm into an apple.

He supposed the stairs would probably be mid-ship, next to the mast or maybe a little before it. Walking the deck in light with the vessel sitting up on one side would've been challenge enough, but walking it in the dark with broken kegs and other oddments lying about was treacherous. He tripped once or twice, and in spite of his best efforts he knocked his shins a good deal before he found the way. If a little light hadn't gotten in around the edge of the hatch that let out onto the second gundeck he supposed he might never have found it. Now, as he stood at the foot of the steps up and the top of the steps down, he wondered what it was that was stuck between the door and the last step. It might be just about anything from what he could see. Whatever it was it was quite large and rather lumpy. Up the steps he went on hands and knees until he could feel it, the old worn leather of a boot and beyond that a trousered leg. It was a man, now dry and nothing but skin and bone.

"Hullo," said the man. "Why are you tugging at my leg?"

Jonas started and nearly fell down the stairs. It was not the cold, empty eyes of a decayed man that were looking at him but the bright, blue eyes of a very-much-alive man, though a moment before he was certain they had been closed. Now they drew open and stared almost as emptily as they *should* have been.

"I think I've been killed," said the sailor. "Have *you* killed me?"

"I haven't," replied Jonas quickly.

" 'Twas a terrible thing," said the sailor with a shudder. "I remember it, I do. It came out of the east and went into the west."

"What was it!" cried Jonas feeling hot as if he'd just come from a fight with his heart racing; and he knew why: because of what the dead sailor was about to say.

"A demon-train!" he croaked, and his eyes became pale.

Jonas caught his breath. "Yes!" he cried, though he didn't really know why. "Yes, a demon-train! Do you know where it's gone?"

"How should I?" asked the sailor. "I think I'm dead."

Jonas searched the man up and down, looking at all his frail, rotted coattails. He felt sympathy but he wasn't sure why. He'd killed many men and even boys, and yet now he longed to be able to help but one. Perhaps it wasn't *so* bad, he thought. Perhaps it could be undone. But had he ever known any man who could undo death? Only wicked magic.

"I am, aren't I?" said the sailor. "I can see it in your face: I've been shot, or stabbed likely as not. I just . . . I just know it."

The mission that brought him into the landed ship (that strange vessel which was becoming less and less pleasant with each second) came back to Jonas' mind. "Is there any food still in the hold?" he asked quickly.

"I don't know," said the sailor. "Perhaps a little, what hasn't been baked by your cruel world. But you don't want to go down there. There's a demon in the belly, a frightful monster with red glowing eyes, cruel teeth, and a thirst for man's flesh. It's ate my mates, I'm sure of it! The captain, he'd know for certain if there's any food left. He was the only one who ever went into the hold. He never feared the beast. But I suppose he's dead, too."

"Not sure I believe in demons," said Jonas. "Wicked men, yes, but not demons."

The sailor sighed. "At least I tried to warn you." And with that and a creak of his weary bones he turned away and did not speak again.

Jonas crawled back down the steps until his feet were on the deck once more. Then he felt for the steps down, and down he went until the rough-hewn planks of the deck below were under his boots.

By some happy chance as he was groping in the dark at the last step he happened to bump his head upon a glass lamp hung from the hull strut. It was only fastened by a hook, and so he brought it down. Even in the dark he could tell it was quite full of oil and the wick fresh-cut. A spark from his flint caught flame, and by its light he could see now rows and rows of hammocks that hung perfectly still in the silence of the hold: he was on the berth deck.

Around he went and down again. The creaky steps made known his coming, the dust parted with his presence. Now he was right on the very lowest deck: the hold of the ship.

Oh, there were victuals aplenty, sure as anything! At both his right and left hand were storerooms filled with long strings of dried meats and vegetables still hanging from the rafters. On the floor were overturned chests, still latched. There were barrels, also, some bound, some loose, some broken, but when he turned them open he found them full of fishes dried and smoked in salt, potatoes, hams, turnips, cabbages – almost any kind of preservable food you could wish for. He could easily pack enough, he reasoned, to get him as far as his back would allow him to get; and of course if Darkfinger were with him now they might carry away twice as much and so feed two hungry fellows for more or less the same portion of time – or probably less.

He stumbled about in the dark for some time, the flame of the lamp only just lighting his way, and he collected as much as he could, bundling it in his things. He even found amongst the odd-ments scattered about the hold a few good bur-laps that time and wear had not done away with.

A good fright now found him when as he ven-tured farther into the hold he came upon a room that at first appeared empty, yet when he went inside he stumbled over the bones of a man lying amidst the floor. These did not speak or stir but lay there looking very wretched and miserable. And he was not the only poor fellow who had met his fate there: there were many corpses, all in iron manacles and tethered into the hull of the ship. A little farther on still he found the iron bars of a cage – a brig, rather: the ship's dun-geons; and beyond that was another, and then another, and in each the iron manacles of slavery and the bones of they who had died there.

At last he understood what this ship was about: it was a slave ship. He'd heard of such things, though never out here in the west. In the east, perhaps, there had once been slavers which took men's lives and sold them for silver *dahlers* across the sea. It was a wretched trade, honour-less, and the thought of it had never sat well with him. Even amongst runners there was one universal truth that everyone understood: men are born for freedom.

It would be best, he thought, if he finished his work and made good his escape. The musty stench of death and decay, an odour he had not noticed before now, was like a fire in his lungs, a revulsion that crept up inside and tried to take hold of him.

He'd all but forgotten about the demon as he searched the hold of the landed slave ship, his mind turned instead to food in his haste to resume the pursuit of the coach-train. But now he saw it as he was making his way back toward the stairs. He didn't know how long it had lain in the corner there, how long it had been watching him; but it was watching him now, its scarlet eyes unblinking in the dark, catching the light of the lamp. Not *a demon*, he thought; *it cannot be.* Some foul and dangerous creature, perhaps, but no demon.

His hands went to his guns at once, dropping the lantern to the deck in his haste, where the glass broke and the oil ignited in a gout of flame. He drew them free of their holsters in an instant; he pulled the hammers and waited. He breathed his prayer: the sacrament of the gunman, but his hand was neither steady, nor was his eye true. And the sound of the chambers of his guns turning in the perpetual shadows in the hold of that ship was loud, much louder than suited him. Every living thing for at least a hundred turns had heard it, said his delirious mind to him. Six rounds each; twelve rounds total: but would it be enough? He didn't know. It might take any number of shots to kill a single foe, if it had good luck and a thick hide, and if he couldn't shoot it through the eye. And then, with a horrified, wretched feeling in his gut he remembered taking the rounds from his right-hand iron before falling asleep, only just to check them to make sure that the powder hadn't got wet when he fell in the creek. But just as a clumsy fool might do he'd forgotten to reload them. Now, instead of twelve shots he was holding only six. And now that he thought about it that right-hand iron *did* feel a mite lighter than it ought. He should've noticed that at the first of the draw.

"Is that two irons you're holding, or just one?" asked the demon from the dark. "Ah, *'tis* just one, ain't it? One *good* one, anyhow. What's got you all up in a tizzy, laddy?"

Jonas caught his breath before it escaped and he let it out slowly. His heart was drumming like the hoof-falls of a running horse, like the thundering *chugga-chugga* of the coach. He'd heard of animals that spoke like men, true enough: a donkey had once spoken to its master, 'twas said, and then again an eagle had cried of the coming doom before the world fell into the shadow. But animals were liars, same as men, and unless there was an ass sitting there in the dark by the stairs then it could *only* be a man, a man with red eyes.

Or a demon, he had to admit. And was it only coincidence he had heard that very voice before but he knew not where?

"What's the matter?" it asked. "You've gone all pale like you've seen a ghost."

"I've seen nothing of the sort," replied Jonas, and his voice sounded like the frightened warble of some bird to his ears.

"Fearless men don't tremble," said the voice.

No, fearless men *didn't* tremble, Jonas agreed; but fearless men weren't the men who won wars, either: those were the men who trembled but still took the charge because in the end they were the men with honour.

"Fancy yourself a hero, do ya?" the voice conceded with a mark of scorn. "You know, lad, you got it all wrong, so ya do. You're running west to catch a coach but it ain't *going* west, you know, it's running the other way."

With this last remark Jonas' blood fell even colder than it had been, for the voice that spoke to him out of the gloom was none other than that of Jonas Arthur, himself. Whatever tremble had taken him before, whatever fear was in his blood, it now fell away to something much, much worse. It hadn't occurred to him he might actually be wrong, that the train might have turned around already. He'd been so definitively certain that it *was* going west, rails or no. And whatever it was that was in the darkness he wouldn't have called it a liar, not even himself.

"Anyway," it continued, "what you want *isn't* to catch it up, either, what you want is to go back east and join your boys again, knock off a few coaches, turn out a few banks: you know, the stuff you runner-boys do."

It *did* sound like good advice.

"Your fellow, Darkfinger, is lost for sure, anyhow, and your other man, Tucker, is turned a yellow-gutty coward. Charlie is dead, as are those brothers you were so fond of. And what is this train you're chasing? A phantom? A dream? Turn around, Jonas, I say, turn around and save yourself this trouble."

Turn around, yes, for Hembridge and Dodge. To lift gold once more. To run and gun. To be free of this burning *need* to follow the thing of his desire. He supposed he longed for that, aye. He supposed it was reasonable. In a few weeks he could have his feet up in a saloon in Dhill as he waited for the next coach.

But neither could he forget the cry of the train running over the hills, and what he said was, "I cannot turn away from my hopes and wants," though he hadn't meant it to be more than a thought.

"Can't? *CAN'T?*" cried the man – or demon. "Let me tell you what *I* can't do, oh man. I've lain in this dark for a thousand years without flesh to tear or the light of little eyes to watch as they fade from me. I can't feel the warmth of the wind nor the turn of the sea. I can't taste the iron of your blood!"

It was on him in a flash. He could feel its claws, feel its hot breath on his neck, see its smouldering eyes. Its wings were unfurled. It was laughing at him, hungry, ready to feed, and he couldn't stop it, it was so powerful. Its serrated incisors tore his shoulder with just a touch. He fired his gun but the light of those ghostly red eyes vanished before him and he knew he'd hit nothing but the cold, empty air and the underside of the berth deck.

Five more shots.

It was before him again, and he fired his gun. Again he missed.

Four shots left. Still he hadn't hit it.

He fired again.

Now three.

Now two.

Then none. And he was dead. He knew it. He saw it, like the light of the stars winking out before his own eyes.

Blam! Blam!

The echo of his gunshots in that narrow place reverberated in his head, and it wasn't until the silence returned that he realized they *hadn't* been his shots at all. The lights of those demonic eyes were vanished, and now the light of a pale lantern was flooding the stairwell.

"Jonas! Jonas?"

A thin, wavering shadow fell down the stairs. "Up 'ere!"

Jonas scrambled after, unable – unwilling – to take another look at what might lie in the darkness.

And there was Darkfinger, waiting on the stairs, the pale light of a lantern swinging gaily from his hand and the muzzle of his own gun glowing red in the dark, acrid with the smell of burnt powder.

"What'as *that*!" he cried, helping Jonas past the last step: his eyes were pallid, his face riveted upon the darkness of the hold.

"Not here, out in the light!" breathed Jonas. "Only in the light."

They made their way to the gunports, and then out they slid and dropped down to the ground. For a time they only lay in the sand that had blown up against the side of the ship, breathing hard and unable to say anything. Jonas' shoulder burned where the demon had bit him, though now he could see clearly that the wound was not as serious as it might have been, barely more than a scratch in the sun. Then, when the fear had fled him and the breath had returned to him, he at last spoke, and his voice trembled even now with the light of the sun and the cool of the morning. "It was a hungry demon,

I think," he said, "put there in the hold to guard the slaves of this ship. It urged me to turn back, Darkfinger, it urged and I nearly listened."

"Was that perhaps its purpose?" asked Darkfinger. "And what'as come about for the slaves, then? And the crew?"

"For its purpose I can't say. I didn't believe in demons until today," replied Jonas. "As for the other, the coach-train came. It came and set the captives free and slew they who held them."

"And I shot it? The demon?" Darkfinger exclaimed.

Jonas shrugged. "I don't know."

For a time they sat in the shade of the shadow of the slave ship for the sun was already climbing high and the heat was beginning to rise from the wasteland in quavering waves that set the horizon to dancing like ripples in a pool. And though in time those memories in the hold *did* fade Jonas never forgot the face of the demon.

In time Jonas said, "I've found food. I think it will get us a few days more, at least."

"Good," replied Darkfinger, "for I've lost mine."

~CHAPTER SEVEN~
THE WASTELAND

As they stood on the edge of the wasteland with the Frontier at their backs and the wiltering sand and sun of the end of the world before them Jonas knew he had always expected to stand here one day. It wasn't a conscious thought; it was something that went on in the back of his mind, like the puppeteer behind the curtain pulling the strings. The only thing that had *not* been in his vision was this slim, dark-haired, quick-trigger of a kid standing next to him, thumbs tucked into his gunbelt, his face still and unmoved. And Jonas had never imagined it would be the memory of a train and the cry of its whistle that would keep him moving forward.

Much of what had happened since their good-byes at the Sundry mining camp already was told from Jonas, but one thing still stood between them.

"How did you get out from under the hill?" he asked.

Darkfinger's tale was sinister and riddled with foul deeds. "Many turns it went down beneath the surface," said he with a shudder to recall those dark and cramped places. "There's a lake down there, a sunless black sea. The water on the shore is sickly and fish dart about, fish without eyes or mouths but great whiskers by which they feel for prey. And I knew I shouldn't let m'fall in, else mine skin would burn away, so poisonous was the water. But the tracks were laid right to the water's edge, and there's where I saw *them*."

"Saw *what*?" begged Jonas, intrigued.

"I don't know," said Darkfinger. "They were many and dead and sick and rotten. And they would've eaten me – certainly, 'twas not for want of trying that they didn't succeed. People I think they were once, but now they're dead and rotten. Green folk, pale-skinned and with lamp eyes. They et mine 'orse and one or two took a nip at m'fingers. And so I shot 'em, one by one, until m'guns were empty and I was the only livin' thing by that lakeshore."

"Gah!" said Jonas, which was supposed to mean *Ghastly!* but didn't come out right.

"And then I found a tunnel," said Darkfinger," and I followed it until I came to a place where a stream flowed in through a hole that was too small to get out by. But I kept by the waters, and then it came out on a nice little sunny bank over a quiet brook. And when I got to the stream I saw yer tracks and I followed 'em over the stones 'til I saw this 'ere ship standing against the wasteland."

"And it's well you did," replied Jonas. "I have always believed in the wickedness of men, Darkfinger, but I've never believed in demons. Yet they are very real, it would seem. I think I'd be dead now if it wasn't for you. You have undoubtedly saved my life *and* escaped your own dark travels."

"Now ye may well believe in demons," said Darkfinger with a rueful grin, "for we have both faced them and proved the better."

The remainder of that morning they lingered on the edge of the True Frontier, unwilling to venture into the wastelands with the sun so high and violent. There in the shade of a rock they smoked a little, and Jonas told stories, as men sometimes do when once they are met with someone with whom they think they would like to be friends but are not yet. He told of the runs he'd made, of the desperate escapes and the bloody gunfights. And Darkfinger, in turn, told of the south lowlands where the fields stretched to the horizon and at times if one stood at the top of the windmill on Crooked Lane one could even see the sea sparkling on the eastern rim. His voice was far away and wistful as he spoke.

In this way they were quite cool and well-rested, both men *and* Jonas' horse, too. And when evening fell and the cool was returned to the earth and the breeze they were not sore of the heat but quite disposed to be about their journey.

Darkfinger told Jonas one other thing which fascinated them both, and they would wonder for some time what, if anything, would come of it. "There was many tracks by the stream, b'sides yers, I mean," said he, "both 'orse and men. They followed yer trail for some way 'til ye came up 'nto the rocks and crags, and there, I think, whoever was following you found yer suit cold."

"You didn't see them, did you?" asked Jonas, hopeful.

"No," replied Darkfinger, "but I've little doubt for who it was: in every 'oofprint was the tri-star mark of Lord Quenn, and I caught their foul scent on the breeze. I even saw what I'm certain were the prints of Jake Weston's boots."

"Then we best make such speed as we can into the wasteland, when it is quite cool," said Jonas. "If they catch us here in the open with nothing but the desert at our backs I doubt even you could hope to get off enough shots to be of any worth. And then Quenn himself would see to our executions, likely as not. Won't be a second hanging, neither."

With the things they still had all bundled up on Jonas' horse (Darkfinger's gear, also, had been lost), they set out into the wasteland with the sun falling before them and the world growing cold behind them.

There wasn't much of anything that still lived in that land. A cactus or bit of scrub brush where the wind and the sun couldn't destroy it, perhaps, and from time to time they'd see some distant thing on the horizon, like a far-standing hill with the ruins of some fort built upon it. But these things always passed away behind or vanished before they could get close. It wasn't until the coming night was drawing the heat from the earth around them that they found anything much more than a rising boulder. And now the wasteland became a thing of much strangety, of pale, shifting shadows and queer lights in the sky that might have been stars but were not. In the dark of night and the moonlight the hills shone as if they were made of cut glass, and there were at times wind-made rises that were sharp and glistened like the pearly waves of some ocean current standing out fierce beneath the Silver Judge. There were sometimes even copses of trees and little thickets of undergrowth standing up like twisted fingers from the earth. But all were dead and withered away, and some, when they were close enough to see, were *not* the trunks and limbs of trees at all but the dead and drying bones of great beasts that had died with their faces in the sand and left their cold bones lying silver beneath the light of the moon as a testament of the hatred of the land that had claimed them.

When the moon was high and their feet grew weary with the march they began to wonder how much farther they might go before dawn. It was then that they saw the shape of a man walking before them at some paces. He kept perfect time. He was always with his back toward them and a long stick in his hand and a hood over his head.

"What is this stalking shadow?" asked Dark-finger, reaching even as he spoke for his holstered iron.

"Aye," replied Jonas. "A man? A stranger? But who would dare to walk these perilous paths but us?"

"Does he not see us?" wondered Darkfinger who was whispering despite himself. "Or *hear* us?"

"Check your chambers," suggested Jonas.

But a moment later the moon was covered for only a brief second, and when they could see quite well again the stranger was gone, vanished like a ghost into the darkness.

"It leaves me uneasy," said Darkfinger.

Jonas agreed, though he said nothing. Strange things sometimes happened beneath the waning moon. One could trust the Judge, for he was strong and true, but he was marching on now about his own errands and soon it would be the Harvester that stalked the endless marches of the sky.

Not long before dawn came they found a sheltered trove between a rock and a stand of deadwood into which at some time long gone some wayward traveller had pushed two heavy-bound chests of cedar, both now rotted and empty. But the ground was dry and comfortable, and so they lit up a fire with the rotted wood and cooked some breakfast. And then, with the sky growing pale in the east, Jonas spread out his bedroll and Darkfinger made his own bed on the sand. Jonas kept the first watch, both his guns loaded and with spare cartridges nestled in a cleft in the rock. But they found little rest during the heat of the day. Even in the shade of the rock the sands of the wasteland returned the sun in suffocating waves from the earth.

Before high noon Jonas knew his horse wouldn't be with them much longer. It'd grown weary, and a day or two more on the hard face of the wasteland with nothing to eat but dry twigs wouldn't lend it any strength.

The day or so that followed were hardly any different. They journeyed on by night and also in the cool of the afternoon and morning, if they could; but when the sun climbed high it became quite treacherous to tread the empty wastes and they sought refuge from the heat. On the third day the horse could go on no more and so Darkfinger shot it with one of his *darkiron* shells, saying even as he did so, "Farewell brother; thank ye for yer sacrifice," as he laid its head down in the sand.

For perhaps a moment Jonas had some misgivings about leaving such a quantity of raw meat to spoil in the sun; but when it came down to it he wouldn't have touched the flesh of such a beast who'd given its life for him, not even to spare his own.

The next day they were wearier and hungrier than ever, and they found no shade; so they buried themselves in the sand where it was cool and covered their heads with their own jackets.

They were nearly a week and a half in the wasteland when they saw the stranger again, pacing along ahead of them in the light of the moon, never turning, never looking back. This time Darkfinger drew both his guns, and Jonas called out, "Aye, stranger from afar, do you bring news from out of the wastes?" But when the moon passed again behind a cloud and came out once more there was nothing to see but the endless glassy shifts of sand. It gave them an ill feeling, as if trouble was upon them.

The next day the sun burned like a crimson furnace in the sky, and when night fell it was much colder than any they'd endured yet. They didn't dare to stop, not even for a moment. The Autumntime was coming, likely as not, Darkfinger said, and much sooner than they could've reckoned. And sure enough that night the Judge did not show his face, but on the night that followed it was the gold of the waxing Harvester that pushed himself over the southern horizon. Another twenty-two days would bring the rising of the Harvest Moon.

To make their troubles worse still, the next night they saw for the first time the itinerant raiders that had so troubled the town of Drayton. By moon they came, first from a good way off and with harsh cries. Darkfinger fired off six shots but they couldn't tell if he'd hit anything. But then, like feral wolves, the wasteland marauders came out of the dark, with wicked, ugly faces and voices like rabid animals, riding great horses and shaking spear, sword and bow in their ebony fists. Jonas shot and killed three, and Darkfinger two (that is they saw the bodies felled but when they arrived at the place there was nothing to be found but dark blood in the sand). Once or twice they were beset on foot and it came to blows. Both were scratched, and Darkfinger even had a very serious cut beneath his eye, a cruel, nasty thing from the blade of his foe, but it healed in a day or two and nothing came of it. In the end the savages left wailing into the dark and they didn't return that night.

The first and second week passed into the next, and though they'd rationed their food and water for fear they'd soon run out, now their fears became reality: they had perhaps a few dried vegetables, a salted pork or two, some dried fish, and a few stale pieces of rumcake still in their bags, everything else had been eaten. When these things, too, were gone they would starve. Another day or so they could persist, Jonas supposed, but not more.

The next morning the sun rose on their weary travels, glittering across that glassy land of dust and hard rock, and they saw in the distance a hill that was no mirage. At the crown, with a little pathway leading up to it, was a house whose timbers were weathered and greyed and whose chimney was broken and crumbling. The walk was all smooth stones and worn earth from heavy travel, but there was nothing behind the dusty panes that stared out at them. It was a *bleak* house, standing very much at home amidst the dry, empty, trackless wastes of the desert. It became no *less* real when they stood before it as when it had been from afar.

Jonas cupped his hands about his face so as to block out the glare of the sun and pushed his nose up to the grimy windowpane.

"Do ye not see anything?" whispered Darkfinger.

"No," answered Jonas. "Nothing."

"Mayhap it's deserted," suggested Darkfinger.

"Not with smoke in the chimney," replied Jonas without turning or looking; he must have seen the smoke when from afar, he thought.

"Smoke?" asked Darkfinger, stepping back so-as to see the chimney. Sure enough there was a curl of grey issuing forth from the red, cracked bricks.

"We should keep going," said Darkfinger.

And it almost seemed to Jonas that it was the only sensible thing to do. But what he said instead was "*What*, and not go in? There may be preserves, and we shall need them if there are." His voice was incredulous, a sound strange to his ears. Then at once it was the only reason to him: he was no coward.

Darkfinger did not reply. He looked ashamed. "Yes," he said at last.

"After you, then," said Jonas. But what good was it to step over that dusty old threshold?

And so the Kid set his boot to the door, and though the hinges were strong the latch was not and it broke from the frame. In went the Kid with his guns in hand, and Jonas followed after as the door banged against its stop.

But it was indeed empty – at least they neither met nor saw anyone there on the threshold save a starved, bedraggled mange-of-a-cat that skittered out of their path. Jonas nearly shot it for his heart leaped into his throat at the sight.

"See? No one," said Darkfinger.

"The cellar, then," said Jonas.

The door they found behind the musty kitchen. They had to cross the silty boards, past countertops and cupboards thick with dust. The discarded oddments of kitchenware were years in disuse, Jonas thought, and lay scattered on the floor. Chair and table, too, were broken and ruinous, and a pantry-shelf had fallen against the cellar door. For good measure they looked inside the old and battered closet when they had stood it upright, but it was empty.

The door into the cellar was neither locked nor rotted, and it opened at Jonas' touch. Beyond was only the forlorn black that accompanies all such crypts and vaults. But when they had fashioned a torch of the leg of the table and doused it with oil from Jonas' box, even the most stolid shadows were chased away.

The cellar was small and much emptier than they had hoped, save for the dust that, as with the rest of that house, had collected on every surface. The only oddments to be found there were holes dug in the dirt floor, holes the size and shape to fit a man of even height. And as Jonas now looked he thought that perhaps not all these tombs were empty. Two still contained the desiccated remains of those for whom they'd been delved. They were both faces familiar to him, that of a young boy and the other of an aging gunman. And the sight brought to him both the memory of the empty eyes of the sailor lying dead aboard his ship and the cold fear of not knowing what it is one faces.

"Darkfinger, look there—" he was saying, but even as he stood in transfixed dread the light went out and he was alone in a sea of shadow.

Panic is always the first response under such circumstances, but a runner trains himself in vigour to bypass this and go instead to the next. And so, though his knees knocked and his hands shook, Jonas did nothing but wait. At the first the demons of his past were paraded before him like some sick mummer's farce. He saw a boy in

Whistletoe who longed to run and gun; he saw his hands bloodied in his foolish need to become a man; he saw the horrors spread before his eyes, both then and now. And just as he had suspected all along he might, he heard them speaking in familiar voices.

"Three's my number, true enough," said the voice of Charles Getworth. "The number I needed, the number I got. Three in my belly, three in my head."

"Was that slimy ol' gunny Arthur," said the other voice, that of Lenant Johnson, Charlie's then closest friend and consort. "Might be he didn't pull the trigger but he landed the shots, just the same."

"Speak nothin' ill of the man," replied the voice of Charles, though even now it was morphing into that of another. "He's as innocent of the matter as you are. Henry Dalton shot 'im, that's the one, shot 'im dead—" Now the voice was truly changed, and it was that of Darkfinger himself which finished: "—I did, killed the great Charles Getworth cause he thought he might be faster'n me. I'd shoot ye dead, too, Jonas Arthur, if ye think ye can best me."

"Darkfinger!" cried Jonas, heedless of his own reality: that but a moment before the voices had changed, and voices had no right to do that but in one's own head. "Darkfinger, where are you?"

"Here—" came the voice of the Kid. "Over here, Jonas," it came from another direction, echoing to him now. And then, simpering, "Jonas, this blighted quest must be the death of us. Surely, ye know this t'be true. Must ye kill me, as ye have let yer friends die? Dead, or left behind."

110

As the Kid spoke Jonas found he could see palely by some sourceless light the face that said the words but it wasn't that of Darkfinger, it was the boy he'd shot in Drayton. The moon was kissing the side of his face as his complexion turned ashen with surprise, his hands even then groping at the hole that had opened in his chest and the blood that flowed down his belly.

"Least ye did it clean," said the boy in the voice of Darkfinger the Kid. "If ye're going to traitor me, Jonas, at least see that I don't hurt nothing more, please, I beg ya."

As the voice of Darkfinger was speaking, though Jonas had been wrapped in fear, sooner or later even fear becomes mundane, and now he edged himself by little to where the stairs must surely be. There he felt the first tread and he crawled deftly up and to the next, intent on leaving behind whatever foul thing was dwelling in that dreadful vault. But when he had climbed half the way to the cellar door the groan of the steps beneath him brought him to a stop and his heart came again into his throat. But he mayaswell have kept going for all the good it did, for next the rotted wood gave way with a shriek and he found himself lying again on the cellar floor.

"Not tryin t'leave me, too, as ye left all yer other friends behind, are ye?" whinged the voice of Darkfinger – or was it Charlie? He could no longer tell the difference. And there were others he thought of, too, as he lay in the earth, others he'd left behind. Others he'd abandoned.

Turn around, Jonas, said the demon. *Go back the way you came.* And it was true, that would've been the easiest. The safest, even.

111

But he couldn't, not now, not even if Darkfinger begged.

He had to get out.

Frantic, he pawed at the ruin of the stairs but there was no way now that he could have climbed it in the dark. And as he lay, resigned to his own miserable end, he felt their cold and clammy hands on his shoulders and neck, groping, pawing. It wasn't the end he would've asked for, not the one he sought. What hope was there, lying in the cellar of a house that all else had forgot?

There was a terrific banging and clangor above him now which brought him from his misery once more. He couldn't have guessed what it was but at once there came the sound of splintering wood and the door of the cellar was thrust open. *Darkfinger!* Jonas thought at once. It had to be – not the dead voice of the Kid that rasped in the dark but the true, real, honest man. A hand was let down to him, and by the dim light of the door he rushed for it and took hold, clawing, desperate to be free of that place. Up he came and into the light, born of a strength he'd not known the Kid possessed. But it wasn't Darkfinger the Kid who stood before him. Rather this person had drawn a hood over his face and he was robed in grey. But it was the flesh of his face and his hands that alarmed Jonas more than anything, for they were stony and coarse, as earth that is baked beneath the sun.

The stranger said nothing, neither in recognition nor reprise. He was rough in his manner as he was in his flesh, and he led Jonas swiftly from the kitchen to the common room, and from there to the hall and the foot of the attic stair. Still he said nothing, but his outstretched finger made known the door above, and Jonas didn't doubt that he alone was meant to open it, though he was terrified of what he would find.

Up he went, nonetheless, and he pushed open the door with a *creak* of it rusted hinges. Beyond was a pale dimness, though not dark, for at the far end of the attic was a narrow window that let in the light. And in its shaft Jonas couldn't mistake the shape of Darkfinger standing still in rapt captivation. What the Kid saw or perceived he couldn't know, but it seemed to him that his flesh was alive as with maggots writhing in the disgusting dominance of death over life. "Darkfinger!" he called softly. "Darkfinger, to me. Quickly!"

Darkfinger made no move, not even to turn his head.

"Darkfinger, it's I, Jonas," he called again.

Now the Kid gave over and brought his eyes to bear, but it was deliberate. Yet when he had Jonas almost wished he *hadn't* for his eyes were alive with the worms that were devouring his soul, and the horror on his face was terrible to see.

When all else is naught just listen, Charles had once told Jonas. And while listening would do little good here for himself, for Darkfinger it might be the only thing left. And so Jonas drew one of his guns and he threw the hammer and the trigger in the calm of the still attic. The shot was deafening. It rang in his ears and for a time he could hear only the silence it left behind.

"Darkfinger!" he cried yet again. "Hurry! Quickly!"

113

And now the Kid shook his head as one does when awakening from a dream. At once his face was changed from transfixion to the fear that Jonas himself felt, but he lunged across the attic floor, just the same. Down the steps they both ran, no longer eager to see the inside of strange houses in strange places. They didn't rest until they were once more in the common room. There the haggard rasp of their breath was overshadowed by footsteps in the corridor. From around the corner came a young girl. She might've been anyone's daughter, might've been anyone's friend, but when she walked it was on legs that shook as if broken and sometimes on all fours like the mangy cat which had crossed their path at the door, skittering and twisting. When she turned her eyes to them they were large and round like eyes that stare and see nothing but terror for too long and then become accustomed to both terror and darkness so that is all they see. When she spoke it was with the *hiss* of a snake. "F-ffry-iteful mee-*sss*!" said she. "W-what-a to-doo-*sss*!" She outstretched two shaking fingers on each hand, looked at them each, and then a grimace widened across her face until they could see each of her broken teeth.

Darkfinger drew and levelled his guns, but those *darkirons* that had always been so steady now shook a little.

"Who-*sss* . . . me?" asked the girl. "Have you *sss*seen mee*sss* . . . kitty? I've loss-*sss* it and I don't know where to find-*sss* it-*sss*! If you'd be so kind-*sss* . . . Kitty! Kitty? Mamma's gonna make-*sss* a nice-*sss* saucer of you!"

Jonas bit his tongue. Darkfinger narrowed his eyes and his hands shook less. The shadows seemed heavy in that place, as if the sun had suddenly been dimmed, though the common room was well-windowed. Jonas could feel it just as he had in the hold of the slave ship.

"Don't like my friends?" asked the girl. "Don't like what they have to say? Terribly lonely. But they keep good company. You should listen."

"Their words are lies," Jonas heard Darkfinger say – the true, real Darkfinger this time.

"Well," said the girl in a dithering voice, "if you don't like them . . . then GET OUT!" She shrieked, her childish face gone suddenly wide-eyed and vicious, her snarl more fierce than any Jonas had chanced to see before. And it seemed to him that a sharp, cold gust of wind took him in the face with her words.

But then, as suddenly as she had changed, she was once more as she was. *"Lalah tralah . . . lalah!"* she sang, and she turned and skipped away through the back door which fell to behind her with a dreadful *crack!*

"Get *out!*" whispered Darkfinger then, his voice and his courage gone. "Get *out*, Jonas, get ye out *now!*"

And they did. Perhaps it was some whisper in the air, perhaps some gentle touch that never wants to be seen, but they felt it and they knew it. They leaped over the broken door, and with guns in hand, their hearts beating quick and the daylight strong around them, they turned at once on that lonely, old house with the desert all around, ready for anything.

But there was *nothing*. They couldn't even now hear the laughter of the little girl.

"I don't know what that was," gasped Dark-finger through trembling lips, "but it *'twas* evil, really, terribly evil. We must go at once! Whatever happened in the ship, whatever you saw, I know my bullets don't kill demons, Jonas."

There was no argument, and so they turned about and made west once more, passing that house at a wide berth and not looking back, not even once. Neither wanted to speak of that place nor what they had seen within. It wasn't until much later they discovered that the Lonely House had once been a waystation for those travelling the rails, but in recent years the wasteland had swallowed many things, and not all had been lost – not really.

~CHAPTER EIGHT~
BEYOND THE WASTELAND

They were a little and not altogether un-pleasantly surprised to find that beyond the Lonely House the desert was much *less* desert and more the hard land of the Frontier once more. "Could we'ave come to the end of the wasteland so soon?" asked Darkfinger, for he was eager for a sight other than the rise and fall of glassy hills. But in truth they didn't know what lay beyond. It did *feel* soon. Perhaps it was only that the wasteland was eternal to the minds of them who had never been beyond the Sundry hills; or perhaps the Lonely House had served to thrust the hardship of the weeks already spent in hunger and toil on the sand and heat from their minds. Now they marched on across dust and gravelly hills littered with desert shrubs, sage,

117

and spiny deadwood that grew in their path like the fingers of death itself still so wantonly trying to claim the dry ground. They supposed then that it made sense if they now should stand upon the westernmost edge of the wasteland, for who would build even a haunted house in the desert? Here on the edge there may once have been life. If the winds prevailed in the west then here on the edge things might one day grow – *might*.

In spite of the climbing day they pushed on, unwilling to rest so near that dreadful home. And anyway, the heat of the wasteland was falling behind them now. About midmorning a skiff of cloud came in from the west to shade their travels, a welcome relief, true enough. Not long after they began to notice a thin layer of haggard grey rising out of the horizon like a mist, still perhaps many days' journey before them. Neither could doubt what it was: mountains, real, honest, blue mountains, probably covered in heather and willow-downs and short alders and hemlock, aspen and willow and birch and beech in the low places. Even the thought brought cheer to their hearts because they both remembered years past when they'd journeyed east of Dodge where all roads wind through the Sleepy Mountains. For Jonas those were fond memories.

Yet another pleasant and unsought-for surprise came when the sun was climbing to noon. They stumbled upon a set of iron rails that rose up out of the earth and ran on ahead of them toward the mountains without breaking or turning away to follow some other course. In spite of the ground in which they'd been laid, the ties were whole and the spikes still firm: lying in the dry sand of the wasteland had served to preserve them.

Darkfinger once voiced his supposition that a coach might've passed by recently. He noted the manner in which the dust had been blown from the way of the train. "I guess we follow in the path which has been prepared for us," he said; and Jonas didn't object.

When the day fell the mountains still seemed no nearer. And when they collapsed next to the rails in the low shelter of a shallow hollow in the ground Jonas wondered how far they might actually have come and how far still they had to go. They gave themselves over for weariness for some hours and arose again still quite fatigued before dawn to push on in the twilight.

When the sun arose at their backs in a dazzling array upon the eastern rim, reinventing life in the wasteland, the mountains seemed to have crept suddenly upon them in the night and now stood at a good distance, no longer a smudge on the horizon. They could make out individual valleys and peaks, some of the latter capped in white. "Two days," supposed Darkfinger; and he was probably right.

They followed the rails. There didn't seem to be any other reasonable thing to do. And when, on the morning that followed, only just as the sun's first flicker came upon the horizon Jonas heard the faraway cry of a train, he couldn't be turned aside. "It's near, Darkfinger!" he cried; and he wouldn't rest.

It was in fact two days from that moment when they two stood in that hard land of hills that grew steadily higher and sharper before them and looked up at the grey mountains standing like a line of jagged teeth. They were in the very shallowest foothills now, and it might be all that night and the next morning, too, before they came upon the lowest valleys where streams came out and were drank by the desert. This was their chief concern, as their own water was in very short supply and what they *did* have had become quite stale in the heat of the wasteland sun. There at the foot of the mountains good water would run like wine, as fine and as satisfying as the heartiest laughter.

There weren't just rails and ties anymore running through those hills; they came now upon several roads that ran this way and that, crossing the rails sometimes, or at others running along parallel with them. Once or twice Darkfinger thought they might follow one of these to see where it would lead but Jonas wouldn't hear of it, so great was his desire to catch the train. Now more than ever he was certain it was only just before them.

It was still a fairly well-placed surprise when they came quite suddenly just about sundown on a platform and rail-station standing right next to the tracks. A road came from the north, and another from the south, and there they joined with the rails. But the station was empty. All the glass in the windowpanes had been knocked out. The old office and lobby smelled of emptiness, forlorn, and mold. And Darkfinger said there was a hatred lurking there, too. "Like in the Lonely House," he said. He didn't want to look farther, but he consented to waiting at the door while Jonas poked about in the empty office. The desk was overturned and filthy, the lashings of the chair all rotted away. Desert hounds had made their home there once, leaving behind fur and pellet; but these, too, had moved on. Pictures on the walls now were so badly faded he couldn't have said what vision they once told. The strong-box was torn open, and whatever secrets it had concealed were coveted away. But something was in that place, something drawing him.

At last Jonas found it: a floorboard that creaked beneath his weight and easily came free when it was pried. He lifted it up, and there in the space beneath the joists was a little metal box with lid and latch but no lock; and when he opened it, inside was a long, cruel knife with an ugly face like a demon engraved upon the handle. There were also strange markings upon its blade, runes which showed nothing in the dim light of the dusty office but Jonas found he could read quite well when he held up the blade to the light in the window. What those letters said he could never afterward recall. Darkfinger wouldn't look at it, said it was filthy and wretched. And when Jonas did he, too, had the most dreadful feeling, as if something were crawling beneath his skin, trying to get out. In the end he put it back and didn't touch it again, for it brought to him memories of the slave ship and the Lonely House, and neither were things he was fond to recall.

As he knelt once more over the smuggler's cache beneath the old scuffed flooring, the knife in hand, Jonas found now he was loathe to relent the weapon back to its resting place as he knew he must. For a time he hesitated, engrossed by its crude design. *Take it for your own*, said his thought to him. *You have need of a new blade.*

The truth was that he hadn't any need of it, for he had his own stout knife at his belt, a tool he'd melded himself more times than he could number.

But the urge was there, nonetheless, however he turned it in his mind.

It was only at the last, and with a tremendous effort, that he let it down into the cache and turned away; and in the end he was glad of it, for even as a boy he'd heard tell of weapons imbued with strange qualities which lent them dangerous properties, and once he'd seen one for himself. Who knew what evil he might've brought on their quest had he kept it to himself.

They were a little sorry to turn their backs on that solid roof and the walls that kept the wind from tearing at their clothes. But in the end they had to, and the thought of that wicked face in the hilt of the knife, its eyes now alive in Jonas' memory, kept them from looking back.

Night was falling and the mountains were still much too far. So they pressed on into the evening, walking at first by the feel of the rail-ties beneath their feet and then by the glimmer of the crescent moonlight on the iron rails themselves when the hour of darkness had passed. On they went, well into the night, until they thought they could go no farther. And as there was no rock or hollow to make their camp under or in they laid their gear next to the rails and pulled their jackets well up over their heads to keep out the wind.

Sometime in the night Jonas was awakened. At first he didn't know what had disturbed him, and yet he thought his dreams had been getting more and more excitedly queer. There were footsteps so close that he could feel the ground trembling. His hand slipped to his gunbelt which was laid at his head, and he sat up, all in a hurry, drawing the hammer and casting about in the dark for whatever it was that moved as a thief. But there was nothing, save the silently sleeping form of Darkfinger.

Much later he seemed to awaken again, as if from a dream, and for a moment he thought that the first had been the dream. But then he knew it hadn't. Then he thought that perhaps *this* was, for there was a fire burning about ten paces from him, and in its light he could see the shape of a man hunkered on his heels with his arms wrapped about his knees. His eyes were bright and his hair was silver. By this token alone it was not the Kid, but Jonas didn't know who it might be. There were even irons at his sides. "Who are you?" Jonas called, the thought of his own guns no longer coming to his mind for there seemed to be no danger.

"I am the Traveller," said the stranger. "I am the Walker. I am the Trainman. I'm going west, you know. I have been for a very long time."

"Have you lost your train?" asked Jonas; and it seemed a very good question, though he didn't know why.

"I've lost much more than that," replied the man. "I'm searching for it, though, you know. I'm looking and looking and one day I'll find it."

"*Where* will you find it?" Jonas asked.

The stranger smiled a bright, warm, friendly smile that made his eyes dance, and he said, "I don't know, but if you want to follow me, I'm going *this* way."

This time Jonas woke up and he knew he'd *not* been dreaming. Nor had the stranger been anything but that same silent person who'd drawn him from the cellar of the Lonely House, he could not doubt it.

The sun was just rising beyond the eastern rim of the wasteland. He got up and walked both north and south as far as he could without losing sight of the tracks and Darkfinger's sleeping figure. There only just to the north of the rails was the remains of a small campfire and two sets of footprints which came from the east, stopped by the fire, and then continued on westward. At the sight of this he shook a little, but in the end he returned to Darkfinger and awoke him with no news of what he had seen. Darkfinger sat up with a start and a look of bewonderment in his eyes, and he said, "Bless ye, Jonas, ye've just awoken me from such a confounded dream!"

"The sun is coming up," said Jonas. "We should be on our way now."

They ate the last of their provisions and drank the last few drops of water in their canteens. And then, empty-jugged and empty-walleted, they turned their eyes toward the mountains and made westward.

All day they went on, hardly stopping, hardly *daring*, for by evening their hunger was returning like a fire and their thirst along with it could not be quenched. Round about four o'clock or so by the sun they *did* stop at a hanging-rock where

Darkfinger pointed out a flowering desert plant on the ground whose petals were good to eat, save for their sharp spines. There wasn't anything like enough, though it tasted quite badly, but they both had as many as they could pull from between the iron-barbed thistles. Then they went on once more.

When they had been walking for perhaps twenty minutes beyond the hanging-rock, the day was declining into the west behind the mountains and Darkfinger exclaimed, "Hullo, what's this?"

Jonas looked, and there ahead of them the hill had risen up quite sharply. Beyond it, with the setting sun still glaring at them through the peaks, they could see the high, forested slopes, ridges, and valleys of the mountains. The nearest spur seemed to come right out into the wasteland toward them. It was from this that the hill-cutting rose up, and there, right before them at the base of the hill with the tracks running right up to it was a long waterway complete with wheel and sluice and a set of narrow tracks emerging from the mountainside by which miners once long ago had hauled ore. Now all was silent, save for the little stream of water which still poured from the end of the sluice box and into the ground where the dry detritus swallowed it.

"Oh, sweet January!" cried Jonas, stooping at once to collect what he could in his hands. It was terribly cold and thrilling and it went down like fire to his parched throat. But it was good, he could not deny.

When he had drank his fill from the little waterfall there at the base of the sluice box, Darkfinger had his; then they filled their canteens until they could fit no more, drank again, and were quite satisfied.

They saw now that there were many roads going this way and that about the mountainside, even running in switchbacks into the steepest places. Many were so broken and ruined by rain and moving earth that they were little more than paths to walk upon. Most ended in the black, gaping mouths of mine shafts. Some went so high they could see no end; some went nowhere at all.

It was the tracks that they were most interested in still, for these went straight on before them through the ruins of the little town that had once stood around that place. There they vanished into the side of the hill.

"What does this mean?" asked Jonas.

"Ho, see the timbers?" said Darkfinger. "Once a tunnel was cut into the hillside and the tracks went on through it, but now it's fallen in upon itself and all you can see are a few logs sticking from the rock. We can follow it no farther."

It was a disheartening sight. Who knew where the way might have led them? But it was stolen away and they could not go that way. "It has gone beyond my reach," Jonas muttered, disconcerted.

"The coach?" asked Darkfinger.

"Aye, gone," replied Jonas. But the coach was not all, he realized.

Darkfinger looked away up the side of the mountain, up the nearest valley where the cuttings could be seen for some way before they vanished into the shadows of the evergreens and the heather beyond. "We might yet follow it," he said reservedly. "These mountains go right up to the sky, I'll warrant, but someone has gone before and they've left a path to guide us. Why shouldn't we follow? We've been in the desert f'days, and our food is gone. Mountains is what we need. Who may know what lies beyond? An adventure. Perhaps even an end."

Jonas considered this a moment. He looked up at the hills and the valleys carved by streams, at the heights capped in snow, at the wild, untameable places where anything might happen, where any danger or monster or demon might be waiting; then he looked back at the wasteland, at the True Frontier now so far behind them, at his home. They'd already gone beyond the edge of the world. They'd already left so far behind anything familiar, anything safe. But then, had his life ever been safe?

The adventure is before, said the voice of the stranger in the night – only now it was in his head. *Come and take it with me, Jonas. Leave everything behind, and come this way with me.*

At that moment there came on the wind a faraway sound, so high, so shrill, so indistinct that it might have been the cry of an eagle or the wind in the trees or some deep groan of the mountain – or it might've been the whistle of a train; and that Jonas thought more likely. It came down from out of the mountains, and then the earth seemed to tremble with the steady *chugga-chugga-chugga* as it pushed its way up some distant slope.

127

Jonas looked back at Darkfinger. "Irons fitting for the journey," he said, "and shells we've few, though more might be cast if we find the time."

"Water in the mountains, rain in the valley," added Darkfinger with a grin and a touch of his forefingers to the *darkirons* at his sides. "Where there's water a man can go."

"Then on we go," said Jonas. "To whatever end we might meet."

~CHAPTER NINE~
THE ABANDONED MINES

As they stood at the foot of those mountains that seemed to be as much a part of the sky as the earth, they quarrelled about whether they shouldn't perhaps have a closer look at the ruinous mining camp. Jonas thought they ought, thought they might find something of use; but Darkfinger said in the end that, what with the state of things and the obvious years that had played on the rotting timbers, they weren't likely to find anything of use at all. Though they might find for themselves a broken leg or neck. Jonas had to agree for time was precious seconds now to both of them and they were eager to make for the heights. And anyway, there might be almost anything lurking in the darker corners of the mines that dotted the hillside, almost anything at all. Who could know? Better to be high in the foothills before darkness came down.

As they went on about their way, Darkfinger said, "I might be able t'take a nice spot in the heather over this tumble of rotten timber. Somewhere with water and fire."

"And food," added Jonas despondently. "Maybe something with fur or feathers roasting on a spit. Even something green would be better than this." He'd begun to ache in his gut, a culmination of days with near to nothing to eat.

So they gathered themselves and made for the start of the road that climbed into the hills.

There were even more mineshafts than they'd at first suspected. Every few turns or so they found the rotting timbers of some picker's hole jutting from the earth. Oftly the hills had come down to hide the entrances, but sometimes these black doorways would yawn vacantly at them, the supports still holding on desperately to their former strength, now so nearly given out.

"These are only the foothills," said Darkfinger in wonderment looking up at the darker heights above. "It's up there that the *real* mineral is." Jonas knew nothing of mines or where to find minerals, and if Darkfinger knew any such thing Jonas never knew how he had learned it.

"Do you think the road goes right over the top?" asked Jonas distractedly: he was still thinking of meat turning on a spit, grisled and dripping. Neither he nor Darkfinger had ever been so high in the mountains before.

"*Something* does," replied Darkfinger in agitation.

They went for some time on the bare, lower slopes where the trees must once have been felled away to make room for the little mining camp. There were only stunted alders and prickle-nuts now spreading sparsely amidst the low Great Willow-herb that browned the hillsides with its dead blossoms. Grass and heather pushed up through rotting branch and stump. It wasn't at all unpleasant, even when once the hill became steep and the road less prominent. But then they came to the treeline that surrounded the ruinous mining camp, and though the road continued upward, it was mostly overgrown with underbrush and thick firs. They left the road then, cutting northward across the side of a gully, then turning to scale a gush of loose stone; and there they came up over a rising ridge invisible to their eyes from below. Now they were up and over it they couldn't see from whence they'd come. The camp was gone from sight and most of the wasteland along with it. They could only just make out the far horizon in a cloud of grey and silver with the setting sun making long shadows of every swell and gullet.

In a low in the ridge they found again the wending road, loitering for a time amidst the Blue Mountain Pine before it made on with its brutal ascent. Up this way, down that way they went, until it was nearly twilight beneath the trees. Then the foothills ended and the real climb began, a steep, arduous trail of loose scree held in place by shrubbery or boulders that wouldn't sustain their weight. A mountain stream came down through a particularly close and narrow valley, and the road went back and forth, back and forth, marching up the side, cutting right through the thinning forest, through balsam, hemlock, alder, low bushes sparkling with bright red berries and much lower bushes with dusty blue berries. Occasionally the twitter of a bird or the chitter of something much furrier would come to them from close at hand.

They were perhaps halfway to the height of the valley when the trail ceased its march back and forth and cut instead straight up the mountainside, so steeply that at some time a stream had come down and carried away the dirt leaving only hard stones to step on. And from there it was always climbing quite precipitously up grass and heather, through brush and bramble and places where the bushes sometimes had the white cotton-fur of some mountain animal tangled in them. Sometimes there were little rockslides that came down through the trees and they'd have to step across them without disturbing the loosely piled stones. Once in his excitement Darkfinger stepped too heavily and too quickly and had to spring away before the stones on which he'd only just been standing were carried down the mountain in a thundering cascade.

Jonas began to feel weary and drawn now. I say *weary* because it wasn't exactly a tiredness: he'd been farther than anyone he knew, save Darkfinger, and he'd rustled more cattle, taken more trains and banks than any other runner west of Dodge City. And yet the climb was doing strange things to him. It stole his breath and the strength from his legs and it left him feeling like each step was the hardest he'd ever made. And just when he thought he'd never put another foot forward, the trail abruptly turned – an honest, real turn, just like a garden path – and he found himself looking into a comfortable little shelf on the side of the mountain, walled in at the front with short fir trees, at the back with steep crags. A trickling mountain stream came down right through the middle of it, and there was ample heather and moss so that any man could be comfortable as if he were sleeping in his own bed.

"At last!" cried Jonas, and he at once sat down in the heather to quiet his aching feet.

"I'm gonna light a fire," announced Darkfinger. "And then I'm gonna shoot something and cook it. What shall I shoot, d'ye think?"

"Anything that moves will taste like a well-roasted side of beef," replied Jonas. At the moment he cared less about food than he did about his own weary legs.

Darkfinger was more than just a man of the irons. His fingers could turn almost anything to his purpose; and so, though nearly all the trees were wet and dripping from the clouds that hung low on the mountainside, he had a fire burning brightly in the center of that little glen in perhaps five minutes – a very reasonable time when one considers that all one has to work with is damp heather and dripping branches. Then he went away with his guns loaded and a last laughing call over his shoulder, "Keep yer iron ready, Jonas; who knows what demons wait in these hills."

Darkfinger was gone for some time. Jonas hadn't counted the silent minutes there next to the fire, but if he had he was sure it must've been perhaps an hour or more before he heard sharp and clear in the mountain air the echoing shot of a *darkiron*. It reverberated and came again, and then a third time, and then he heard it racing away, faint in the distance. Evenso, it was quite dark and even the memory of the setting sun was fading when Darkfinger stumbled through the trees to the south, three of his chambers empty and his knife bloodied. But he had on his shoulders the carcass of some animal freshly killed and peeled.

"What is it?" asked Jonas.

But Darkfinger shook his head. "I d'know," he said. "It was white, I think. I couldn't rightly make it out when I shot it, and when I found its body 'twas mostly muddy and bloody: the shot was not my best. So I skinned it right away."

"You've been gone so long," replied Jonas. "I was beginning to wonder if you hadn't yourself become prey." He supposed Darkfinger might think he was joking but he wasn't.

But then Darkfinger replied, "I found nothing that breathed in the dark nor spoke with a voice nor refused to die when I wilt it;" and there was no jest in his eye.

As they sat roasting the meat of the wild animal on long spits about the fire, Darkfinger said quite presently, "I can feel the pull, Jonas, the pull of the train. It drives me onward. I think I know how ye have felt all this time. Now yer longing has become my own. I wonder why I didn't see it t'begin with."

"I think it's each to his own nature that determines what we see," replied Jonas quietly. "We may look unheeded, but it's our hearts that tell us the truth. And now I wonder what it is *really* that's drawn us to follow and if it isn't this stranger in the night that is actually before us."

At this Darkfinger became silent and moody, and so Jonas changed the course of converse. "Did you get any sight of the higher slopes?" he asked.

"I wish I 'adn't," replied Darkfinger.

"Are they bad?"

Darkfinger was silent for a moment, thoughtful; and then he said, "I ne'er shied before any obstacle that stood in m'way, Jonas. I've crossed great rivers, climbed high hills. I've killed men and bears. I've carried *darkirons* for most of m'life and I've proved to m'self perhaps a thousand times that I'm worthy of this burden." He looked Jonas hard in the eyes. "But I'm no mountaineer. I'm a gunrustler, a murd'rer and a thief."

At this Jonas laughed; he couldn't help it. A picture had come to mind of Darkfinger, the fastest gun west of Dodge, the murdering king, turning aside from the mountains, his guns useless, returning to the desert and the wasteland, back to the True Frontier – and that was comical. Even Darkfinger grinned a little – or perhaps it was a sneer.

As for himself, it was no joke for that was not far from the truth that Jonas felt.

"But do you think we can make it over?" asked Jonas persistently. "Do you think we may yet stand a chance?"

"I think we'd be the greater fool t'be turning back when we've come s'far," replied Darkfinger. "My fear-a going back still is more vast than all the heights above." He gave a drawn-out sigh, rummaged through his pockets, and brought out his pipe which was really Jonas' spare because Darkfinger had lost his own in the mines. And while he filled it with tobacco he said, "I did see a way, I think. It went up and up, so high that I couldn't quite see where it went over the high pass, but 'twas sound to my eyes – no trail, but sound just the same."

"No trail?" asked Jonas. "Do these roads not go over the mountain, then?"

"Nay," replied Darkfinger blowing a smoke ring that went over the fire, the sparks popping up through it. "I've seen: perhaps halfway from this place t'that where there are no more trees there is a cut in the mountain and many mines comin' out from the side of the hill. The road goes no farther."

"That isn't good news," replied Jonas. "I'd hoped for good roads and easy walking until we were well beyond the mountains."

"There may yet be other ways higher still," replied Darkfinger encouragingly, though they both knew it was a fool's hope.

Silence fell between them then and they listened to the sounds of night in the mountains: the drip of the trees, the thunder of some distance cascade, the trickle of their own brook where it came through the glade, the crackle of the fire, the call of some strange animal they had no sight for. And always the still calm that filled their heads with madness.

Jonas lay back in the heather. He was content for the nonce, he realized. For the first time in he-did-not-know how long.

Darkfinger laid back, too. What he was thinking Jonas couldn't guess; but after a time he began to sing in the far southland melody, and the song was one that Jonas had heard before in the saloons in Jemrock. A stoneborn song, Jonas understood the words but didn't know what they meant. Still, he listened to the Kid's song.

In Dodge-town loft met I a boy.
His hair was white, his fingers thin.
Holstered guns upon his hips,
The weapons bestowed by his kin.
A high-born lad, I thought he was,
But proved the better heretherein.
I watched him as he made the streets,
From Gov'nor's Hill to Wasteland Strands,
And in the slums of City Dodge
He took an apple from the stands.
And then the Bridge-guard came for him.
They bound him by his wanton hands.

Their fists were cruel, their errant pain,
They beat the cobbles red.
A lofty childe, a skilful man,
He took it naught instead.
Then to the stonehouse thought they had
The boy by bond and thread,
But errand lost, their lord a'well,
And he there stole by good and rent,
Their lord he took by bond of coal,
And More t'ould dwell in horr's of lent,
A thief, I thought, and they aswell,
A youth of ill deportment.

Jonas listened well, intrigued. The southern men were known for their songs, and he'd suspected Darkfinger could sing. He wanted to ask

137

who the boy was, but then the song changed, taking upon itself a new quality he was not sure he liked as well.

> *But then I saw the irons dark,*
> *The ones he carried at his sides;*
> *And when he drew them,* skybolt-*fast,*
> *I knew 'twas more than met the eye.*
> *A runner? Never, could not be.*
> *A lad, perchance, of worthy si'e.*
> *But runner? Nay, it'd never be!*
> *'Twas just a boy with gunny steel.*
> *But as I saw, he taught the best,*
> *And duel was won with heedless deal.*
> *Then out the gate that boy 'id fly,*
> *And with his terrier at his heel.*

The words were within him, Jonas realized then. It was the magic of them. He knew them well for they were very like those he himself had sung to himself. The mountain cascade turned itself into a fire within him, a fire for the life of the runner, for the heart of the boy – the boy he'd once been. He dreamed of a hundred duels in the streets of cities as big as Dodge, and some much bigger which lay to the east. He dreamed of hold-ups and daylight robberies, of running and gunning, swagging, furtive escapes, daring rescues, of glory, of honour . . . and Darkfinger's voice went on, lifting higher with the climbing rush of the wind.

> *A runner once, a runner be,*
> *To roam the wild mountains,*
> *Cross the fartherest deserts.*

To run in the hills,
To cry on the wind,
A runner, wild and free.

And Jonas drifted off to sleep with his head on his bedroll and his feet up by the fire, faraway lands and tales of violent charges, bloody wars, and mighty heroes filling his dreams.

~CHAPTER TEN~
TO THE LAST TREE

The next morning was cold. Jonas awoke with the dreamy realization he'd been freezing within for some hours, the chill working its way into his bones like the coming of winter frost. In sleep it might've taken his warmth until he no longer could awaken: that sometimes happened on the Frontier when the days grew short and the Harvester took as he saw fit. Jonas tried to remember where his dreams had led him but he couldn't, they were a muddle of icy delirium and gelid fancies. He was feverish but he could hear quite well, the fever had not taken that from him, and what he heard now was a deathly, muffled silence. He opened his eyes to a world of frosty white: it had snowed during the night.

Darkfinger was gone, his few belongings neatly tucked beneath the nearby branches of a Mountain Ash. In the heather, now lightly dusted with snowflakes, the ghostly image of his body lay; but he was risen.

The fire was cold and dead. Not even a wisp of smoke would stir nor a coal glow. Jonas brought out his flint and tinder from his wallet, but the wood was wet and his hands too cold to work his knife.

Just at that moment the sun came up in the east, casting long, colourful rays across the vast emptiness of the wasteland. It sparkled on the horizon like a perfectly-cut gem. Then the rays reached the glen, high on the side of the mountain, and they set the snow to dancing with glittering droplets in a myriad of different colours, though none as brilliant as the wasteland itself.

Darkfinger came in through the trees along the trail, a bundle of fine-cut sticks in one arm and something furry hanging from his closed fist. When he saw Jonas a light flickered in his eyes and he said, "The good graces of the Fall t'place this mantel upon us, Brother."

The wood was dry, and when Jonas had sat on his hands for a moment or two he was able to catch a few chippings alight. The fire was slow to build but it *did* take, and soon it was burning brightly, chasing the cold from his blood.

Darkfinger said the thing he'd shot was a coney, though Jonas thought it was more like a hare. Whatever it was, it tasted just the same, and they were more than sated before they again consented to collecting up their things and resuming the climb. By then the sun was ascending at their backs and the mountainside began to thaw out little by little until there were trickles here and there and the leaves shimmered with dewdrops. The climb became at best a scramble. The road was a sharp cut that went up and up, so steeply that when they looked down the world seemed to fall away; when they looked up, the mountain stood up so tall and impeding above them they wondered if there was a top to it at all. In places the pathway was so eroded and worn by time and weather they found themselves stepping across little creeks, gullies, and places where the ground had simply given out, and each so treacherous and misgiving they both longed for it to be over, the climb *and* the tremble in their knees. Back and forth the path went. They were now so high they could see the place where they had made camp so far below them it seemed not more than but a nook in the mountainside. And now it was becoming a little less steep, and at each turn there were heather and lichens growing on the level and little blue flowers that trailed across the ground.

"We are nearly to the highest mines now, I think," said Darkfinger, stepping across a little stream that cut down the hill, plummeting toward the shelf where they had spent the night. "The last cuts and the end of the trail."

And he was right. They'd only just come around the next bend and there before them was a narrow cove cut back into the mountainside. In it still stood the timbers that supported the shaft. A slat of corrugated tin served as a roof over the entrance and the wood was still sturdy enough that they might have stayed there and been warm and dry, had they the need. Beyond the standing supports was still the open mouth of the shaft itself, yawning black and empty, not very large but big enough that one person alone could creep inside if he was careful. There were no rails but a gently chilly breeze was coming from it and a little trickle of water dripped over the loose scree. And neither was altogether unpleasant.

"I wonder are they all still open up here?" said Darkfinger curiously. "Or have the tunnels collapsed?"

A little farther on, they passed another that was much the same. A rusty hammer, an axe, and a shovel were lying about, all in various states of decay, and a number of spikes were piled and corroding in the earth. Then not far beyond that they came to yet another mineshaft. This had no roof, but the supports here were also strong and the opening was big enough that several men could easily walk in abreast. A dreadful foul stench was coming from its opening, and it brought to Jonas' mind images of foul creatures and horrible things that might live in the dark.

He hurried past.

"How many mines did you count from below?" he asked when they were beyond these and had come to another turn-about in the road.

"Ten, perhaps a dozen," replied Darkfinger. "Hard t'say from such a way. And I could see nothing f'certain, only sort-a wide places in the path where the shile has been dumped. It makes me wonder t'think of the men who cut this, so far up on the side of the mountain, and how they got the ore down when once it'd been unearthed."

"Carried it, I suppose," replied Jonas. But even as he said it he chanced to look again down the slope of the hill and the height and the sheerness of it took his breath away and left his head spinning and feeling not altogether comfortable.

Around the next turn they were quite pleasantly surprised to find a narrow shelf on the hillside with perhaps half a dozen more mineshafts cut into it, all quite close together and with enough space in front of them that Jonas could still make out where the rails had once run along the side of the hill. The ore had been dumped, cart-to-cart, and then wheeled away, but to where he couldn't tell. And this was the end of the road, for even though they searched about both north and south along the mountainside, there was no path higher, not even the smallest. If there ever had been it was swallowed beneath the heather and lost for good.

"From here we must make our own way," said Darkfinger, looking up to the peaks above.

It really was a sight, to be sure. They were now so close to the bare crags that one got hope that it might be possible to make it up and over, if one found a valley accommodating to the needs of those without wings. But now as Jonas looked closer still that hope was destroyed. Little valleys here and there were filled with loose and crumbling rock wherever the heights had let it fall, and the pinnacles in between were sheer and so steep that even the most skilled mountaineer might be hard put to find good places to hold to. Some way above them the last gnarled, twisted alder grew feebly from the rocks, and so for some way yet they might make good climbing, even steep as it was, for the sparse mountain foliage still held the hill in place. But beyond that point what should keep the stones from shifting and them from plummeting to the valleys below, if the mountain should give up their footing? Perhaps it was only some force of magic that had kept the mountain standing for so long at all. To their eyes it seemed the smallest disturbance might break its delicate hold.

"We should climb to the last tree at least," said Darkfinger. "Perhaps from there we may see a better way."

So up through the heather and brambles they went, up through the little valleys and ridges that marked the heights, holding to alders and hemlocks that were stunted and gnarled with the brutality of the mountains. The moss was slippery and the rocks were coarse with the lichens that grew upon them. Their boots were ill-equipped for mountain travel, being hard and tanned against the elements of the Frontier and smooth upon the footing so as not to catch in the stirrup. But both Jonas and Darkfinger were strong and hearty from a vigorous supper and a restful night's sleep, and there was little to come against them in the clear morning air that they couldn't master by strength alone.

When they were nearly to the last tree the clouds moved in close around them, a rolling sea of cold white that when they were right in the midst of it was so thick they couldn't see more than a few paces before or aft. It was wet, too: Jonas could feel it clinging to his flesh. Now they could see neither the peaks above nor the valleys below nor anything in between. Everything, tree and shrub, became damp with the mist and slippery to the touch. It soaked into their clothes as they climbed, and the air, too, was colder than it had been. It got into their skin and brought a tremble to their knees, even with the vigour of their chore.

Now Jonas began to wonder how they might make for the peaks when they couldn't even see their way ahead. "Darkfinger!" he called. "We must stop or we will be lost in this fog!" His voice echoed a little and it came back to him sounding dead and sullen.

Darkfinger was a little way ahead but he stopped and looked back. The same fear that Jonas felt welling up inside his gut was reflected in the Kid's face: his hands were shaking and his breath came in short gasps. "Jonas," he said, "I don't know what t'do. My mind says t'keep climbin' or we shall ne'er make it over but mine spirit says t'not to!"

"See, this is the last tree," Jonas replied. And it was: a twisted, muted little tangle of coarse bark and fibrous leefage that grew up not more than a half-half from the broken, piled stone of the mountainside. Upwards of this there was nothing green or good but more broken stone, all piled up so steeply and treacherously (so precipitously in fact that they stood with their hands on the upground and hardly had to stoop at all). It went up until it reached the sheer crags high above them from whence the mountain shook off from its shoulders little bits at a time. Even now, as they stood in the relative safety of the last trees, little stones were dislodged and sent spinning away down through the brambles below, and every time Jonas was certain that the entire mountainside would simply let go and slide away beneath their feet. He said: "We can go no farther if we cannot see the way, and even if we can see it will be a treacherous climb across rock and boulder and wet moss, Fall-willing we make it at all! How long will this cloud last, do you suppose?"

"Might be all day," replied Darkfinger. "And up here there's no place to sit down and put one's feet up, not with the rocks so steep above and the bush so shallow below and nothing to stop you if you fall. If we have to wait it mayaswell be where I might stretch out my toes before a fire."

Jonas agreed, and though neither of them relished the return journey down through the tangle of stone and bramble, they both knew it was better than sitting there on the side of the mountain with the cold mist rushing by them all the time. And so they climbed back down again, and a slow journey it was, until they were standing once more at the mouth of the last digging, feeling very cold and frustrated with the fruitlessness of their work.

"So what then?" asked Darkfinger sharply, sitting down on a boulder and grinding his foot into the earth.

It was not a good feeling to be defeated so easily, and Jonas knew it. "I wish I knew," he answered. "It seems we're destined to be turned away. I cannot even recall when last I heard the cry of the train."

"There might not even be a way over, at all," said Darkfinger. "It might be impassable, if the miners never sought occasion to pass it."

"No," replied Jonas. "There *must* be a way, there *has* to be."

Darkfinger was silent for a moment. "Because the coach is still ahead?" he asked at last, hesitantly.

Jonas nodded his agreement.

"If only these infernal clouds would move away," said Darkfinger. "We might at least have a better look about, if only we could see." He arose. "And this climb has made me so thirsty. Is there no water to be had?"

"From that last mine," replied Jonas recalling a gentle trickle that had flowed across the path.

As Darkfinger returned to find it Jonas gave himself to the earth for the sake of weariness. He wondered where the train might be. It seemed forever since he'd heard the cry of its whistle, days since it'd gone beyond his hope, into the mountain. It seemed now as if it were all a dream, he chasing a fool's hope. But that was all the hope he could muster.

~CHAPTER ELEVEN~
A WAY THROUGH

The fog was lifting. The clouds weren't exactly moving up or down but just *away*. Jonas could see some way in any direction now, but it was like looking up at the sun from under water. A good way above him the clouds had split apart and there wheeling in the gap was an enormous bird, black against the sky. It wasn't a bird he was familiar with: much too large to be an eagle, much too small to be a chestine. It didn't circle, either, as any other bird might but cut across the sky and then came back again, making ragged turns and straight lines; then it returned the way it had gone the first time. And with each turn it was so graceful that it hardly seemed to move at all. As it came back yet again it gave a long and piercing cry that seemed to hang in the air and throb deep in the earth.

"It's a gorfalkon," said Darkfinger who seemed to have come up silently while Jonas was watching the bird turning this way and that.

"How do you know?" asked Jonas in reply. He'd never seen any such creature before, not in his entire life.

"I know it by the way it moves," replied Darkfinger. "I've never seen one b'fore; there've been no gorfalkon in the Frontier or in the Southlands since b'fore I was born. My grandda remembered them only in stories. But that's one, sure as anything: almost an eagle but much too big."

"Aye," agreed Jonas. "What do you guess it's doing?"

"Hunting I s'pose," replied Darkfinger; "that's how eagles hunt. It's searching for something, anyway."

Jonas' hand unwittingly touched his gunbelt and he was aware at once of the tremble in his fingers. Excitement or fear? He wasn't sure. The uncertainty scared him, so fear was close-enough to the mark.

"It drives such a fright within me," said Darkfinger, still watching the gorfalkon wheeling to and fro in the gap. "To see something no one's seen in a 'undred years or more."

"Does it?" asked Jonas. "It does the same to me, but I almost wish it would land here."

"I feel quite the same," agreed Darkfinger. "Just that it would land. Perchance it would eat me; I don't know. Perchance it would speak; I don't know. I just wish it would come down so I could see it."

"Do you see where it's going?" asked Jonas, for the gorfalkon had indeed turned once more and vanished into the clouds.

"South I think," replied Darkfinger. "Toward the peak."

Though he hadn't consciously noticed it earlier, in his memory Jonas knew what that peak looked like. It was perhaps the highest in the range, and it was separated from them by a narrow saddle in the mountain and a deep ravine lined with firs and hemlocks. With the clouds so close and only his memory to serve him, it seemed to him now it might be only a few hours march at the most to make the crossing through the valley in between. But rationality told him it would be much more difficult: things in the mountains usually were.

But the more he thought about it the more it seemed the thing to do, like some voice inside him was saying, *Cross the ridge, Jonas; follow the gorfalkon.*

He was acutely aware then that he'd been staring silently into the mist. Now Darkfinger aroused him from his thoughts with a sharp, almost-surprised laugh and the rustle of his holster as he drew his *darkiron*, absently checking the chargeholes; it seemed he'd struck upon some insight.

"What is it?" asked Jonas.

"I think we should follow it," replied Darkfinger with a glimmer in his eye, a gleam like hope. "I think we should cross to the next peak. I've a *feeling.*"

"So have I," said Jonas. "If only this Fall-damned fog would let off a little."

But even as he said it he was aware that the clouds were, in fact, moving back little by little still until they could see at least into the next valley – not the one dividing them from the next peak, of course, for as any good mountaineer knows there is no end to the little valleys and ridges on the slopes of mountains and you never quite know where you are until you're there. It wasn't much of a sight, but Jonas already was beginning to feel hope returning.

"It couldn't hurt to have a look," he said. Anyway, up had done them no good, and returning down was certainly no good at all. So south it was.

The going wasn't easy. The trees were short and thicker than ever, sprouting up on the slope of the hill in coarse and dense copses. They were wet and dripping with the still-melting snow, and though their roots went deep and they offered very good support to keep one's self upon the hill, they got in the way and bit at the arms and face in sharp slaps.

Still, from the mines they made good time, and gradually the trees and underbrush thinned until Jonas found himself beyond the next ridge, lost from sight of the mines and looking south onto open hillsides with little rocky outcroppings, ridges here and there marked by slides and cascades of water and the green of the heather. And the best part of all: right before their feet was a narrow, worn trail that went up and down, over rock and bush, twisting this way and that. It was well-travelable.

"Animals, I think," said Darkfinger. "Perhaps like the one I killed."

"Perhaps," agreed Jonas.

It seemed to go the same direction they were making, in a more or less southerly way. So they followed it without question until Darkfinger said excitedly, "Jonas, look!"

Jonas leaned against the side of the hill to see past Darkfinger but all he saw was the hump of the next ridge and the indigo late-summer blossoms poking up through the green of the heather.

"There's someone ahead!" cried Darkfinger.

Jonas' blood went cold. Who could be climbing through the mountains along those treacherous pathways but madmen following the whistle of a train? Or perhaps it was something worse. Whatever it was couldn't be good, he was sure. But Darkfinger was running now and with much more agility than Jonas could hope for, given the youth the younger gunslinger still held in his supple frame. Up the trail he went, over rock and boulder, never missing his footing until he, too, was almost lost to sight.

"Darkfinger!" Jonas cried in alarm, suddenly uncertain of what it would mean to be left alone in the mountains. "Darkfinger, wait you stony fool!"

And then Darkfinger was gone, vanished beyond the next ridge.

The panic set in. Jonas wanted to hurry himself to keep up but he knew he would fall, and on the open slope with nothing but sharp rocks and heather to catch him to fall was almost certainly equal to death. He wanted to draw but there was nothing to shoot that would be of any use. "Darkfinger, you fool!" he yelled again. His voice sounded dead in the air, though not so dead as the gunshots that rang across the side of the mountain like a thunderstorm. Perhaps they were the discharges of a *darkiron* revolver with notches etched into the blue of its hilt or perhaps they were something else, he couldn't tell. But the thought of falling forever down that hillside was nothing like the dread of those shots. It set a fear within him like a disease, and he started to run clumsily over the little path, his boots slipping on the grass and heather. More than once he nearly lost his footing or missed some rock.

For a little way the trail went up and down but mostly more up than down, winding this way and that. In places there were little humps and bumps in the side of the hill so that at one moment there would be a sharp hill up on the right and a dreadful drop down on the left and then at the next Jonas would be stumbling over fairly level ground with perhaps a rock or two and a bush on his left to steady himself upon. He hardly looked up. The adrenaline was hot in his veins and he had only one thought: find Darkfinger and find him fast. It was all panic and alarm and he knew he wasn't thinking straight but he didn't dare stop to collect himself.

Over one ridge and then the next he went. He thought he heard someone yell up ahead but he saw nothing. He kept running.

Much later he remembered looking up once to realize that he had no idea where he was or how long he'd been frantic. It was all strange valleys around, and though his feet had followed the path as plainly as it went he was alarmed to realize that there were *dozens* of these little paths, though much less plain, going in all directions here and there about the mountainside. Some climbed up, some down. And all followed their own fancies.

There was another ridge ahead, he now saw. It was exactly like all the others, just a steep rise of heather in the mountainside with little bits of moss and grass here and there, a flower or two, and the occasional rock jutting out. But Jonas supposed that if he got up to the top it might lend something of a view.

The trail wound round the bend of the ridge, and here Jonas caught his breath because it almost ended. For a moment there was only a thin line in the heather, and then he spotted it again just some few paces ahead. It came to a spot in the side of the mountain where there was a great hump sticking up and a valley between it and the uphill side. A copse of trees had found rooting on this little knoll, and there, where the path went down into the valley, on a particularly large rock was the gorfalkon, preening itself as if there was nothing more pressing to attend to.

"Watch yourself, Friend," it said in a cool voice looking up at him interestedly.

Jonas fell in the heather, out of breath. But worse than that, the reality of the moment was settling itself upon him like a hand squeezing his breath away.

"Don't worry about your fellow," said the gorfalkon, resuming its grooming with an impartial note in its voice. "That *is* what you're all bothered about, isn't it?"

"I thought—" said Jonas – but it occurred to him that he was, in fact, speaking to a bird, and then it seemed the more prudent thing to draw his guns, so he did, aiming them at the gorfalkon and training his eye. He didn't know where its heart might be but he supposed it must be more or less in its chest and its chest must be more or less in the midst of all that bright, gleaming plumage. It was making no effort to shield itself: it would be an easy kill if it came to that.

"Oh, put them away," said the bird, still with that fair-minded drawl in its voice. "I won't hurt you, you know."

"How can I be sure?" said Jonas, still catching his breath. "You're a gorfalkon." And even as he spoke it occurred to him how silly it sounded.

"Well spotted," replied the bird rudely. "Actually, I'm a corgrief, if it pleases you, and even if it doesn't."

"What do you want?" asked Jonas, guns still in hand.

"Oh, I was just flying beyond the mountains when I noticed a couple little humans crawling upon the wall of the earth," it said. "Foolish of young chicks to climb so high."

"Beyond the mountains?" asked Jonas excitedly. "Where are you going?"

"To war," drawled the gorfalkon. "There are many of us still. It's time to come down from the heights and go to battle."

"What battle?"

The gorfalkon laughed aloud. "Never you-mind, funny human," it said. "You best get after your friend now. In there. They're waiting for you." It directed him to the mouth of a cave quite close to where he lay. He had not noted it before for the heather concealed it in such a way that you could not see it rightly until you stood before it. It was closed off by a heavy stone door, but this was not latched and it swung easily at his touch. "Best keep those irons in hand, too," the bird said. "The Hill People are funny folk and not to be taken lightly."

Jonas turned away. It didn't seem to him to be very wise to go into a crevice in the hillside without properly ascertaining the full volume of the situation. Of course, he'd never been so high in the mountains before but he knew that such dark, deep places often are home to very dreadful things. But there didn't seem to be anything for it, not if he wished to see Darkfinger again. He checked the chambers of his guns, and then, fully loaded and with hammers drawn, the darkness plotted itself before him.

He needn't go far, he now saw. Almost at once he was aware of a little light ahead, and it got brighter and nearer until it was a thick, black candle burning in an iron sconce on a narrow shelf in the rock. The cave turned by little to the left, running true and well-cut, and Jonas realized it had clearly been *made* that way, not merely torn, as mountains sometimes are, creating vast and treacherous holes. And the thought of what might be inside, if it had been carved by skilled hands, sent excitement racing up within him. It might be something nasty and unpleasant, yes, but the very worst things always *found* nasty holes and preferred it if they didn't have to do the digging for themselves. It was usually *men* who took the time to carve such things and only men who used candles.

A little way ahead was another candle, and beyond that another. Jonas was beginning to wonder just how far the cave went then when he realized that the next light was *not* that of a candle but more like a fire burning on a hearth. And sure enough, next thing he knew he was stumbling through a wood-framed door which was standing only just ajar, and beyond was a bright, fire-lit chamber. It was furnished as a bedroom, sitting room, kitchen, and pantry all in one, and there were three others present.

"Hullo," said one cheerily. He was a short man with bright eyes poking out from his burly face, and he was sitting before the fire with his hands outstretched, as if to warm them.

~CHAPTER TWELVE~
FRIENDS IN CLOSE PLACES

"Who are you?" asked Jonas. He tried to sound cantankerous, but it caught in his throat: the warmth and the hearth-light were working wonders on him, as only a cheery fire can. All the fortitude made on the doorsill was quite slipping from him, even as he spoke.

"I'm Brimhallow," said the stranger without looking; instead he turned a kettle that was just beginning to sing on the fire. "This is my brother, Goran."

Jonas was somewhat alarmed now upon this realization: that the two men seated before him were, in fact, not much taller than boys. Yet they were stout and strong and hairy, and their faces were grim, just the same.

Now the third person spoke: "Oh, Jonas!" he said.

And quite at once Darkfinger was there also, his eyes shining and a beaming smile stretched across his face. "Jonas, I'm sorry," he said, turning the raised guns in Jonas' hands aside, the guns Jonas had quite forgotten about.

"Sorry?" asked Jonas. Thoughts of hot water, warm fires, comfortable places, and the smell of coffee had quite sent his mind running, and he hadn't even any idea what Darkfinger might be sorry for.

"I meant t'go back at once when I saw, but, I, I don't know, the fire and the warmth and all were just—"

Jonas shook his head for he too understood well enough, now that he was standing there by the fire. The thought of returning back out through the door of the cavern onto the open mountainside made him cold and feverish.

"Well, come-come then," said Brimhallow. "Put away those tools, Sir. Join us for coffee, if it please you. A spot to chase away the fear and anger. We're all good men here."

Jonas *did* put away his guns but he never let his hands stray far enough that he couldn't have them again from their holsters in a hurry.

"Who are you people?" he asked when Brimhallow had offered him a steaming mug.

"Most folk call us *The Hill People*," said Brimhallow. "I suppose that name is as good as any. There aren't many of us, anyway, and we're not very fond of strangers who come tramping through these parts—" The implication was apparent. "—not that they come often. But still, we're hospitable-enough."

"I'm grateful," said Jonas.

"There's meself, and Goran, and our brother, Turkish," said Brimhallow. "Goran brought this other one in all wet and bruised from his tumble down the heather. Turkish now, he went out hisself to see if he couldn't spot you when he learnt there was another, and maybe also to find some supper, so we'll be expecting him back shortly."

"Again, I'm obliged," said Jonas.

"So you are trying to get beyond The Demon's Teeth then?" asked Brimhallow when they were all seated much more comfortably about the fire and with mugs of hot coffee in their hands.

"What's *The Demon's Teeth*?" asked Darkfinger.

"These mountains, of course," said Brimhallow. "They run from the Swile in the south to the Duranges in the north. It's an impressive range, so my father said, for he has journeyed as far north as the Teeth go and as far south, in the other direction. No small measure, for the Teeth are much greater even than the Silver Mountains in the east."

"The Silver Mountains?" asked Jonas. "What are *they*?"

"You can see them," said Goran now, speaking for the first time with a dour voice, not unlike a snarl, and dim eyes that looked and looked but never seemed satisfied, "when you stand at the top of the pass on a clear day. They're tall, far beyond the desert, like a line of broken looking-glasses."

163

Jonas knew of no mountains in the east, save the Sleepy Mountains, and they couldn't be compared in height to The Demon's Teeth.

"We've never been so far east, though," said Brimhallow. "My great grandfather went away across the desert once many, many years ago, before I was yet born. But we've not crossed the Great Desert since. Is that where you've come from, across the desert?"

"Of course it is," said Goran darkly. "It's the only place the tall men come from these days, and at that precious few."

"Why so few?" asked Darkfinger. "Are there not men living in these mountains any longer?"

"Men?" asked Brimhallow, surprised. "There has *never* been men in these mountains; not on this side, leastways. Not what *you* would call men, strictly speaking. There are the drizzle, of course, but they are no more men than the pale people are! And they are friendly to no one, not even the goblin, and the goblin are friendly to any with desires as foul as their own. And then there's gremlins, I suppose, still living in the Duranges, but there's been none in these parts in perhaps a hundred years or more. No, the drizzle are our only neighbours now, and they're something very different from men. They ride out into the desert, or sometimes north to make war with the Babylonyan, as they once did."

"But what has made all the mines we've seen?" asked Jonas.

"Oh, surely not men!" laughed Goran, and even his laugh wasn't a pleasant thing to hear. "It was the people of Thelnor who bled the mountain, but there are no more of their kind so far south anymore. Once they came in the winter. Not men like you, you understand, but wicked, dark-hearted people who dig deep into the hills and steal from the earth. Many, many years ago they travelled to these parts in search of metals. They cut deep holes, they rended the stone with fire and broke the mountain open. But then the drizzle came to make war. They fought bitterly. Now the Thelnorian have left and will not come again."

"But young sirs," said Brimhallow in such a way that it was obvious he had grown uncomfortable with the talk, "you want to get beyond the Teeth, yes?"

"Aye," replied Jonas warily, wondering if they might ask about the train and hoping that the opportunity would arise, like a door thrown wide.

"I shouldn't know why!" growled Goran. "There's only grim tidings beyond in recent days. There's rumour the goblin march on Jericho and the pale people, too, are going to war. Babylon itself is let off her chain."

"And the train is riding the rails ever westward," said Brimhallow. "We've not seen it but we've heard it, three nights past. Must be well beneath the roots of the mountains by now."

"The train!" cried Jonas, quite forgetting himself. "*You* know of the train?"

"*Satta*, heard of it, yes," replied Goran. "Rides the rails, sometimes. Comes and goes, mostly. In the time of the Thelnor when these mountains were teeming with devils and monsters the train would come often. It came to do war upon the drizzle, for very bad men they are. It came to bring freedom – or so it was said."

"Yes," agreed Brimhallow. "But then it was silent and didn't come this way for perhaps a hundred years."

"Until now," said the Kid.

"Until now," agreed the brothers.

Jonas then asked, "The train is then a good thing?"

"Ah, don't you see, friend?" exclaimed Brimhallow. "It *is* good; it always has been. *Very* good, least to us mountain folk and to the men who live beyond the Demon's Teeth. But now it comes and goes in the darkest of times. No one seems to know why but it's brought the pain and suffering to this dreadful place."

"The waters run poisonous," said Goran, "and the Autumntime comes on too quickly. Nights grow cold and chilly, and the snows come early. Always was that the first winter brought the shadows. It's something bad, and it begins with that war in the west."

"Yes, and we've got to be *going* west," said Jonas. He'd realized in the darkened silence of the cavern that time was creeping by, and he already couldn't be certain how long they'd sat in the firelight talking.

"But *why*?" asked Goran, showing for the first time what might have been something other than bitter resentment. "What is there in the west, now that the road to Jericho is no longer open?"

"The train," replied Darkfinger, and he turned his watchful eyes on the brothers. Something was glittering behind them, like cold sunshine in the bed of a brook. "We're following the train," he said. "From over the desert. Please, tell us how to get after it now."

The brothers looked at each other, as if they'd shared a thought. "Well, there *is* a way," said Brimhallow. "It's a *dangerous* way but it might be the only way. There used to be roads, see, much farther south that climbed through the lower passes and over, and that was the way to find Jericho. But the goblin watch all those old ways now, and in the high mountains one never knows when one might run in with much fouler enemies. Fyvorns even lived on the peaks at one time or another. No, the only way to make it these days is here in the heights, right in the very steepest places: you must use the West Gate."

"Yes, the West Gate!" exclaimed Goran.

"It's a long, dark journey," said Brimhallow, "right down beneath the mountains. But it comes out on the other side in good time and at such a height that it will be as safe as anywhere. And the doorway is well hidden. No one knows about it anymore save but ourselves and the corgrief."

"The gorfalkon, you mean?" asked Jonas. "The one perched outside?"

"Ah, yes. They are very good folk, if not a little hot-tempered and edgy sometimes," said Brimhallow. "But they're the grunts you want on your side when it comes to blows 'cause there ain't nothing as fierce as a corgrief in a pinch. Why, I seen one tear through thirty goblin or more and get nothing more than a broken claw for his trouble."

"But now they're all going away to the war," said Goran. "And undoubtedly it will cost them dearly."

"But *why* are they going?" asked Darkfinger.

"Because they've an oath with the men of the valley, that's why," replied Brimhallow. "And they keep their oaths, rain or shine, slick or slim, you can count on that!"

Just at that moment there was a sound in the passage and they all looked up at once to see another someone coming in, stumping on short legs, his bushy beard which once had been yellow but now was white with snow tucked neatly into his belt. He was leaning on a long-gun, almost as long as he was tall, and there was a heavy axe stuck in his belt next to his beard. A large, silver cat with bright eyes and black markings on its fur was stalking behind him.

"No meat," said this third as soon as he'd come into the cavern without so-much as a 'Hello'. "But plenty of berries and roots and even a few mushrooms — what the slugs haven't spoiled."

"So *that's* what took you so long," said Brimhallow.

"Yes," said the third brother. "We've gone down as far as the Upper Gate where the caps sometimes grow in the moss."

"Did you see anything else?" asked Goran.

"The corgrief are all moving west," said Turkish, for that is who this new fellow was. "They're flying in ones and twos as they usually do, and one even said the King has taken to the skies!"

"Then this war is a very serious matter," said Brimhallow. "The king of the corgrief wouldn't fly west if it was not of dire need."

"Yes," replied Turkish, "very serious indeed. The corgrief *did* mention that the white men were in the path of the train, said he'd wait for these if they wanted to take the West Gate. He has volunteered to make certain it's safe on the other side."

"Yes, the West Gate," agreed Brimhallow. "We'd only just thought of that ourselves."

"We'd be very grateful!" said Darkfinger.

"I'll take you as far as the last lamppost," said Turkish, "but you must understand that nothing you can say will convince me to walk the shores of the lake with you."

"What lake?" asked Jonas feeling a cold chill at the word, feeling it was not a *good* lake. He could only imagine what foul memories were brooding in Darkfinger's mind at the mention of it.

"It's way down beneath the mountain," said Goran in a voice much colder still. "The water's black and the shore is black*er*. No light will shine down there. It's a fearful place."

"Is it *safe*?" asked Darkfinger who had never shied from danger, as you have seen, but neither was he keen about going into it without first knowing where he might end up.

"Safe?" asked Turkish. "Who can say? Who knows what lives down in the deep places? The Thelnor dug far in their lust for stone, and once all these holes were fresh and wholesome. But bad things creep in, you understand; they always do. Still, it's a *firm* road, true enough, and many have walked it, myself included. But that was many years ago and I've no wish to go there again. And so if your mind is quite made up I will take you to the last post, and from there you must make your own path."

And so it was agreed. Turkish, who was the eldest of the three by some score of years and obviously the decision-maker, said it was perhaps an hour's walk to the last post and from there darkness until the West Gate. But the brothers insisted that Jonas and Darkfinger wouldn't be plodding blindly onward, stumbling into holes and tripping on stones. Two torches were procured, as well as an ample supply of greasecloth, and these things were packed into Jonas' roll. Then several hard biscuits (which the brothers said were much better than the few dry cakes that Jonas and Darkfinger had brought with them) were packed into Jonas' bag, along with some other dried things. And finally Brimhallow insisted they have a spot of the soup he'd been cooking up on the fire before they leave. They did, of course, meaning no disrespect; and then, with a hearty good-bye from Brimhallow and a somewhat more rough and grim one from Goran, Jonas and Darkfinger followed Turkish and the silently-pacing silver cat down into a low door that let out from one side of the cavern and into the darkness below.

The East-west Passage as Turkish called it was dark enough, to be true. The floor was smooth and worn from years of feet upon the cuttings, and at somewhat lengthy intervals there were lamps fastened to the walls and burning brightly with an electric light. Jonas wanted to asked what made them burn and how long they would remain lit, but now Turkish took on a much darker, sulkier mood, more like his brother Goran. Neither Jonas nor Darkfinger felt any excess discussion was to their favour.

When they were quite deep by the warmth of the air Jonas realized he could *feel* the silence. It sounded in his ears like the sharp ring of a smithy's hammer. It was so quiet he imagined he could hear noises coming to them that must surely be from far, far away. Once or twice he even was certain he heard the distinct *slosh*, as of waters upon stony shores. Days of that and the voices would begin to raise their own soft chides, he knew. And it wasn't just the silence that was getting to him: the flicker of the lamps on the walls made him drowsy. He wasn't a man who is fearful of dark, cramped spaces, but being so far underground for the first time in his life was working horribly upon him. Certainly, it wasn't bothering Darkfinger nearly as much: the Kid was taking the path in a long gait, his eyes stealing the dark.

They passed only two other tunnels, both of which yawned vacantly at them. The first Jonas realized was the way by which this deep road had been cut down from the surface; the path from the brothers' cavern was in fact only a side road, and they had just come onto the main way. It smelled quite earthy and fresh, not at all a dark, dank underground sort of feel. But the next that they came upon was a small and ill-conceived hole. It smelled of deep, foul things, and no matter how they broached the subject Turkish wouldn't tell them to where it led.

It was an hour, perhaps, since they'd left the three brothers' comfortable cave when the stairs began and they came to the last lamppost. At times on the journey in the dark the lamps had been quite far apart, and sometimes they couldn't see the next when they had already left the last one behind. But this time they knew for certain the light flickering next to them was the end: the darkness beyond was so complete, so dead and silent, and the air too smelled stuffy and still as if nothing had breathed in it, proba- bly *ever*.

"This is it," said Turkish.

"That's our path?" asked Darkfinger, wide- eyed at the descent into the darkness below. A single set of narrow steps was chiselled into the stone and descending so steeply that you might have argued it was more akin to a ladder than a stairs. "How should we be able to find our way?"

"It's not so difficult as you might think," re- plied Turkish. "There are stones to keep you by, chiefly along the lakeshore where the road goes this way and that. So long as you don't lose your- self or let the light go out then you *will* come out the West Gate in good time, I'm sure."

But something in his voice was not so certain.

"Lose ourselves?" said Darkfinger with a note of perplexity.

"Has anyone before?" asked Jonas.

Turkish was quiet for a moment, thoughtful, stroking the ears of his great cat. "Yes," he con- ceded at last. "In the Hill Wars there was one, a Thelnorian. He went into the mountains, making for the West Gate, and he never came back out again. He was lost in the dark, we think, and his mind along with him. Down there he may yet dwell in some dark, silent hole, eating naught but the blind fish that are born in the stone."

"What a miserable end!" grunted Darkfinger, his hands straying to his holstered irons. "I

172

should say I had lost it all already if I could put one foot upon that step!"

"You'll make it if you keep true," replied Turkish. The briefest glimmer of a smile tugged at the corner of his lip, and that in that cold and dank place warmed the heart more than ought else.

There were no good-byes this time. Turkish turned and was gone back up the passage with the cat stalking at his side and the shadowy flickers of the lamps playing on his back.

The passage below wasn't getting any less dark. Away from the lights that were so warm and comforting Jonas began to *feel* the gloom as plainly as he felt his own heart beating in his chest; and the cavity below them, like the maw of a ravenous wolf, was vivid in his mind, whether he saw it with his eyes or not. It seemed more an empty, gaping *nothing* now, a demon's den that would swallow him whole. The smell of the air down below was warm and suffocating.

"Shall we feed this monster?" asked Darkfinger even as he bound up a torch and lit it with Jonas' flint and steel. "Aye, if it even is possible." At that moment a shiver ran up Jonas' back with the cold of death and silent slumber beneath the mountain. What might be down there? It certainly wasn't friendly.

"Nothing for it," replied Jonas. He tightened his pack and belt, gritted his teeth, and with resolve, and his hands on his guns, he stepped down into the deep beneath the mountain.

Those passages below the last lamppost were the darkest places Jonas and Darkfinger could ever remember: even they were darker than the

Sundry mines, Darkfinger said. You haven't really been lost until you see that blackness. It was like ink, so complete that even the torches struggled to remain alight. They went at most times with their hands upon the walls, *feeling* rather than seeing because there wasn't much of anything *to* see. Looking at the struggling flicker of the flame hovering in its little world of darkness was rather a claustrophobic feeling.

They were always on stairs that went more or less in only one direction: down. It was at times an easy-enough climb to those with tired feet, but more than once the steps had been cut so steep and so narrow that it really *was* more like a ladder than a stairs, if indeed it had ever been as a stairs. And they hadn't gone very far before they couldn't have said with any certainty how far they'd actually come. It was disorienting in the dark. It made one lose one's head. And now they began to understand what Turkish had spoken of.

Down and down, little by little they went, always in that cloud of inky blackness. Hours it seemed, and they stopped to relight their torch once or twice.

But sometime after that Jonas thought he heard the lap of water on stone.

"Do you hear that?" he asked, stopping to listen hard.

"The lake," replied Darkfinger. "It must be close."

"I'd like a drink if we could get to the water," said Jonas.

But Darkfinger replied: "I wouldn't dare."

And when Jonas thought of it he agreed; one never knew what things might be lurking in a lake so deep beneath the mountains. Certainly the water must be oily black like the darkness, sickly to the touch and greasy on the lips.

The stairs ended then. The walls were wide around them. It felt open, as if they were in a great and vast hall, perhaps with an immense, carved ceiling high above their heads. But it was a dead, stuffy kind of openness. The air was perfectly still, not at all like you might expect in such a wide open space. It was so calm it made one's skin crawl with how unnatural it was, and the constant sound of the water on the shore, water unseen in the dark going *slosh-slosh-slosh,* was not at all pleasant as it should have been.

They would've lost the path for certain if it hadn't been marked in stones as Turkish said it would be. So now they went along with their noses to the ground so as to see the markers, and Jonas nearly walked right into the murky depths of the lake lapping on the sunless shore.

"Hi! Darkfinger!" he cried, stopping up quite short with his boot-toes beneath the waves. "I do believe we've come to the lake at last!"

"On the right?" asked Darkfinger who was standing behind with the light in hand and looking blindly ahead. "Good, then we're on the right path."

By the water they walked until the sound of it lapping on the rocks was the only thing pounding in their heads – pounding like a thunderstorm in the silence. It must've been hours, always plodding forward, no sight nor sound, just the *slosh* of the lake. Jonas began to wonder if

Turkish's warnings held any merit at all. That is until another sound wore its way amidst the steady plodding of his feet. For every one of his footsteps there was another that echoed it, not quite in time and not late enough in the stride that it might be Darkfinger's. And anyway, he could hear the Kid's quite plainly. No, this was something else, and it was almost on his heels.

His hands were on his guns before he had quite properly thought of it. Then he was standing motionless in the dark, hissing at Darkfinger. "*Shhh!* Did you hear that? We're not alone!"

In a moment Darkfinger was about with one gun in hand and the torchlight flickering on his stony face. "Where!" he whispered fiercely, his eyes wild; it seemed he'd been wondering himself if that footstep perhaps wasn't in his head after-all.

"Behind me just now I thought," said Jonas, his voice shaking a little.

"So 'tis not the voice of mine own thoughts," said Darkfinger. "Then come ou' with you, ye demon! Show yer wretched face!"

A noise as of many flat feet falling on smooth stone came to them from a long way off, but it sounded so near they could touch whoever made it, so complete was the silence everywhere else. Something was flickering nearby like their own torch but much redder, much darker– or it may have been a trick of the darkness, as a desert mirage.

"Check your chambers!" said Darkfinger, turning his own cylinder out and then snapping it shut and pulling the hammer of his *darkiron*.

They waited in silence now, listening to the sound of whatever was in the dark getting steadily closer, nearer, and louder, neither quite knowing what facet it might take. But it never came. They waited and waited, and still they stood there, their fingers trembling a little, the sweat standing out on their faces.

And then it beset them, not from in front but behind. Darkfinger cried aloud and dropped the torch to the floor. In the dying light of the flame Jonas thought he could see the Kid writhing in turmoil on the earth. Something clung to his back. Darkfinger was trying as he might to turn his gun around to shoot it but long, spindly arms were grasping at his own. "Jonas, help me!" he choked. "It's got me by the neck! Shoot it! *Shoot it!*"

But Jonas didn't – *wouldn't*. The light was bad and he might just as likely shoot Darkfinger as the enemy in the dark. Instead he holstered his gun and drew his knife from his belt, not really thinking, of course, because a gunrunner *does* not *think* when things become serious. But before he could move something struck him in the back and he fell hard on the floor.

177

~CHAPTER THIRTEEN~
PASSAGES IN THE DARK

When Jonas awoke again he wasn't by the waters of the sunless lake. He knew because the incessant lapping of the water on the shore was silent. Aside of this, he hadn't any idea where he might be at all. The darkness was complete. He passed a hand in front of his eyes but saw nothing. He drove an elbow into his thigh, just to make sure he was awake, and thus discovered he was bound hand and foot.

The next moment the stolid shadows dwindled before his eyes, giving way to a harsh, red flame that flickered in and out, like an old man whose life has led him to the end of this world and now he stands on the platform waiting for his coach. And then a voice was whispering in his ear, "Ah, dear, sweet Gutter, what has he brought? A nice little boy with big iron? A *Good-to-eat*?"

Another voice answered the first: "We mustn't eat it, Mother!"

"Don't think Gutter would miss just a mouthful to keep his old mother on her two weary feet," replied the first, and with these words, an old, leering face came into the light before him. It was so twisted with time and decay, so sagging with age that if it had been entirely human he might have guessed its age well before the turn of the century. Its ashy skin and bright eyes beneath its mats of ebony hair were like those of the demon that crawls from the crypts. Its twisted, knobbly knuckles that pawed at Jonas' shirt and belt were like the dried-out roots of old trees. "Maybe it doesn't want its eyes, either," she crooned, for it was in fact an old witch of a woman, bent and doubled with age. "Maybe I'll poke them out for jelly."

"They aren't to be touched until Gutter gets back, Mother!" cried the second voice. "He will be frightfully angry. You don't want that!"

"No, he shan't!" replied the first. "He shan't even notice. He doesn't look at its eyes, does he? And anyway, when he gets back with that other one he won't care two stones about this one. Know why? Because he's gonna be hungry, ever so hungry hisself. When has our old Gutter ever passed up a chance at supper when it came walking so willingly down from the demon's hole where the day shines still?"

"Never," said the other distastefully.

"For true. Now help me pull apart his neat little corpse so we can have some supper!" She pawed again at Jonas with long arms and fingers that stuck in his eyes and mouth and she felt all over his shirt, purring at times as if she'd found something she liked. There came from her a terribly foul stench like meat that has sat in the sun and gone afoul and he could hear her old joints rasping as she moved.

He choked back the terror rising in his gut. Oh, if only he could reach his guns!

Just then there was a shuffling in the dark and another voice was raised, a much deeper, gruffer voice than either of the first two, perhaps younger than the old woman's though much older still than the other. "Hail! Mother, what is this? Not yet suppertime and you're already helping yourself?"

"Just give me a bite, you wretched boy!" the old woman cooed. "All I want is enough for my teeth, perhaps a toe or two for I'm starved like you wouldn't believe!"

"No!" replied the younger in the dark, his voice like tempered steel. "Not even *one* bite, not till I catch that other slippery thing!"

"You didn't get it?" asked the other voice.

"No," said the third. "Caught it away down 'ear the grotto but it slipped before I could get my hands round its ugly neck."

"What if it comes back?" asked the second voice with something like a tremor of fear.

"Then I stick it with my spear and hang it o'er the fire!" cried the old woman. "It shan't get away again!"

"If you hadn't let go of it—!" indicted the second.

"—and if you hadn't knocked me head with that great stick o' yers!" she wailed in return, holding a spot on her head where a sizeable welt might've been visible through her sparse and grisly hair. "What did you want to do that for, anyway?"

"Shut it!" said the third, his voice accompanied by a *whack!* that must surely have been his open hand on the head of the younger. "What of *that* one?" A long, ugly finger was jabbed at Jonas. A leering face, pale but hard, scarred and ugly as the finger it accompanied came out of the darkness, wide-eyed and twitchy. It had sharp teeth poking past its cracked and greasy lips. "Smells a'right dudn't he!"

"Like supper!" shrieked the old woman. "Let's eat him!"

"I told you, not 'til I catch that *uthuh* one!" yelled the third, and again with his voice came the *whack!* of his hand but this time it was on Mother's head.

Now it was apparent to Jonas what had happened. The misery of it made him sick. But Darkfinger was still out there somewhere, and with his guns, Jonas prayed. Whatever dreadful people these were that had made themselves a home beneath the dark of the mountain Jonas didn't think he'd mind shooting them himself if it came to that. He'd smelled evil before in the hold of the ruined ship, then again in the Lonely House in the wasteland, and that was how this smelled: rotten; foul.

The old hag and her two sons, when they'd grown tired of bickering and hitting each other, sat down some way off around the dull red flame which might've been a fire in a brazier but a fire that burns some kind of wood which isn't found in our world or east of the wasteland where Jonas was from.

And now Jonas, given at last a few moment of peace, began feeling about in the dark as best he could, for his hands were knotted together before him and he was lying on his side on cool, dry stone. Yet the knot was not quite as secure as it might've been and he thought he might get it loose if he tried. Even one hand would let him reach for his knife.

It *did* loosen, the cords relinquishing their hold by little and little. But when he put his hand to his belt where his knife ought to have been there was nothing there. Of course he'd dropped it when the second brother hit him in the back as he and Darkfinger waited in terror on the shore of the lake. He felt for his guns, too, but his holsters were empty.

"At least I can get out of these knots," he said to himself, though his heart was despairing.

By the fire the high, shrill voice of the old woman became a cackle and he caught bits of what she was saying. "—tied him up all snug-like and put pins in him till he started to squeal like a stuck pig, I did! . . . and then when the fire was quite hot and right for cooking . . . what a fine feast that little guy made! Who knew you could get so much meat from—" (Here there was a good deal of yabbering, little of which made sense in any language, Jonas thought). Then Mother was saying, "—might've shot him myself, had I known the *buggar* was packing those nasty irons."

183

"Shot it, Mother?" asked the younger brother in amazement. "What, with its *gunners*?"

"Aye!" cried Mother. "Duntchee doubt it, Sonny. I would'a shot it dead, I would'a."

"Shut your old, foul rotters, the both of you," snarled Gutter. "Shut it before I knock you both on the head again."

After that Jonas couldn't make out their voices anymore. His hands were free, anyhow, so now it was just his feet still tied in the knots. With his fingers he made short enough work of it.

Just about the time the final cords were coming free Jonas heard again the raised voices of the witch and her sons. They were squealing, bumping about in the dark: something was going on. Maybe Gutter was clobbering them both on their heads again. Jonas could only hope it was true.

The knot came free and he scrambled away from the stake that had been his imprisonment. Now what was he to do, he wondered. He had no idea which way let him out of this place. And who could say what *this place* was, at all? There might be walls close by, or it might be all wide open spaces as far as the lake. He didn't dare to make a run for it, not without first knowing what he might bump into in the dark. And if he *did* know which direction was which, the moment he ran they'd be after him quick as jackals, for undoubtedly they could see much better than he in the dark, being used to the shadows beneath the mountains.

Their voices were coming to him quite shrill again, terribly excited about something, though at first he didn't know what. Neither could he see anything but their grotesque shadows leaping on invisible walls, cast by the wicked glow of the fire.

"Over here!" cried Mother. "Went this way, I saw!"

"No, not that way, you stupid, old, brainless thing!" yelled Gutter. "It wouldn't have gone back to the lake."

Jonas' heart jumped into his throat with excitement. At last! A heading! Now if only that old wretch would get out of his way. He marked the direction of her voice and crawled back from the stake and the fire until he thought he was as far as he dared to go for fear of falling into some hole.

"Then why don't you go'n check the other one," said Mother. "Maybe he's ready to be talkin'."

"Send Sonny," answered Gutter. "I ain't yours to be telling me what to do. I'm going after this slippery little fish and I'm gonna spear him, you see if I don't."

By the sounds that came to him after that Jonas guessed Gutter must have run off in the other direction while Mother, meanwhile, went back to the fire. And the latter, at least, was true because a moment later she began screaming. "It's gutted him, it has! Cut his belly right open and spilled all his worms out!"

But Jonas barely heard this because he was running now as fast as he dared with his hands out before him, groping wildly in the dark, making for the direction of the lake. If he got to the water, he reasoned, he'd be able to find the path again and make for the West Gate.

But at that he stopped cold. What of his guns? The thought of leaving his irons by the fire so that old wretch of a woman could paw over them for a time and then end up shooting her own sons, likely as not, well, the thought made him choke up all over again. Sure he wouldn't mind if those ugly, wicked people who ate anyone who passed by were shot, but that old woman touching his guns . . .*ugh*! He couldn't abide the thought of it.

And then a truly dreadful thing occurred to him. What of Darkfinger? Had he also gone on to the West Gate? Supposing he hadn't. Supposing he was waiting around in the dark, unsure of which way to go. Jonas couldn't leave him there on his own, for the voices in the cellar of the Lonely House still plagued his memory. But on the other hand he might spend hours searching. Maybe he'd even get caught again, and then what would he do?

He stood for a moment in the dark feeling the world so big and wide around him, feeling the warmth of the air, feeling the stale sting of it in his lungs. He felt helpless, oh so helpless. *What would Darkfinger do*, he wondered?

But the answer was apparent almost at once. They were hardly friends – companions, certainly, but hardly friends. And Darkfinger had killed many more men than he and was likely the faster shot – though since their faceoff in Dodge had ended in a frantic scramble to get out alive this would have to be left to the jury. But Jonas was convinced now that Darkfinger possessed a certain honour that he himself had never thought of before. And he knew at once what the Kid would do.

He turned around, turned his back to the lake and the air flowing down from the sunlit ways above, the air that smelled a little less fusty than that before him. He turned back to the dull, dead glow of the fire and gave up all hope for despair.

When he was close-enough to the flames that he thought he should be able to hear Mother and Sonny talking, he was alarmed to hear nothing at all. The air was perfectly still. Closer to the fire he crept until the heat of it was on his face. He surely must be just beyond its glow, just close enough to see anyone who came or went but not so close as to be seen himself. There he'd wait for them to come back, though he hadn't any idea what he might do when they did.

Something caught his eye, something lying close to the fire, something that didn't move. *Darkfinger!* he thought. Oh, what had they done to him? He crept in closer. Nevermind if they spotted him. But it *wasn't* Darkfinger, either: it was Sonny lying dead, his face on the ground and blood pooling around the slash in his gut.

Darkfinger! It had to be him. Only the kid could've done it. And if he'd killed Sonny then he must still be close. Maybe he'd come back to help. Maybe he was looking for Jonas right now!

The sound of running feet came to Jonas again as he sat there by the fire and with it came the scream of the old woman. "Gutter, Gutter!" she cried. "Did you get him? Did he get away?"

187

"Spear him quick, Mother, and I'll shoot him dead!" yelled Gutter in reply. "Quick, before he gets past and out to the lake!"

Even as Gutter yelled there came in the dark of the cavern a violent, resounding, roaring gunshot, and Jonas knew it wasn't his own gun that had been shot but Darkfinger's big *darkiron*.

"*Arrh!* You little devil!" screamed Mother. "I'm going to cut you up! You gone and killed both of 'em!"

The sound of running feet was close now, not the flat *slaps* of the dwellers but the hard *knocks* of a booted gait. And then Jonas could see Darkfinger, wild-eyed and with both his guns smoking, running low to the ground, right into the circle of light around the fire.

"Jonas!" he cried, and it was both excitement and alarm in his eyes. "Jonas, where 'ave those monsters put you?" Darkfinger couldn't see him where he crouched at the verge of the pool of firelight.

"Darkfinger!" replied Jonas in but a whisper, the happiness that only the reunion of close friends can bring filling his heart. "Where is the old witch?"

"Close, *too* close," replied Darkfinger. "Here, I've your guns. Took 'em off that *thing* when I shot it. But I'm 'fraid I've lost yer knife, and yer bag, too."

"Nevermind!" hissed Jonas. "You're safe, that's all that matters. Let's go before that *cani* comes back."

They ran now like they'd never run before. Jonas feared at any moment they'd run into a wall or trip on some stone in the floor, but Darkfinger seemed to know the way, even in the dark. Of course, thought Jonas, the first thing any sensible person would do was to get his bearing so as to make a hasty getaway if the need found them. Certainly he himself should've known better. How many times had he only just made it out of some camp before the *droges* caught up because he was foolish and didn't plan his escape?

"Slow now," whispered Darkfinger suddenly in the dark. "I think we're almost to the lake. Here, down on the ground: help me find the road!"

They both got down on their hands and knees and searched about for the stones that marked the edge of the path, but before they'd found it Jonas put his hands in the water at the edge of the lake. "Too far!" he whispered. "Back the other way!"

But they were startled by a shrill voice in the dark. "Where are you, dear sweet little boys? I'm going to find you and peel the skin right off your fingers, I am, and then I'm going to roast you up all nice and proper like I should'a done a'ready!"

"Hurry!" whispered Jonas.

"It's here," replied Darkfinger.

And sure enough, Jonas' hands had just then touched a standing rock that could only be one thing: the edge of the road beneath the mountain.

"Up then, and keep moving!" said Darkfinger.

But now, as they ran on the path as fast they dared, feeling with their hands for the markers at its edge, the voice of Mother came to them once again. They couldn't make out what she said, it sounded more like a cry of glee than any-

189

thing else, but there could be no doubt about it: she was ahead of them, making for the West Gate to cut them off.

"We'll never get out if we can't get past her," said Darkfinger.

"We have to try," replied Jonas. And they both knew it.

The path began to go up a little now and it seemed to Jonas it was wending to the right, around the edge of the lake. It never stopped climbing.

Once Darkfinger put a hand on Jonas' shoulder and whispered fiercely in his ear. It might've been the wind for all that Jonas heard, but perhaps a moment later Darkfinger's meaning was clear for he heard the sharp slap of Mother's feet coming quickly and quite close. It seemed she was running parallel with the road but not upon it; they heard her voice saying, "Catch 'em at the stairs, that's what we'll do! Hide in the dark till they're quite close then stab out their eyes!"

When she'd gone on they kept moving, always upward, always forward. But now a nasty thought was growing in Jonas' mind: supposing they didn't hear her. Supposing she hid so well they went right into her trap. He couldn't shoot what he couldn't see, and even Darkfinger's guns would be no use then.

The same thought must've occurred to the Kid because he was moving slower and more cautiously than ever before. Quite suddenly he wasn't moving at all and Jonas could feel as plainly as if he saw Darkfinger gripping the hafts of his guns. "The steps are ahead," he whispered in Jonas' ear.

"Then where's the witch?" Jonas asked.

But Darkfinger's voice cut off his thoughts. "Quickly, hide!" he hissed.

They passed the line of stones that marked the edge of the path and, fumbling about in the dark, they found a boulder beyond that was so large they both could crouch behind and be out of sight. And now there were voices coming to them that were certainly not of Mother or either of her wretched spawn. These were new voices, hoarse and gruff, the hungry voices of wicked men, and Jonas couldn't have guessed *who* or *what* they were.

There was a hurried scuffle on the stairs and then came Mother's voice as she sprang past them, saying, "Oh, those awful, nasty, wicked creatures! What do they want to come down here for? Fish, sure. Are there no fish in sunlight or moonlight? Ugh, I'll spear them from behind one at a time, that's what I'll do, and we'll have goblin for supper, if we can't get those slippery devils in the dark! No, of course we shan't. They'll get out soon enough, so they will, wretched creatures!"

Then she was gone and from above and much higher up they could hear quite plainly the shuffling of many footsteps in the darkness. Only it wasn't quite dark anymore, not as it had been in the deep. With the footsteps came a light, the dry, warm glow of torches held up in shambly hands that are hardened and scabrous for gripping in rough places. "Fishes, fishes in the dark!" they sang as they marched:

Fishes, fishes in the dark!

191

Tasteful things.
Yummy things.
We want them for our supper.
Nothing like a tasty fish,
Fishes, fishes in the dark!

Jonas slipped one eye around the edge of the boulder and counted the goblins as they passed. One, two, three . . . he was to fifteen, and then Darkfinger was grabbing his shoulder. "That's the last one," he said. "Quiet now and we'll get by alright, what with all the noise they're making."

So they went as quietly as they could round the back of the boulder, then up the steps until the loud, rough voices of the goblinfolk were far away and far below.

Now the going was much easier than it had been because it was very obvious which way was forward. One had only to follow the steps, and though each step was steeper than the last, so that after only a little while they were climbing with their hands as much as with their feet and trying not to think of what was behind and below them, it was quick. It seemed only a very short time before the breath in their lungs was quite fresh and there was a little more light ahead. Then Darkfinger cried, "Look, Jonas, look at it!"

And sure enough, streaming down upon their faces was a cold, pale radiance, not the light of day, but perhaps something else.

"What have we come to now?" wondered Jonas, exasperated. What could make such a strange light?

But only a few more steps brought them to the end of the stairs, and now he understood.

They were standing in the mouth of a mountain cave, much like the one they'd come in by. Low down in the north-western sky was a bright-gold moon, not yet full but perhaps a few nights past its first quarter: it was no longer a crescent but a half-winked eye looking down on them. And it was certainly one of the most beautiful things Jonas had ever seen.

They were both so weary with the dark and the climb they would've lain down and fallen asleep right there on the threshold without even blanket or fire, had Jonas not reminded them both the goblins might come back before dawn. Having goblins tripping over you in the night would be much worse than a few more minutes yet on their feet.

With the moon so long down about the horizon, dawn was undoubtedly near already and this brought them to wonder just how long the journey beneath the mountain had been.

They went beyond the mouth of the cave, though not far. A short walk to the north brought them through a stand of firs into a secluded hollow, barely large enough for the both of them. But it was surrounded on all sides by hemlock and alders, and unless someone was to walk right into the midst of it they might pass within a matter of paces and never know they were there. So they lay down back-to-back in the heather. It was not very comfortable, and they had no pillows for their heads (all their things were gone, except for Jonas' flint and tinder which he kept in the pocket of his jacket next to his pipe). But they were warm enough with their jackets pulled up snug around their necks and their backs together. They were asleep before the moon touched the horizon.

~CHAPTER FOURTEEN~
THE OTHER SIDE OF THE MOUNTAINS

Jonas felt he must've been moments from freezing when he woke. It wasn't only that he'd lost his things and however warm his jacket was it just wasn't warm *enough*: the sun was well up already but of course it was on the east of the mountains and they were on the west face now. With the lateness of the year and winter coming on apace the nights were getting cold. If he didn't find a new bedroll before the snow began to creep its way down the mountainside winter would be bitter and arduous at best.

But there was nothing for it now. When you wake up cold on the ground it's nearly impossible to be warm so long as you lie there and so you must get up. He did this now and he cursed the dark when he remembered his knife was no longer stuck in his belt. Darkfinger still had his, however; it was longer and sharper, and what with a few dry sticks from beneath the trees and his own flint and steel, Jonas managed to light up a low, crackling fire. Now, if only there was something to eat. He supposed he might be able to find an animal but he wasn't sure he dared to shoot. Who knew what nasty creatures might be skulking about still. The goblins, perhaps, or maybe even the old witch from under the mountain. And anyway, what with the cold of the night still in his bones what he really wanted was a good, hot mug of soup; but he hadn't a pan or water.

Darkfinger woke up just then, none too glad for the fire, and when talk of food came up and around he brought out of his jacket some dried meats and fruits the brothers Brimhallow and Goran had given them. He'd felt he might like a thing or two on the dark road and so had smuggled a little inside his jacket rather than Jonas' bag. It wasn't nice eating cold things like that when the air around them was already so frozen, but it was better than being hungry, true enough.

Darkfinger said he'd heard a stream the night before and he thought it must be quite close, so Jonas went to find it, and it was. It was a bit of a climb to get down to it for the water came tumbling from out of rocks that had once fallen from some higher place and now were piled in a great and scathing heap. The water was terribly cold against his fingers but it was oh-so-refreshing, and when he'd bathed his arms and head in it he put his shirt on again and had a good long drink. Then he tended the fire while Darkfinger went down for a bathe.

When they both were back at the fire once more, as there was nothing else to be done they started to think about where they should go next.

"We might find the place where the tracks come out," said Jonas, "because then we'll know where the coach has gone and be able to follow it."

"Of course," Darkfinger agreed.

But they weren't entirely certain of where they'd come out relative to everything else. Was the old road that had run under the mountain, the road by which the coach had passed, north or south of them?

"We must climb up a bit and see if we can have a look around," said Darkfinger.

There was a rocky ledge on the mountainside not far from where they were. The stream flowed from beneath it. It was a good scramble to get up, but when they were at the top they stood on a spur that struck out in a point of mountain-bone. Now they could see the lands that surrounded spread out like a map, vast, even unto the western horizon.

They were high on the side of the west face of the Great Peak and before them was a long valley that ran north to south with the Demon's Teeth, backed by lower hills of evergreens on its western side, the side opposite them. It joined another valley a little farther south that ran west, away from the point where the Great Peak was joined up with the next peak in line; and that, Jonas reasoned, must be where the old road had come out, right in the low of the saddle where the peaks were met.

They were climbing down from the rocks again when a bird, black against the sky, flew low over the heights and came slowly down toward them, circling little by little, until it passed quite near over their heads.

"Jonas!" exclaimed Darkfinger. "Did you see that?"

"Yes," replied Jonas feeling his own hopes rising, for the bird was a gorfalkon, and unless he was quite mistaken, it was the very same creature which had spoken to him the day before outside of the brothers' hole (or perhaps it was three days? he didn't know).

They stopped at the foot of the rocks and, sure enough, the gorfalkon came back, swooped down and alighted on a rock, himself very excited and quite out of breath. "I've been searching for you two all morning," he exclaimed. "Took your pretty time getting through, didn't you? What foul thing befell you beneath the mountain?"

But Darkfinger would surrender no tale. Jonas could only reply grimly, "If it's just the same to you, I think I'd prefer not to return to those dark places so soon."

"Very well," replied the gorfalkon. "Nevermind that. I've flown far south this morning and I've seen many things. Goblins are astir in the hills and also many Darklings. Do not enter this valley, for the pale people are making their way south from Mount Tyran in the north and many have camped where this valley runs into the Jericho Valley just *there*. They 've joined with the goblin: the forces of Babylon are marching on Jericho."

"How shall we get through then?" asked Jonas.

"Not having a wing or two about your person does make things quite difficult," said the gorfalkon. "But I think if you make your way south a bit, and are very careful, you may creep by the goblins. Have you still your weapons?"

"Aye," said Darkfinger. "No demons or darkness could carry away our guns."

"That is good," answered the gorfalkon. "But I warn you just the same, be wary. I shall watch from the skies as best I may, but soon I and my brothers must fly to the battle, for already the scouts have returned and announced that the city is besieged! And there are many more foes yet on the move. For us this war begins below in the field, for we are ordered to harry the enemy on the road."

"*Where* is Jericho City?" asked Jonas.

"Right this way," replied the bird, directing their gaze down the valley to where it joined the other. "Follow the tracks and they will not lead you wrong. They say the train is once more on the move!"

"The train!" Jonas and Darkfinger exclaimed together.

But the great bird had already lifted itself on its wings and made for the sky with a last, long cry that echoed on the wind and seemed to come from everywhere at once.

They made their way back to the mouth of the West Gate and Darkfinger took a moment to examine the bare ground there. He had only some meagre skill in the telling of tales in the earth, and Jonas professed none at all, but it looked to them both like a great many someones had been through in the night. And then – and this was the most disturbing of all – Darkfinger found in the loose earth a set of prints that cut sharply off to the left, the prints of someone crawling on all fours. Jonas needed little imagination to see the witch with her nose to earth say, *Which way did ye go, ye little vermin?*

The hills on the west side of the Demon's Teeth were all up and down, even as high as they were. There were little valleys of broken stone here and there with ridges rising up in between, and all of them were covered in aspen and alder and hemlock forests with little creeks running this way and that through the heather and over the tumbled stone. And though they could see far into the valley below, standing there on the side of the mountain made one feel so small and alone in the world. Jonas at times was certain he had been a fool all along to chase after the coach when he realized how large a place the world was. It might've been days and days to climb down from those heights, if there was a way at all.

They went south now, keeping to the edge of the mountain. "Only a matter of time," said Darkfinger, "till we see down into the Jericho Valley." And then they would undoubtedly be able to make out the rails, stretching away into the west, and Jericho somewhere at the end of them. In his mind and hope Jonas imagined a terraced city of white walls and grey streets, cascading down over the moss and heather of the farther hills; but when he thought of it seriously he supposed it would be more like the Drayton camp: a dingy circle of old shacks and tents, hardened foresters with pick and axe and shovel, feeble horses, and perhaps a weathered wall of stakes that wouldn't keep out a hungry stag.

About midmorning they stopped in a shady glen of spruce and aspen. They had seen neither wandering goblin nor skulking witch and the gorfalkon hadn't returned bearing any ill tidings. "I s'pose the goblins have gone much lower 'nto the valleys where the forests're thicker and the sun doesn't shine s'much," said Darkfinger thoughtfully.

They lit up a low, smokeless fire and spit-roasted a wild hare that Jonas caught in the rocks with his bare hands. It wasn't anything like enough but it would have to do. Then, standing on the southern edge of the copse, Darkfinger pointed out a silvery thing shining in the valley below just where the two were joined.

"The camp of the Darklings that the gor-falkon spoke of," suggested Jonas. "But whatever it is, it's unnatural for something to sparkle like a diamond against the deep of the woods."

"Looks t'be right in the place which we need to cross the valley floor, too," said Darkfinger disgruntled. "Would feel a mite better if ye had still yer things. Without food, and with the fear of those dreadful people upon us at all times, it'll be a terribly long road to Jericho."

"We could go back," said Jonas quite thoughtlessly, looking back at the mountain and thinking of all those dark, dreadful places beneath it.

From Darkfinger's angry glare *he* hadn't forgotten, either.

They returned then into the thicket to trample their fire, but they both came up short only just in time: a moment later and they would've been standing in the midst of a crowd of people, some with dark, gnarled, ugly faces and others who looked rather like men but there was something in their eyes that was cruel and wicked. It is quite likely that, if it wasn't so dim and shadowed there in the trees they would've been seen at once, but as is was they were still well back in the shadows and concealed by the leafage.

"*Shhh!!*" hissed Jonas who had seen first what awaited them.

Darkfinger's eyes became wide and for a moment he looked like he might be sick. He at once made good to get from sight amidst the undergrowth, and his hands dipped to his guns. He was thumbing the hammers before either of them had drawn a breath. They were both thinking the same thing: Goblins! Darklings! And so much the sooner than either of them had hoped.

The goblins were speaking in loud, angry voices, for which both Jonas and Darkfinger were thankful. A few of them were pawing carelessly through Darkfinger's jacket which he'd left by the fire. "That's my pipe!" Darkfinger whispered fiercely as one drew it out by the stem. "Scoundrels!"

"They's close," one of the goblins was croaking. "Everything smells with their stink." In antipathy, he spat on the ground.

"They won't make it far," said one of the Darklings. "Har! Here's one of them boots!"

"And here's the other!" said another, for Jonas had in fact taken off his boots as they'd taken their early lunch and had been procrastinating the unbearable process of pushing his sore feet back into them: the cool air was quite a relief.

"Smells something horrid, it does," grunted a goblin. "Nasty little slobberin' devils! My, what a stink they make. Let's do make all good speed and get away as quick as we can!"

"Frightened, little rats?" cackled a Darkling. "The Chief did tell us that you people took fright at everything but I expected a little more gut in your bellies."

"Not frightened!" croaked the goblin. "If only the Golden Traitor wasn't so bright."

You may've read in other books that goblins and other such evil creatures don't like the sun. I'm afraid it's quite true. They have no love for anything bright or good. The sun they will often call the Golden Traitor for they've been taught to believe it once was a goblin who fell in with the company of men and ever after sought to brighten the world against its own kind. They make a point of not coming out of their holes during the day at all if they can help it. But Darklings are very wicked men and they don't fear the sun but will mock it and curse it if they must. Now the Lord of Babylon was calling forth his hordes, and the goblins feared the wrath of their master much more than they feared the light of day.

"You'll stay, just the same," the captain of the Darklings was saying. "You'll not go back to your holes till I say you can or I'll see that the Chief himself deals with your treachery! We'll find them, we will. Any Jericho *gdull* are to be delivered to the Commander with their throats uncut and their guts still in their bellies."

Jonas was growing very uncomfortable. He thought at any moment the nearest goblin might turn around and look right at him, its queer smile shining through its yellowed teeth and its bright eyes wickedly spiteful.

"It's lost," he whispered to Darkfinger through a grimace. "Let's get away quick!"

Darkfinger gave a last look but he didn't turn away. His eyes dropped to his guns. "Common, Jonas," he whispered, something edging its way into his voice, something Jonas had only ever heard twice before: once in the streets of Dodge and once again in Drayton. "We can take 'em! 'Twixt you and me, we've got through much worse."

"No!" hissed back Jonas. "Shouldn't make more noise than we need to."

"Then we take 'em *quiet*," replied Darkfinger, drawing his knife. "I'll catch that one from behind, and you nab his nicker; then we'll take the rest."

Jonas didn't like it but Darkfinger was right: it didn't feel right running away. And anyway, he needed his boots, didn't he? Least that was what he told himself to quiet the doubt of his mind.

The closest goblin, the one Darkfinger had marked, was standing not a turn away. The scabrous flesh of the back of his legs and neck was like that of a tree and his hair was coarse and black and matted. Jonas hadn't ever seen a goblin before save a dried-out corpse hung on the wall of a saloon in Manter, but now he found himself hoping it wouldn't turn its head for so much the worse was its face in his mind.

Darkfinger stooped low beneath the edges of the trees, poising his knife to strike. When he did, the goblin went down without a cry for he'd placed his knife true. Before Jonas quite saw what happened Darkfinger was thrusting the cruel goblin blade into his hands. It was at least as long as his arm and marked with a wicked, crooked edge that would tear more than it cut – and not that it was dull, either. The steel was smoky-blue and engraved, and he couldn't help but wonder if the knife in the waystation's smuggler's cache had not perhaps been forged by goblins.

"Now!" Darkfinger whispered, and together they leaped from the edge of the glen.

It's hard to say what the goblins thought at being taken by surprise, for their faces are so hard and stony, you see. Certainly they only just had time to see one of their company slump down in the heather and, although they often will fight with and kill one another, to see their own dead at the hands of a man always makes them bitter angry. But the Darklings' faces grew angrier still and their fists tightened on their weapons. "Cut their throats!" they cried. "Kill the little men!"

Darkfinger took the first. He proved in a moment that his hands were as deft with a knife as they were with a gun, and the raider went down with his long blade in its throat. Then the second was on Jonas, and in the beat of his heart he had to teach himself to wield the clumsy goblin blade. Even so, it proved handier than he had expected

205

and the goblin fell without its head, for the edge was long and cleaved the air at every stroke.

Then all the rest of that vile crowd was bearing down upon them. Darkfinger felled two goblins and a Darkling, and then the knife was knocked from his fist by a wicked thing with bright eyes that screeched and hollered in delight at the sight of Darkfinger ringing his bleeding hand. Jonas took three goblins, too, before someone stepped on his foot and someone else scratched his arm. Then they were on him and all over him and he was fighting tooth and nail to get free. He made heedless strokes and couldn't tell in the tumult if his thrusts were true or not.

In the midst of the mad scramble that followed he was certain he would be killed – certain, that is, until the clear morning air was split by the *bang!* of one of Darkfinger's guns. Then Jonas was up, both his irons in hand, and he was shooting (he wasn't even sure *what* he was shooting, his mind had been set aside and it was instinct that had taken over, the instinct of a runner to shoot and kill without discretion when the need arose: it was *battlefire*). Six shots with his right hand, six with his left. He dumped the shells and reloaded, as slippery as a fish, quick as a wolf, and he emptied both guns again, save the final two rounds in the left.

They were lying dead around him in heaps, goblin and Darkling alike, the dead lying upon the dead where his bullets had taken them.

He holstered his right gun, keeping his left in hand in case he needed those last two shots. He had to find Darkfinger, he simply *had* too.

The Kid was there, lying beneath the body of a Darkling raider. The nasty, twisted hilt of the marauder-knife protruded from between his ribs. His *darkiron* had been knocked from his hand, the chargeholes all emptied.

~CHAPTER FIFTEEN~
STRANGE COMPANY

"Darkfinger!" he cried.

He would've drawn the knife free right there but the Kid stopped him. The effort he exerted to raise his hand brought tears to the Kid's eyes, though the pain was all mixed up with some semblance of a smile that might actually have been more pain. "Told you we could take 'em," he said; and now he was not just smiling but grinning as well. He coughed and blood ran from the corner of his mouth. Had Jonas been a man of medicine he might've known then that Darkfinger had just seen the first waystop on the road to the Last Station.

"We can make it to Jericho!" said Jonas then, for he was *not* a man of medicine and hope was still paramount. "I'll get you there if I have to carry you myself. And we'll find a medician who will fix you up. There must be men able to bind the wound, even beyond the wasteland."

Darkfinger laughed and wheezed and choked up more blood that spattered on his chin. "Maybe if ye help me up I can walk a bit," he said.

"You're going to *have* to," replied Jonas. Every goblin and Darkling in the hills must've heard the firing of the *darkirons*; every enemy for a thousand turns or more would descend down upon them.

Jonas still wanted to take the blade out but Darkfinger wouldn't let him. "Doesn't feel right," he said; "feels like a piece of it's digging into m'heart every time I move." So they left it in and bound it round as tight as they could to seal the wound and stop up the flow.

Jonas helped Darkfinger to his feet then and, though the Kid hacked up more blood and his face congealed, when he was standing his breath came evenly and his resolve strengthened.

Still, the going was slow, *terribly* slow. It was pain and torture for Darkfinger: Jonas could see it in the Kid's eyes with every step he made. But Darkfinger didn't complain, and it was only from time to time he'd demand they rest. And it was a wonder then, for the farther they went the stronger he seemed to get.

The land around them was mostly highland hills, ridges, and valleys now. The west side of the Great Peak descended with less vigour into the valley below than the east had done, and so it wasn't altogether unpleasant country to travel in, even for Darkfinger. There were more and more shady glens and low places where the moss and heather grew thick beneath the underbrush and the trees grew higher and higher. This was good, and Jonas felt the easing of the nerves that comes with knowing one is in safer confines. Fewer unfriendly eyes to mark their passage.

But still there came a time when a deep ravine – or perhaps more like a canyon – opened up before them. Both north and south slopes were steep and littered in loose shale that wouldn't support even a child's weight, if one had chanced to test it. Waiting at the bottom were only sharp rocks, tempered by years of wind and rain into crenulated bastions.

To make the matter more difficult still, to their right and the west where the slopes of the Great Peak fell away into the valley below they now found themselves standing on a wide sort of shelfland, perched on the shoulder of the mountain. This barred their descent, and so neither could they get around the gorge by traversing the lower slopes. If Jonas and Darkfinger had known, this place would've been called the *Risen Gall* in the tongue of the eastlands, for the dead sometimes walked there, it was said, and those who fell into the gorge rarely came back.

Jonas supposed they might climb up and thereby get across the top of the ravine where the mountain shed its load little by little into the valley below. It would be a dangerous, strenuous climb, even for a strong man such as he, and he doubted if Darkfinger could make it at all, what with the strength that was draining away from him. But it also seemed the only way to cross.

"I'll wait," said Darkfinger when they'd talked it over, "whilst ye climb as quick as ye may

211

across to the other side; and there, perhaps, ye may find a way through. In the very least ye shall be across and can go on without me t'slow ye down."

For that last remark Jonas scolded the Kid. The idea on the whole didn't seem a very good one, but it was the *only* one. So in the end he agreed. He laid Darkfinger beneath a tree with both his guns loaded and his knife close at hand, and then, with one last, long, despairing look back, he took to the heights once more, nimble with the exhilaration and fear still fresh and in equal measure.

It proved not such a dreadful climb, afterall. True, the crossing at the height of the gorge was treacherous, and more than once Jonas paused, his breath caught stiflingly in his lungs as the shale and scree beneath his feet shifted then came to rest again. His boots were planted wherever the slope looked most stable and his hands were on the uphill side to disperse his weight. In this way he could look between his boots and see where the slide of loose debris went over the edge and into the gorge below. If it should move he too would go over that edge, and if that should happen he knew his chances would be nothing but spitshine in a roaring prairie fire.

But soon enough he was standing soundly on the southern ridge and looking back, thinking that somewhere over there Darkfinger was hunkered up beneath the trees on a bed of moss and heather, if only he could see him. He hoped the Kid was alright.

The ridge ran down little by little, all hilled and thickened by underbrush; and when it could go no farther it ended in a steep climb down into the valley, far below. Jonas made his way down it slowly now, for in spite of the brush that grew thick as blood up through the settled stones it was still uneven ground and ill-suited for walking. He was now perhaps half-way down the ridge and he'd seen no easier way across nor place by which they might get lower down. The valley below was opening before him, and he could look far up Jericho Valley, a good way into distant dales and hills far off on the western horizon where grey-blue mountains stood tall with ice-capped peaks. And there, on the eastern edge of a hillock, with the valley falling away to his very feet beneath it, sparkling in the high sun, was the city of Jericho. The sound of a bell peeling came to him even now from so far off, and it was perhaps the most beautiful thing he had ever heard.

Maybe it's shameful to mention it but at that moment Jonas thought of nothing but that city, nothing but getting *to* that city. If he could've flown across the valley he would've done so, leaving Darkfinger behind.

Now he supposed he could climb down to the end of the ridge. From there he could see quite properly what kind of a town it was, if it had a wall or if there were many houses or people or roads, for his eyes were sharp and could see well at such a very great distance. And there would probably be a path by which he might descend into the valley below, for all manner of wild creatures must live on these slopes and where they go often paths are left behind. From there it would be a straight walk to the gates of Jericho.

213

He hurried now, paying little attention to his bruised shins. He scrambled from one rock to the next, slipping under brush and over logs, always moving down the length of the ridge. Alders grew thick and strangling in his path, high clumps of them overwhich he could not see and he had to work a path that wound in, out, and amongst them from time to time. The sweet scent of juniper was upon him and a mountain ash nodded before him, as if in some friendly greet. A creature in the rocks on his left let out a shrill whistle that hung on the air for a moment before subsiding: perhaps it was a rodent or a bird, he didn't know. He climbed past a stump that was charred and blackened, probably the recipient of a skybolt. A bird gave a sharp melody on his right but it wasn't quite right for a bird, he thought, it was too low and too *cooing*. Another answered somewhere ahead of him only this one was rather more like a soft *hoot*.

And now he knew what it was, for the wildmen of the prairie grass often spoke thusly to one another, and he knew it was too late. The shrubbery on his left moved. A small rock was dislodged behind him and it skipped past his shoulder. Then the thicket in front of him moved, too, but it wasn't really *bushes* that were moving, it was a tall man in dry trousers and an emerald-green cloak keeping low to the ground and moving so quickly that if one wasn't sharp they wouldn't see him, at all. He went like a shadow and was gone in a soft flutter of the trees at his back.

214

Jonas froze. To himself he laid all manner of profane curses for he ought to have known better, he ought to have seen.

"Stay, stranger," said a soft voice behind him. "There are many of us close with arrows strung and we don't miss readily. As you value your life *you will not move.*"

Before Jonas a man stepped out with hood drawn and mask pulled well up to his eyes – cold, fierce eyes that would spear you as soon as look at you. He was covered all in deep green as were his friends, and his gloved hand was gripping the carved hilt of a longsword bound round in an intricate scabbard of burnished silver. "Who are you that walks this land as a spy?" he asked. "Are you a Darkling? Some servant of they who pillage and burn? Or of their foul allies, the hill goblin? Speak or I will slay you where you stand, God-willing!"

"I am not a spy," replied Jonas quickly. His voice shook but he pushed his guns deeper into their holsters and drew his hands away quick as he could to show he meant no harm. "And if the Darkling and goblin are your enemies why then that makes us friends, I should think. They've wounded *my* friend, and though I've killed all of those that attacked us he now lies hurt and dying on the far side of this gorge. If I cannot find a way to bring him to Jericho I fear he may die!"

At this the wood-wary stranger gave Jonas a curious look from beyond his hood, and then his eyes were turned to someone who now stood behind Jonas, as if for some confirmation. But none was needed. A strong hand touched Jonas' shoulder, and now a man much fairer than the rest and with a strong face that made you want to trust in him stepped forward and said, "I am Anhil of Jericho and these are my rangers. If you are an ally we would know this for certain for allies are scarce in these days. If this friend of yours lies hurt, as you say, we'll know what foul deed it was that felled him, and then the truth shall be yours – or your deceit shall be met with a swift vengeance."

There were six to the company, Jonas saw, and he had the idea there were many more he did *not* see. They didn't give their names, save Anhil, but they went with their hoods up and faces masked and weapons at the ready. And now, as they led him back to the edge of the ravine Anhil told Jonas many things.

"These hills are all presidance of the county of the Gallidros, presided over, thusly, by Jericho City," he said. "They have been for time out of mind, and it is by our strength that they remain so. Goblin and Darkling both would take them from us, and then the very stones beneath our feet if we let them. Babylon has long-since hungered for the breach of our walls; they would make this vale a part of the waste that stretches forever over Akotar. But there are none who know these hills better than the Rangers of the Gallidros. We come like the wild animal, swift as shadows in the night. We've been many days in the hills hunting goblin, Darkling, and many more foul creatures. But now the defence of the city is called and all men must return to their arms. The siege has already reached the gate."

At the edge of the gorge they came to a halt and Anhil pointed up toward the peak perhaps twenty turns or so where a number of stakes were driven in between the rocks, each with a dark, grisly lump set atop. "This is the penance that Jericho demands of its enemies," he said. Jonas suspected there was a wary message in those words.

They were right on the edge of the gorge now, Jonas, Anhil, and those five who accompanied him plainly. For a moment Jonas thought they would walk right off the edge. *Are you mad?* he was going to ask. Did they not see there was no path to get down? But at the very last they stepped through a hedge of close firs and a narrow ledge opened up before them. He saw now there was plainly a path, hardly more than that of a wild animal. It went right over the edge and, clinging to the wall, it made its way by little and little down into the divide. Then, at perhaps fifteen turns, it vanished quite suddenly into the rocks and was gone. But when they now came to that place Jonas saw it did *not* vanish as he had thought but instead it went through many low places, winding this way and that way, always with the very largest and heaviest boulders on his right so that if the mountain above gave way and let slide a great load of its stone they would be well protected, and likely as not what *did* come down would pass quite harmlessly over their heads.

When they came again where they must resume the hill a narrow pathway had been cut into the stone. It went up the side of the ravine in narrow steps, well chiselled but steep and treacherous to anyone who didn't know the way. For the rangers of the Gallidros it was a well-trodden path and they seemed to walk it as easily as if it were fair-levelled.

Very soon they were beyond the gorge and walking amongst the highland hills once more. "You'll see, it isn't far now," said Jonas when they were nearing the place where he'd left Darkfinger. A great relief was coming upon him – and also a dread that Darkfinger might not be where he'd been left, only a soft indentation where his body had lain. But when they came into the glen, sure as anything, there was Darkfinger, asleep on the heather, his guns still held tight in his fists. "Darkfinger," said Jonas, shaking him gently. The Kid opened his eyes and smiled, though it was only with great effort.

At once Anhil was there and one of his men was with him. "This is Ahkair," said Anhil. They looked first into Darkfinger's eyes, then at his hands, and finally they drew back the bandages and looked at the wound. "The cut is that of a goblin, and clumsy" said the ranger, and Anhil agreed; "but the blade is that of a Darkling, and that bodes ill."

"What ill omen?" asked Jonas.

"The Darklings mark their weapons with poison that grows black in the blood until even the most resolved man would fall and turn on his own," replied Anhil. "If your friend doesn't reach Jericho before the moon has risen at the Wintercome he will die – but first he will take as many of us as he may."

"Can we make it?" asked Jonas. "Will you help us?"

"We are indebted to any who slay so many of our foes," replied the rangers: many were looking on Darkfinger and Jonas with a new wonderment, at the wounds that marked their valour and the weapons that were their friends.

"Of course we'll help you now," said Anhil. "But you must understand our caution is our own just cause, and what counsel we hold even now is our own by rights. There are servants of the enemy at every border, their spies walk among us, and we choose our friends more carefully than we choose our enemies."

Two of the company slipped away quietly then and made north for the field of battle where the dead still lay. "They will mark the place with the heads of the slain," said Anhil, "and no goblin will dare to tread that ground for as long as the bones remain."

Then they that waited still with their captain made ready to leave. Ahkair, who had examined Darkfinger's wound (for he was a physician of the woodman's fashion), applied a golden leaf between the Kid's teeth and then removed the blade with such steady hands that it hardly pained Darkfinger at all. With ointment from a purse he carried beneath his tunic he bound the wound with strips of cloth and made fast the knot so it wouldn't loosen. From a flask he forced a draught down the Kid's throat. Then Anhil himself lifted Darkfinger's arm over his shoulder, and Jonas took his other, and in this way they made south once more.

There was a place, the rangers now told them, where many could lie safe in the dark. It was a refuge of the men of the Gallidros. There were many like it scattered through the hills, sacred places by which the rangers could harbour in their own lands. It was perhaps some hours away still, and even though it was high time for lunch they would have to travel hard if they were to reach it by dark.

~CHAPTER SIXTEEN~
THE TRAIN

The day slipped by, and by the time the sun was sunk into the west, now gone below the horizon, the company descended into a hollow on the south side of the southern ridge (Gald-inspur, as the rangers called it). It was sheltered on every side by the forest which now was thick and twisted with thorns and bracken. The way they'd come was the only way to enter the hollow if one didn't want the prick and the tangle, so Anhil explained.

There was also a stream flowing through the midst of the dell, a laughing little brook that ran over clear, blue stones and was cool and delicious as any mountain stream that flows from the heights. Each of them had their turn to drink and wash as much as they wanted, and now a good many more of the rangers came down by ones and twos until their number had grown by half a score. Then a fire was made and food was produced: fresh meat roasted over the coals, cold venison and dried fruits and nuts, even berries, freshly picked. It was wonderful to anyone who'd been out in the mountains for so long and the desert before that, and Jonas and Darkfinger were quite famished.

When everyone was well fed Anhil called many of them together. To some were given orders specific; but to most he commanded the watch. Then they dwindled away, vanishing one by one into the forest again at each side of the hollow until there was only a handful still around the fire. And then those, too, drew away to different corners of the dell until it was just Jonas, Anhil, and Darkfinger who remained near. Jonas was weary; but as for the Kid, he looked much the better, likely as not due to the ointment of the rangers.

And now Anhil asked, "Where have you come from? And to where were you going? And what mission has brought you so far? For I know that there are no towns in the vales near and there are no passes in these mountains south of the Duranges, not since the goblins closed the road through Snowstone and Idenhall. Not without a great host could the high roads be retaken and the watch-fires rekindled."

"We've come not from over the mountains," said Jonas, "but *through* them."

"Through them?" exclaimed Anhil. "Are you then some apparition by which you can pass through the stones the god has laid in place?"

"No!" laughed Jonas. "We came by a dark road. It was called the West Gate by they who set us on it."

Anhil's face clouded. "I've heard of that road," he said. "An old passage all but forgotten to us, though we know still its hated mouth. And maybe it is well that time has left it for it was always a dangerous place, deep, and full of dreadful things. My kin have long called it the Sunless Road and never gone in thereby. Ah, but I believe what you say; I can see it in your eyes! And early this morning, before the sun was yet up, my men captured an old witch, a nasty wretch of a demon who spoke dark tidings of dark places and people with bright eyes who whisper curses in the night. Undoubtedly she has crawled out of that hole on your scent to murder you in your sleep."

"Mother!" whispered Jonas, horrified.

"Yes, I believe she did call herself that," said Anhil thoughtfully. "Though what child would permit her company I wouldn't dare to guess."

"What did you with her?" asked Darkfinger who seemed to have taken some interest in what was said at this point.

"Tied her to a stake on the hillock where we found her," replied Anhil disinterestedly. "When daylight came doubtless she went mad with the fright of it, for you understand the creatures of the dark do not love the sun. Surely she got herself free and returned to her hole, but I doubt she'll ever venture out again, not so long as she lives, which may yet be a very terrible long time."

"You ought to have cut her throat," replied Jonas bitterly.

The ranger regarded him with reproach. "*Ought* has nothing to do with it," said he. "It's the goblin and Darkling we hunt, not vermin from the underground. Life for such a creature is wretched and miserable in suffice. There is no sense killing what doesn't need to be killed, not when it did us no harm. It is for vengeance and honour that we slay our enemies, not pleasure."

"Just the same, I would like to see her dead," replied Jonas; and he was very bitter.

"But you still have not answered all of my questions," said Anhil then.

So Jonas answered: "We came from across the wide wasteland – the True Frontier, we call it. Beyond is our homeland."

"What is it like?" asked Anhil.

Jonas thought for a moment, thought of the dry prairie grass that would rustle in the wind this time of year, of the rolling hills, of the low valleys and rivers where the fish tasted of rot and decay, or the towns that grew hot in the heat of the day, where bodies were often lying in the street where they were shot, until the carrion came to feed on them.

"It's a hard world," he said, "a hard, dying world without forests. A world where the air is stale all the time. There we don't kill for honour or glory or freedom but because someone else has something we want. My world has been left behind."

"Sounds a wretched place, indeed," replied Anhil, though his eyes were on the fire and it was impossible to say if he was disgusted by what he heard or not.

"To tell you the truth," said Jonas, "we're not really certain *where* we're going. We've come across the wastelands, true enough, in pursuit of the coach; but we've no idea where it's gone now or what we should find before us. And now we've been delayed so many days in the mountains that it must be well beyond those far hills by now, if it came this way at all."

"It is *not*," replied Anhil, though he didn't look up. "It's not gone, it's in the valley below as we speak. It came this way some nights ago, and it's partly for the sake of the rail-bourne that we men of Jericho are going to war. Indeed, if my fellows and I don't succeed in the defence of Jericho then it won't be gone but it will be lost to you, just the same."

"What do you *mean*?" asked Jonas and Darkfinger at once.

"Do you not know what it is?" wondered Anhil. "Don't you know what rides the rails from here to the eastern sea and back again?"

Jonas and Darkfinger looked at one another but neither replied.

"It's the *Fera*!" said Anhil. "The *One* Train. Don't you see? It's *thee* train!"

When he had said this Jonas felt the growing horror he'd known on the platform in Little Puretill. He could see still the glowing, demonic lamp on the train's caboose as it vanished beyond the hill. But there arose within him a longing to follow in its wake, to walk the rails and see where it would go. And then he began to forget that he'd ever been frightened of it, at all, and all he felt was that longing to go where only the rails would lead him, to know the wonderment of it, to feel

225

the deep rumble of it in his bones, to go beyond the farthest horizon.

"It's a symbol of freedom," said Anhil, still starring into the flickering flames of the fire. "It guards this land from those who would wish it evil. It's kept for so long our foes in the north at bay. But more than that, it's hope and deliverance for my people. It awakes in each of us the will to fight another day. Though our walls have been assailed for many years we've always held firm *because* of the hope the train brings."

"Is it then just a train?" asked Darkfinger with a note of disappointment.

"A train?" asked Anhil, at last looking up. "Are you mad, man? Do you not see? It is not *just* a train, it's so much more! Wherever it goes the captives are freed and justice is dealt with a swift hand. I'm telling you it's *thee* train! Did you not wonder at the stirrings that arose in your heart when you saw? I said it delivers to us *hope*! When it passes by any who hear its cry will remember their dreams, remember their purpose, remember the young man they once were. You, Darkfinger the Kid, have lived your life as a warrior who doesn't lay down because that is but a small part of your purpose: to fight for freedom, even when no one else will, the same honour that your father bestowed upon you. But more deeply than that, you must go home. You are a stranger in these lands. You cannot fight for a purpose not your own. And you, Jonas Arthur, it awakes in you firstly a fear because you've been running your whole life from that which you know to be true: that you are a man of honour, not a murderer and a thief. It calls you to follow because that's who you are, a warrior strong, a warrior proud."

Darkfinger's mouth was open and his eyes blank in wonderment. Jonas himself couldn't quite believe the things this ranger of the mountains was saying. How did he know so much about them when they'd told him so little?

"It's late," said Anhil when some moments had passed and still neither Jonas nor Darkfinger could find any words. "Best to let dreams take your thoughts. Tomorrow we'll go down into the valley. Five more nights to Wintercome."

Jonas set down with his feet to the fire and his head in the heather, but he lay awake for a very long time thinking about what Anhil had said. At last only two things had occurred to him: either Anhil, humble ranger of Gallidros, was what they'd sometimes called a *seeing-man* in his homeland, or Jonas Arthur had experienced for the first time in his life his own *rivening*; and if the latter were the case he knew he'd never be the same again, not as long as he lived.

Sometime in the night something disturbing entered Jonas' dreams. He saw a long hand reaching out of the trees at the edge of the hollow, fingers waggling for the hem of his dusty trousers. And in his dream, though he tried to move he couldn't: something held him fast, though he had no idea what it was. A voice called to him softly: *The train, Jonas; where is the train?* And he knew that the hand would take the coach away unless he could stop it somehow. Then he awoke in a cold sweat, feeling the freezing mountain air tingling in his skin, and part of his dream turned out to be true: he couldn't

227

move. At first he panicked, but when he began to come to sleepy terms with the world around him he realized it was not a groping, shrivelled hand that had disturbed his dreams but people all around him going this way and that and speaking in hushed voices.

"Did you see it?" asked one. "How big was it?"

"*Big*," replied another. "Biggest I've seen this far south."

"Where was it?" asked someone else.

"Just up the ridge, standing in the moonlight."

"But it isn't the Wintercome yet."

Jonas sat, his arms and legs and back aching as they'd never done before. The dream quickly faded, sleep gone with it. It was cold. Maybe that was why he was stiff all over, even to the bone. The fire was built up but it was fresh wood and it crackled loudly. "What's going on?" he asked a ranger who was sitting quietly nearby, his bare sword laid across his knees and his eyes watchful in the darkness.

"There're monsters in the hills," replied the ranger. "Go back to sleep. We'll keep the fire burning and they'll not enter the hollow."

Jonas lay back down. His mind was racing in different directions, as of a train that comes to a fork that has not been properly set. He wondered now if sleep would come again, at all. He longed that it might to shut out the thoughts that taunted him. If only for a moment.

~CHAPTER SEVENTEEN~
FALLEN FRIENDS

Jonas didn't awake again until the sun was up in the east. It was greying light for the sun was still behind the mountain. Mist hung low in the valley, and the peaks were laden with fresh snow. The hollow was cold, the grass and heathery white with a light frost. In spite of what the ranger had said the fire was out, but Jonas awoke warmer and far more comfortable than you would expect for having slept on the ground. Someone had cast a thick cover of fine furs about him. Darkfinger, too, was sleeping in skins, an elaboration of tawny-grey and charcoal-black, the adornment of whatever animal they'd belonged to. He had a bundle for a pillow, and the look on his face was peaceful. That did Jonas good, to see serenity in the Kid's face.

The hollow was nearly empty. One ranger, and not one Jonas thought he'd seen before, sat opposite him on the bank of the brook running a whetstone down the length of his blade in slow, even strokes.

"Good morning," said the ranger, looking up when he noticed Jonas was awakened.

"Good morning," replied Jonas: and in the eastern fashion, "How do we fare?"

"There's been much excitement in the night," said the ranger. "We've travelled far in the dark and killed many foes. Even now Captain Anhil is some ten and fifty leagues north tracking those goblin-carrion back to their holes."

"Goblins is it?" asked Jonas. "Have they come here, too?"

"Nay," said the ranger; "but nearly. One we shot just there beyond the trees, and another fell with mine own arrow in its back on yestereve's road."

"By the Fall!" cried Jonas. "Are they really so close?"

But the ranger laughed. "Not as close as you'd think," said he. "They could come within a *furth* of this place and never know it. Don't worry: you're as safe here as if you were within the walls of Jericho itself. Soon Anhil will return, and then we'll move on."

The ranger wouldn't rekindle the fire: the risk was too high. But he was possessed of some cold provisions, dried meats and the bread of the men of the Gallidros. This brightened Jonas' spirits, as only a good, hearty breakfast can, and he found he was quite ready for another day, though he prayed it wouldn't follow the suit of those that had come before.

Sometime later Darkfinger awoke in a delirious fit. He was pale and weak, his eyes were dark, his skin deathly cold, and he wouldn't move. When Jonas lifted his head he cried out in pain and thrashed about.

"Let him be," said the ranger who was sitting on the bank of the hollow smoking weed rolled in a leaf. "Better to let the poison fester for now or it will kill him all the quicker."

It was perhaps some hours hence then, though Jonas wasn't truly certain of the time. Anhil and those that were with him returned. First the brambles on the verge of the hollow were disturbed, and then through the underbrush crept a dozen or so of the men of the Gallidros with Anhil coming along behind, his sword bared and bloody. They looked weary. All their blades were messed, and their faces and hands were marred with the passing of their quarry. Those among them with quivers and bows now had few arrows or none at all. Anhil was the grimmest of the lot: he'd taken a hard knock to the head, caught a bolt with the flesh of his right hand, and an enemy had drawn blood through his coat of leather. But his mood was bright and he said as they entered the hollow, as if it were a competition, "Forty we've slain. Perhaps three parties, maybe four. And also a band of the Darkling."

"You've left us to muck about while you get all the glory!" cried another of his men.

"How long have you been out?" wondered Jonas, for the sun was now climbing toward the time of morning that normal people in normal places would call breakfast time.

"Since half-night," replied Anhil. "It feels as if the day has already been spent!"

"And that wolf has done us no good," said another ranger who let himself down wearily into the heather by the cold ashes of the fire. "Four months we've been away from Jericho and not in all that time have we seen so many goblins in the hills, and not a single *wer-shadow*."

"And he was a big one, too," agreed another.

"A wolf?" asked Jonas. "Did you kill it?"

"Alas, nay," replied Anhil. "We followed it far up the peak, even right into the high crags, and there we shot it three times in the flank; but we could neither make a clean kill nor bring it to battle. It got away."

"A shame," said Jonas who was thinking of times long past when hunger had grown and the meat of a wolf had been a wonderful thing in a pinch – aye, even a treat. When he was a boy he'd once shot, killed and eaten a great grey-back raw, as he'd been starved for some days and had no means for a fire.

But Anhil shook his head. "Would not eat of the wolf, not to save your life," he said. "This wolf was not like the creatures that *you* call wolf. It was the demon that walks by the night and robs babes from the cradle. It is possessed of the craft of shadows."

"A *dakher*, true," agreed the others.

No proper meal was made to break the fast, for it seemed the rangers had already eaten to keep up their strength. But instead they made way to leave. Darkfinger, of course, was of concern for his delirious cries would've awakened the dead and drawn any wandering foes. But Ahkair said to Anhil, "The venom has festered; it *must* be drawn out."

"And you would do this for him?" asked Anhil.

"I would," replied Ahkair. "Let me do it, and you must let me alone with him for the quarter of an hour and keep his friend close, for if I don't render what is left now he will die."

The medician was in earnest as he said this, and so Anhil made them leave, every one of them, even Jonas, though he gave his protest. "I want to stay with my friend," he pleaded.

But Anhil answered, "It will do neither you nor he any good."

It was a hundred turns at least through the underbrush that Anhil led them before he called them to halt. And there he made them wait. "I'll willfully put to death any that defy me," he said wearily.

"Why must he be alone?" begged Jonas.

But the captain of the rangers replied, "There are arts amongst men who practice medicine that are better neither witnessed nor known by us." And though the captain of the rangers was somnolent, his eyes were dangerous, and Jonas didn't dare to test him, though he would've given over much to be near Darkfinger now.

When at last Anhil said, "We should return," Jonas was anxious and perturbed, and he was the first to enter the hollow. There on the earth lay Darkfinger, just as they'd left him. Ahkair hung over his body. The wound was bound, Darkfinger was deep in a fitful sleep, and he didn't awaken. "I've given him a medicine of mine own make. It takes the pain and brings sweet dreams," said Ahkair.

When Anhil saw the Kid he at once ordered the march.

From the hidden dell of the rangers they followed secret ways only those of the Gallidros knew well and no other living creature could find. They went up and down, over hill and through ravines and valleys of sharp rocks kept by the Teeth's weather. But by little and little they were descending, chiefly, and soon they weren't walking on the high shoulders of the mountain any longer but in the gentler, rolling ridges that fell ever away into Jericho Valley below.

Still the entire company of rangers was not present. Jonas thought it like walking with the dead, for many were missing, and yet he felt they were close.

When night came again they made camp once more in the hills. It was at such a place that the thinner forests of the heights were becoming the very thickly wooded lowland forests of the valleys. Anhil said they should make it to the rails before high noon of the following day; presently, however, safety was on the edge of those forests rather than near to the cuttings of the rails where they could be easily discovered. And Jonas was just as glad for he was far wearier than he had ever been since he'd found himself upon the road with Darkfinger the Kid.

As there was little cover in those hills and there were no such hidden places as the hollow in which they'd spent the night previous, Anhil posted many of his men to watch during the hours of darkness. Those who were not called unto the watch bedded down on the very edge of the forest with their faces to an open meadow. But Ahkair said now to Jonas, "Come with me."

The ranger led him deep into the forest where the thickets were close, and then he said, "There's a golden flower that blooms low to the earth. Its leaves are crimson below and as green as my cloak above."

Deep beneath a coppice of thorns they found the plant, and Ahkair instructed Jonas to pluck as many leaves as he could. "Talhorn it is called," he said, "and I've no more in my stores to treat your friend with."

Then he said: "There is another herb that I must have. It's called Oakras, and while the vegetable is as poisonous as the venom of the Darklings, the root has many healing properties."

This second weed they found sprouted at the edge of a brook. Ahkair drew it from the earth and concealed it away in his wallet. And then he said, "You understand what it is I've done for your friend."

Jonas replied, "I can never show the gratitude I owe you."

"It is more than you know, I fear," replied Ahkair. "I've drawn from your friend the venom with mine own lungs, and if it should fester in me I will die in his stead."

Jonas was horrified at this, and he looked at the medician ranger as he never had before. "Why have you told me this?" he begged.

Ahkair shrugged by way of reply, but he said, "Were it my debt I'd want to be told."

They returned to the company then, and Jonas lay down with his eyes on the meadow by which they camped. He might've fallen asleep at once; his eyes were nearly closed when quite close there were voices speaking and men moving about. "Lie still," said Anhil, who had arisen. He and some few others made off through the shadows with sword drawn and bow bent. But Jonas didn't see them return for he'd fallen asleep.

The next morning they ate sparingly, as they had done before. Jonas wondered if these wry rangers of the wild ever ate more than what they could without breaking stride. Again, it seemed, many of their company had been awake in the night, and one even had suffered a very serious wound at the hands of some enemy. Jonas saw the blood on the man's brow and wondered how deep the gash went, but Ahkair ushered the ranger away and Jonas never knew the truth of it, even if the man had lived or died.

Before the day was yet warm they broke and made south once more, following the curvature of the hill. It wasn't such a great distance to the rail cuttings, Anhil said, but he'd amended his resolve during the night: the woods were thick and ill-suited for travel and he wouldn't bring them there so early on in the day. The rails were dangerous now that the goblins kept the South Pass and Idenhall.

It was coming to the noontime when they stopped in a shady place on the lower slopes of the mountain. Here a meal was prepared and they all ate what they could, which wasn't much. Then a few of the rangers were sent on ahead to scout the land. Carrn, who was Anhil's Second, was their captain, and Jonas accompanied them.

As they went this small band of men made themselves known to him, and he learned each of their names and positions, many of which made no account. There was one thing they told him, however, which he thought worth remembering. Near a month before, as they'd made north on the edge of the Teeth, scouting the goblin presence, a dozen or so of their company had fallen into bad attendance with the enemy and been taken. But when Anhil had discovered this he'd ordered the pursuit, and they'd tracked their enemy low down into the valley where the roads come from the north, from Babylon. There they'd fallen on an encampment of Darklings and goblins and beset them. The fray had been bitter and bloody. Though they'd slain all of their foes, true enough, many of their own had taken wounds, and some score had lost their lives, either hewn down in the conflict or to the venomous blades of their enemy. Anhil still was bitter over this, they said.

Not long after that the underbrush thinned, the hills gave way and they descended a dell toward another widening valley which ran away west and into Jericho's own breach. It was all valley forests now, easy walking on sore feet, through moss and spent needles. Then they came out on a hillside that was covered with short aspen and Great-willow Herb, and for a moment Jonas felt some longing within him for something long-past, but he couldn't recall what it was. The rangers told him as they went that they'd be coming on the tracks presently and the roads that went out from the valley to various places. They didn't know what they might find there. Goblins perhaps, or a band of Darklings, maybe. Whatever it might be Jonas shouldn't fire his guns for any reason, they said. If there was battle to be done it would be with the sword and the arrow. So they gave him a long-knife, noticing he had none.

Sure as time, they came over a low hill and into a stand of firs, and there, not fifteen turns down a steep bank, the rails ran straight on through a cutting and up the Jericho Valley, gleaming a little in the high noon sun. The air smelled of oily tar and hot iron and the song of some insect carried to them now.

As they waited on the edge of the embankment Jonas listened to the rangers in their high speech, which was rather like his own language but it sounded much more eloquent.

"Nay," said one whose name was Illachir, "they were stationed to guard this pass. I know this because my brother was amongst them."

"Then perhaps they've already returned home," said another. "Everyone's been withdrawn, afterall. I'm sure Dendros is safe. I wouldn't worry about your brother."

"Or they might've moved south to better cover," said someone else.

"There will be signs to tell us what's happened," said Carrn. "We'll go down together while you set arrow to the string from here, lest any enemy be waiting."

And so the captain Carrn and Illachir made their way down the embankment. The earth was loose: it slid beneath their feet and sent a cascade before them. Then at last they stood at the edge of the rails. There Carrn stooped low to the ground to examine something in the earth. There were words between them (Jonas could see their lips move but they spoke too softly to be heard). Then Carrn turned back and made signs with his hand: two fingers extended, then against his palm, then against his chest; and finally he placed them against his arm.

"Four south, two east, company west," said another of the rangers who lay near, reading the message.

"What does it mean?" asked Jonas.

"For the two and the four who can say?" replied the ranger. "But for the company that went west it bodes ill on all accounts. All roads into the valley are held by the enemy. What madness drove them west I cannot say, but they most certainly have been slain. But come now, if there were enemies near we would've seen or heard them. Just the same, we must be wary." A look amongst themselves and the rangers divided: two went silently to the left with arrows nocked to the string and another two to the right; then Jonas, with those few who remained, descended the edge of the cutting to meet Carrn and Illachir at the railbed.

Illachir was distraught: his sword was already in his hand. "We must avenge them this fate!" he cried.

But Carrn replied firmly, "No Illachir. We'll discover what's befallen them kill those who've done it, if we may; but we'll not walk into the arms of the enemy, not so long as the god is before us."

They went west on the rails then, moving slowly. Carrn ordered scouts to both the right-hand and the left-hand, and they went deftly as a breeze through the trees at either side of the cutting. Perhaps two hundred turns they went on, and there they came on a pike struck deep into the earth at the edge of the rails; and then another, and another. On each was a grisly, hewn head – not that of a goblin or a Darkling but those of men. The expressions on their faces were dreadful Jonas could hardly bear to look at them.

"These were guardsmen!" cried the rangers in dismay.

It wasn't long after that they came upon the scene of the battle. A slew of discarded armory and nocked arms riddled the railbed and the adjacent embankments. Bodies lay this way and that, both men and goblins together in the cruel and twisted agony of death, their flesh pierced by arrows and swords. It was dreadful, even for Jonas, though he'd seen battles before and bodies lying rotting and bloated in the streets.

When they were in amongst the bodies of the fallen the captain of the rangers stooped and examined their sigils. His face fell in dismay. "These are *not* guardsmen of the vale," he cried. "They're the Watch of the Baron of the Gallidros! What foul errand has brought them here?"

"Perhaps they came to meet the train when it came through the passes," answered one of the men.

"The baron's own son, Balin, rode with them as their captain," said Carrn. "Now they've fallen, and who can say of the train or Balin? We've been routed!"

Even as he spoke Carrn was becoming violent, and when he looked around at the faces of the men, he cried, "Find the Balin! If we can't undo this evil at the least we should return the body!"

They each went from one body to the next, turning them over to look into their silent faces. Jonas didn't know what he was looking for but he supposed Balin would look somehow nobler than the rest, if in fact it was possible for any man to be more noble than those men. But as it was he needn't have concerned himself with this, for when every body was turned and their faces seen Balin wasn't amongst them.

Jonas looked around at all the bodies. They hadn't been noblemen but they were still men, he thought. Doubtless most had families at home waiting for husbands and fathers they'd never see again.

A terrible cry startled Jonas from his thought. He turned to see Illachir knelt over the body of another man who was certainly his brother, though the blood on the dead man's face and the gash that killed him had made him equal with his brothers. The ranger wept bitterly and shamelessly.

"Then Balin has died in the hills, perhaps, or made safe from this place," said the captain wearily when they'd made certain they hadn't missed a single body. A few of the rangers searched the bank and bush near at hand for signs of a trail leading away, but none was found.

"It was possible that Balin was never at this slaughter," said one.

But Carrn was already counting his men quickly, and he said, "Tend your blades, count your arrows. If your quivers are light then take what you can from the ground. A goblin shaft will do in a pinch. And when we're ready we'll go west and fall on those foes at the crossing."

~CHAPTER EIGHTEEN~
TERRIBLE MISTAKES

At a word from the captain they were moving, not all in a line or even in a party but spread out in ranks, some in front with blades already drawn and some behind with arrows fitted to the string. They went quickly and silently, and even Jonas had his sturdy knife in hand. Hateful words were passed along, and some of the rangers vowed terrible things if they found the enemy with the blood still on their swords. The *battlefire* was consuming all of their reservations, and Jonas was afraid. The only one of them who showed any doubt was a boy named Ashe. "Captain, shouldn't we even now stand here and await Anhil?" he asked.

It was a sound idea, Jonas knew, but the captain shook his head. "Onward," he replied. "There's no glory in turning aside." Jonas wondered if maybe they didn't think a little too much of their honour and glory. It was the same reason that Darkfinger lay dying.

They came upon the first of the enemy perhaps several hundred turns down the rails. A few goblins were huddled beneath the branches of a low-hanging tree. They were under the very eaves of the southern wood where the sun barely shone, but even so, they seemed distraught and anxious at being out during the day. They grumbled amongst themselves, saying, "Why must we be left out to bake beneath the Golden Traitor when there is a cool wood at our backs? Even the guard of the bridge is not entrusted to us!"

Another said, "*Nagh*, given to the Commander's dogs."

"Faugh!" spat another.

And the reply was, "But of course those great darkies do what they like, yes they do. We shouldst kill them ourselves but the masters shouldn't like that, now would they? Always the goblins who get the dirty work, so it is. And starved, too!"

When Jonas saw them he knew at once what task they were about: wiping clean soiled blades.

"Fie!" cried the captain in anger.

An arrow struck out from Jonas' left and one of the goblins fell with the black-feathered shaft in its throat; then there was the sound of another bowstring on his right and another goblin fell, one of his foul, yellow eyes all but gone out.

"For Jericho, for the Gallidros!" cried the captain; and behind him came Illachir, screaming, "For Dendros!"

They fell on those few goblins who remained. The captain's sword flashed in the sun and Illachir's fell next to it; and the battle was over as quickly as it had begun. Not a cut, not a scratch: the rangers were not even hard of breath as one might expect after such a fight. Many of them looked much younger and ready for war than they had a moment before.

"On!" said the captain then. "We must find the rest of this rabble and finish them quickly. Pray the god has left them all divided, and this will be a swift victory!"

They ran on, round one bend of wooded highland and then the next. The tracks always ran on ahead over the ties and the crushings that kept back the forests. The sound of their feet on the gravel was like the thunder of a storm.

They came on another party of goblins just beyond, and this time Jonas was the first in the assault. Three arrows passed him as he ran swift and sure, and when his knife killed a goblin clean already five others were dead from the rangers' volleys. Then the company was with him and they cut down those that remained, even before a squeal could escape to alarm any other foes who might be near at hand. And there *were* others. One of the rangers cried out, and then an arrow was strung and a goblin that was lurking near fell with the feathers in his eye. Then there was another cry. One of the company was pointing up the opposite bank, southward, toward the thickets of tangled underbrush. "One has gotten away!" he cried.

"Fetch him quick and make him dead," replied the captain. "Meet us at the first crossing!"

Four of the rangers with bows at the ready vanished into the forest. The rest went on once more. But all were growing wary now, and Jonas wondered all the while what might await them around the next bend of the rails. Never once had it crossed his mind that he might turn aside from the task.

He was just wondering what the captain had meant by "crossing" when they came through a low cutting with high walls of stone on either side and there before them was a deep ravine with a noisy river tumbling through it. The rails went straight on ahead, right out and over the water, held up on thick timbers that though they were weathered and patched were not anything like as old and precarious as the trestle over the Drayton River had been. Certainly they would've permitted a party of men or the passage of a train.

Now the company came to a halt again and the rangers were speaking in low voices as they stood in the shadow of the forest.

"There's three on the bridge," said one.

"More below, likely as not," said another. "We shoot those there and all the others will come out in swarms like flies."

"They'll be blind in the sun," said one of the men. "We shall have the advantage."

"Nay," replied another, "those are not goblin-folk, they're Darklings."

"Likewise," said the captain, "the ones above will see us if we try to get below. I doubt if we can even see those others in hiding without revealing our own ground."

"We might go downstream and get into the ravine," said someone, "then reconnoitre they're position."

"No good," said another. "The edges of the Rabbish are covered in thickets and thorns as long as my hand. You can't get down the edge, except at the bridge. Believe me, I've held this post under Ildir."

Now Ashe spoke and there was something in his eyes, something Jonas hadn't seen in any of the other dull-grey eyes of the men of the Gallidros until now. It flickered and flamed violently but it wasn't the excitement or vigour of *battle-fire*. "We shouldn't – we *can't*!" he said. "We must go back at once to meet Anhil and the rest of the company before this madness has slain us all!"

There were a few murmurs and nods from amongst the small band but the captain stood forward and his face was dark and angry. "*Madness*?" he growled. "Friends, we are cowards all if we do not face these criminals! We should shoot those and then we meet the others that will come with our swords drawn, or the deaths of those that lie in the sun are for *nothing*!" He grew stern and commanding, and he added, "The next man who would turn away will fall by the blade of my sword."

Fear gave way to loyalty – or perhaps to greater fear – and though many still voiced their concerns none would've stayed behind when the captain stepped out toward the trestle and the waiting enemy, goblin and Darkling both. Several bows were strung, and four or five arrows struck the pale people that waited on the bridge. One of them fell with a cry but the others never spoke a word, so speedily dealt were their deaths.

And then the secret was betrayed. From the shadows beneath the trestle came the cries of the enemies, so recently alarmed. They came out in an angry horde, ready for battle, the yellow eyes of the goblins flashing, the shadowed eyes of the Darklings even *darker* still. Their weapons were in their hands, and some had bows. An arrow sung over Jonas' head, and he was reaching for his iron before his reason had once again become him. Another arrow or two was loosed but when your enemy stares you in the face only a knife is practical. Jonas now drew his, not *only* a knife any longer but a part of his arm and flesh.

And then the battle was joined and the lines met in a horrendous *clash* of goblin steel upon those of the men. Jonas had no time to count his friends at his sides, only the enemy before, and he killed with a will. In the swollen air of the quickening day the brawl of battle was all that he could hear. Edge upon edge. The cry of they who'd been not as quick as their adversaries. The *ring* of steel. At his side was a man who'd drawn his sword but a moment too late: the Darkling who met him drove him through without a moment of hesitation. There were the songs of bows, and several enemies before Jonas were dead as impulsively as they'd been alive, long, black-feathered shafts in their throats – those four of the company who'd chased the goblin into the woods now were returned and hidden somewhere

high up in the thickets on the southern embankment, shooting their arrows into the fray.

For a moment Jonas was certain it would be a
sure and easy victory, as smooth as one could ask
for. But when the battle was hottest and most
violent every one of the company was quite suddenly awakened by the long, wending *baarooooh*
of a horn. A Darkling, wild with battle-fright,
had stepped out of line of the archers in the trees
and he'd raised a great, twisted horn to his lips
to wind it. At once arrows were nocked, swords
were turned. Time itself ground to a halt, show-
ering an array of sparks like glow-flies, and
Jonas cut down a goblin in his frantic haste to
stay the inevitable hand, knowing even as he did
so the hour had already grown too late. The Darkling was feathered with the arrows of the company who'd even thrown their swords aside in
their haste to shoot him, but that didn't stop him
from sounding one last long blast that resounded
in the valley.

The battle that remained was quickly over,
the last of the goblins cut down with their dreadful cries still in their throats and the Darklings
were scattered into the woods where they, too,
were shot and killed or left to run wild. All those
of the company now were standing about with
blood on their swords, saying things like, "Do you
think they heard that?" and "That horn really
echoed, didn't it?" But Jonas was certain that
nearly everyone for a hundred turns or more had
heard the sound of that horn. Still, the worst
moment of all was when there came an answer-
ing blast from ahead of them that seemed to echo

from one hill to the next, until their ears were nearly throbbing with it.

Now the faces of many of the rangers were pale and whatever *battlefire* had been awake in their eyes a moment before died away to fear.

"How many were gathered at the crossroads?" asked the captain.

"Two thousand, I heard," said someone.

"Nay, it was *four* thousand," said another.

But Ashe spoke, and he said, "No, it is *ten* thousand strong. I've seen it myself, perhaps a week ago, an army of goblin and Darkling gathered under the banners of Babylon."

"We cannot stay here," said the captain, who was quite decided all at once. "We've made a terrible mistake in coming. I'm sorry, Ashe, I should've listened to you when you bade me to return to Master Anhil. We must now make all haste. He will know what to do."

"Are we to leave Ithar and Edrin for the enemy to devour?" asked someone.

But Carrn's reply was hurried and sharp: "We've no choice. They'll be upon us if we linger."

And so they now all went back the way they'd come, the rangers who'd been on the hill having had come down to them while they were speaking amongst themselves. They returned to the place where they'd first come upon the rails. They all paused at once beneath the embankment down which not so long ago they'd all scrambled, each person realizing the same terrible truth. For perhaps a minute or more there had been deep, throbbing hornwinds at their backs, all the while growing steadily. They'd been so low at first, almost at one with the earth,

Jonas hadn't noticed – or at least not understood what they were. But now everyone's faces grew pale, and the captain said, "Quickly now, up the bluff and through the trees!"

They all scrambled up the embankment from the rails, and there they were held at stay amidst the underbrush by a ranger, hooded and cloaked, crouching low and with an arrow nocked.

"Where is Anhil?" demanded the captain at once.

But Anhil and the rest of the company came quite suddenly from the forest with their weapons readied, as if they'd heard.

"We've seen," said Anhil solemnly – grimly – "or rather *heard*. Come quickly: the Darklings watch the roads west and we've seen many in the hills, too, some even in the south. If we've any luck still it must be to get ahead of them before they close off the way. If we've none then the god guide our blades—"

As he'd spoken this Anhil had been numbering those present and seeing their faces, and now he cried, "Where are Ithar and Edrin!"

Carrn was downcast, and he replied, "Fallen, Anhil, they are *fallen*."

For a moment it seemed to Jonas that Anhil would certainly draw from his scabbard his longsword and cut his captain down, even then. For an enduring moment it was only fire that burned in his eyes, devouring Carrn . . . and then came the *barrrrooooh!* of the horn once more, and Anhil at once was both grave and certain.

He said, "We'll mourn and chide when we're in the deepwood. Quickly now Evenhorn, you are

251

van. Down the bank with you and scout the far woods."

They went with a sense of urgency down and over the rails. The coming out of the forest into the open of the cutting was not as nice as it had been before. Jonas felt naked, as if unfriendly eyes were always upon him there in the open. He imagined with every throbbing wind of the horn a new set of eyes would look out from the shadows of the forest somewhere, like the glowing orbs that haunt the corners of children's rooms. But then they were up the other bank and into the thickets.

Now they went south and always uphill, always in the darkest places, always in the thickest forests. And although Jonas had felt before the company of rangers was much larger than what made themselves known, he now saw just how many they were: perhaps three-score men strong, all in grey garb, hooded and masked, and each carrying their gear of war. They went all in line save a small vanguard before, moving silently as ghosts in a single rank, and a rearguard came behind as if they were shadows. And Ahkair bore Darkfinger, for the Kid was now passing into dreams that held like a grasping hand.

They were well up on the south side of the valley now, with the rails far behind them, and before them the hills climbed steadily away, not as steeply as the north but thickly wooded and dense to anyone who walked within. Jonas saw only occasionally by some gap in the forest what lay the land had taken around them; for all the rest of the while he felt as if he'd been folded and blind.

As they came now under the eaves of a forest of bright, red maples, from behind came the sound of strung bows and the ringing of steel, and one of the rearguard hollered, "They are behind us!"

"Lead on!" said Anhil to Carrn, "until you are beneath the eaves." Then he and those others with him drew their swords and turned about to defend their flank. Jonas went with them.

The goblins had come up silently at their backs. Two men they'd already killed before they were discovered, and now those few of the rearguard who remained were hard-pressed but they held their ground. Anhil came amongst them to strengthen their position, and he killed a goblin with the first stroke of his sword. He gave the instruction, his voice ringing with authority: "Retreat but do not *flee!*" Then his men fell into rank, hewing down the enemy where they stood. When the enemy was dead they turned and followed in pursuit of the rest of the company.

The red forest grew sparse, and then it was replaced by heavy boughs and moss-covered trunks. The undergrowth grew thick and the canopy heavy, and then the forest went black, all together. You cannot understand just how truly black that forest was unless you have seen it for yourself as Jonas did. In quiet words the rangers spoke of that land, calling it *"Racka Ickari"* or "the Demon's Lair" as translated by Anhil himself. "The Demon dwelt in these hills and bared his teeth against the desert," said Anhil; or such was taught by the men of old. But they also told other stories which may've been nearer the truth: once the Demon's Lair had been filled with a horde of vile monsters, they said. In a long and bloody war the men of the vale drove them deep into the mountain caves, but at times they'd creep out again, and at such times you'd hear rumours of frightful beasts, ghouls, and *dascari* that stalk the darkest parts of the forest." And it *was* dark, so dark Jonas began to forget about the sun shining on the mountains or fading into the west. It wasn't hard to imagine that place being full of hateful eyes shining in the dark.

How long were they under that blanket of darkness? I cannot say. It seemed hours to Jonas. He grew weary and sore from the march, and when the sun *did* go down (though he could no more see it than you can) and it began to get truly black beneath the cover of the forest, he wanted for nothing but to sit and rest. At last Anhil called a halt to the company, and at his word low fires were lit, fires that burnt down beneath the roots and rocks of the forest floor and gave little heat and less smoke. Then he sent scouts on ahead and also some back the way they'd come to be certain they weren't followed. The rest sat down to make supper.

Anhil at once called Carrn to himself and together they went a little way off where none could hear their words. When again they returned to the company Carrn was solemn and grave and his eyes were heavy. Anhil, likewise, said little, and Jonas thought there was a deep and weary sorrow in him that hadn't been there before: he looked old beyond his years.

It was an hour, perhaps, before the first scouts returned. By their word the forest behind was silent and nothing stirred, alive or otherwise. Then, when another half of an hour had gone by again the forward party, too, returned, but their news was much more dire. Goblins, they said, were beneath the shadows of the forest and watching all the ways, and Darklings, too, were with them, big men, much larger than any they had seen before, and these carried great axes or broad-bladed swords; some even had guns. They were the wood-dwellers from the far north and had no fear of the forests.

"Is there no way through?" asked Anhil.

But the scouts were discouraged for they'd found none.

Jonas heard all this from the shadows around the fire where they'd laid Darkfinger who still was asleep at the hands of the medicine. He felt despair sinking in upon him. They might return the way they'd come and be lost or run afoul of some evil thing in the woods, or they might press forward and be caught between the spears of the goblins and the swords of the Darklings.

Sometime after all this had happened, while he still was sitting by the fire, Darkfinger awoke from his delirious dreams.

"Jonas?" he called; and Jonas was close. He went to the Kid and helped him to sit up with his back to a tree.

"Where are we?" asked Darkfinger.

"In the forest," Jonas replied. "South of the rails. There was trouble: enemies on the road. Our position is betrayed and they are hunting us now."

"Are we going to make it then?" asked the Kid hopefully.

Jonas shook his head because he didn't know. "There are enemies between us and the city at every turn."

"I'm sorry," said Darkfinger after a long silence between them.

"For what?" asked Jonas.

"I was righteous and arrogant," said the Kid. "I shouldn't have led you in the attack."

But Jonas again shook his head. "No need," he said. "We are all righteous and arrogant men, Darkfinger. You would be less a man if you were not brash in your own right. I cannot mark you by your mistakes. Much more important is that you've saved my life many times. I am indebted to you as much as you are to me – or more. And by any accord, they say you will be alright as soon as we reach Jericho. They've given you a medicine to slow the poison."

Darkfinger laughed and winced with the pain. "I can feel it," he said, and he touched his hand to his side where the blade had pierced his flesh, "like a bullet, biting and grinding into my body, trying to get into my heart. I don't think I'll make it."

"You will," replied Jonas with some indignation. "You *have* to!"

"Perhaps," said Darkfinger. "Perhaps not. If I'm meant to die here then here I will die, Fall-willing. But you, Jonas, you will reach Jericho and you will find the train and you will know what it means for you and for me."

Jonas shook his head again. "Be quiet," he said.

Darkfinger smiled and laid his head back. Very soon he was asleep again.

Sometime later Ahkair came by to enquire as to Darkfinger's state.

"Well-enough," Jonas replied. "The dreams have faded."

But the ranger looked ill rather than relieved. "That isn't good," he said. "While delirium holds the battle within him still is fought, but when the delirium is gone one side or the other most certainly has won."

"Then the poison is gone?" asked Jonas hopefully, believing that this is what the ranger of the vale was saying.

Ahkair was silent and Jonas wondered what it could mean.

"How do you fare yourself?" he asked then tentatively, dreading the question as much as the answer.

Ahkair was by nature a jovial man, but he didn't laugh. "It has not beset me," he said only.

He cleaned, washed and redressed Darkfinger's wound, then applied a salve he'd boiled of the Talhorn and Oakras. And when he was done this he took a little root and leaf from his wallet and chewed both until they were a pulp in his mouth and the red of the leaf stained his teeth. This Jonas understood well and he felt a rising sickness within his gut.

Much later Anhil came around again also, and the sadness and weariness that was upon him before was now much less. As they sat about the fire he turned to talk of the company's condition. He didn't want to linger in the forest. Certainly it was reasonably defensible, and with a sizable company so skilled in the ways of the wood they might hold out for days against an attack, fighting in and out amongst the great trunks of the trees and their twisted roots. But the reports of the scouts that came back got only worse. The enemy was moving, they said. There were parties abroad, and some quite close. There were brief scuffles, too; one or two rangers had not come back, at all.

As Anhil spoke Jonas began to realize the men who lay dead behind them weighed heavy on his mind.

But there was very little for it because no one relished the thought of returning through the forest in the shadows of night, and Ahkair made it very plain to Anhil that Darkfinger would not survive another delay.

Jonas fell asleep with his back against a very large root and the light of the low fire in his eyes. But his dreams were dark and dreadful. In most there were goblins on all sides, poking their ugly faces in upon him.

~CHAPTER NINETEEN~
THROUGH THE RACKA ICKARI

How long they'd been beneath the perpetually black shadows of that forest is impossible to say; Jonas never knew. It seemed it was days, very *long* and very *slow* days. They made little ground for all the wood had to be scouted and re-scouted before they could. The darkness and the stale smells of bark and moss and molding things in the shadows became stifling and heavy, made worse because such a wood ought to have been alive and growing but this was not. There was fear in everyone's eyes by the time it became painfully apparent they would be making their third camp soon. More than once Jonas caught the perpetuating sentiment amongst the ranger company that Anhil was foolish to allow an outsider and a sick man to hinder them, for it was largely Darkfinger's condition that inhibited their progress.

It was difficult to get any sleep. This contributed to the length of the days, for time goes on forever when you don't sleep. It seemed the mind simply didn't want to let go in such blackness, perhaps for fear the night would still be there when it awoke again only the blackness would be on the *inside* rather than without. But on that third night (if it was in fact night, for Jonas didn't know for certain what time it might be), he actually found himself falling asleep quite willingly next to the low crackle of a fire he'd lit between two great roots of an especially gnarled and twisted tree – an *elderun* the rangers called it. Darkfinger was near at hand. He'd been getting worse, and Jonas could no longer deny himself that truth. But as Jonas slept he dreamed of glaring goblins and the brightly-glinting eyes of the Darklings peering out of the wood at him. It was a dream that came readily beneath the eaves of that forest.

He awoke, his hands on his guns. He couldn't be sure how long he'd been asleep. He expected to see faces staring at him through the darkness but there were none. His little fire was all but coals now, and it cast no light at all. But by the light of torches which the rangers had lit he could see the Gallidros company going this way and that through the shadows, and all in a bother of excitement. "What's happening?" he asked one who chanced by. "Are we under attack?"

"Gordru!" the ranger replied excitedly. "There are gordru close! Their chief is with Anhil already."

Jonas had heard about gordru, as I'm sure you have, too, but east of the wasteland such things were rumours and wild tales that only children hoped were true and later believed they'd been silly to do so. A month before perhaps Jonas himself wouldn't have believed such a thing, even if he'd heard it said to his very ears; but neither would he have believed any story about gorfalkon and goblins. Now he arose in a flurry of excitement.

All throughout the camp the fires were burning low. But one was stirred, and some of the rangers were bringing wood; others of the company were gathered around: Ahkair and Carrn and Evenhorn were there, and Anhil was in the very midst of them. They were sitting by the light of the flames, their faces ghostly in the dull glow of the embers. The gordru chieftain was with them. Hardly more than a looming shadow in the dark, he stood back from the fire. Jonas thought he could see the creature's wide hooves, round and solid like a horse's and with great coarse tufts of deep silver hair flowing down from its fetlocks; above, its legs were heavy and muscled. Jonas could only just see the light of the gordru's eyes and the glow of the fire on its wide chest when the sparks sprang up.

Then their voices came to him. Anhil was speaking; then the gordru was replying, and in a deep voice like thunder, it said, "There is no way through, not for men who go about making such a noise. But for someone else, perhaps, there is a way. There are still many paths and roads by which the goblin do not travel, deep roads in the forest under leaf and root. They go from here in many ways, and one might – just might – go as far as your city. But you would be wiser still to return the way you have come."

"We cannot return now," replied Anhil. "We already have lost many, and one of our company bears the stain of the Darkling. Jericho is now in the hands of the god if we cannot reach the walls before they are breached."

"There is war in the vale, then?" asked the gordru. "We'd heard it was so, tidings brought to our ears by the over-zealous corgrief."

"Goblin and Darkling have risen up," replied Anhil. "The dreadlord has raised his standard against us. Babylon is emptied."

"Are the corgrief then joining the fight?" asked Carrn hopefully.

The gordru gave no hint of any emotional devotion one way or the other when it said, "They are oft away on their own missions, for they've their own wars to attend to. But the king of their kindred has come forth, it is said, and this would not be so if he didn't intend to meet all his enemies in the field, once and for all. Yes, soon he will come, if he is able."

"We have the need *now*," replied Evenhorn imperatively.

The gordru was silent for a time. It shuffled its feet, it stamped its hoof, and then it said, "We've no desire to ride in the wars of men; but neither do we care for the goblin and Darkling, and if your passage would help to remove their taint from this land then we'll help as we are capable."

"We wouldn't forget it readily," replied Anhil. Then to Carrn he said, "Wake the men and get them ready to move."

Jonas was up and away in a hurry. He returned to Darkfinger, awoke him with a shake, and made him get up. "We're going, Darkfinger!" he said. "There are friends nearby who will lead us through. We're going to Jericho!"

The entire company was astir very soon, for the men of the Gallidros can come from a deep sleep and be ready for battle in an instant, as any good warrior can. They were all moving by the time Jonas and Darkfinger had gotten their things together. And as they walked, Anhil didn't come to them, but Ahkair did and he accompanied them now.

The only light to guide them was that of dim lanterns the gordru carried. These cast a silver glimmer like the moon. But it was enough to see by, and it left the forest in deep shades of shadow so that one thing looked like the next and if one was not careful all things began to look the same. "Anyone beyond the light sees only pale shadows," said Ahkair. "This is the way the gordru dwell in secret."

As for the gordru themselves, they were not many but they spread themselves at intervals amongst the men. They were silent and heavy, pacing quietly with the company, their faces solemn and bold, their eyes dark, their chests broad and tawny. They never spoke, save their chieftain who was at the head of the column with Anhil. But one was quite close to Jonas and

Darkfinger, going with its great head bowed. Jonas was surprised to see that it wore no armour nor ring-coat, nor even a leathern hauberk. Its flanks and chest were bare. But it did wear a silver harness at its sides, and from these there hung great, long scabbards which bore its swords, blades much too heavy for a man to lift. On its back was a quiver of long, black darts and a long bow made of some wood that shimmered like water in the light of the lantern.

"What are they?" asked Darkfinger who was walking next to Jonas in a dreamy daze even though many had offered to bear him.

"Gordru," replied Jonas.

"It's beautiful," said Darkfinger.

How long the march lasted Jonas never knew. Once or twice the line came to a halt. The rangers around them brought news that something was astir in the wood. Anhil came by with a few of his men. Everything was alright, they said, but they implored everyone to keep still and quiet.

Sometime later when again they stood motionless, hardly daring to breathe, three of the gordru with their flanks glistening in the light of the lamps stepped by them nearly silent, their proud heads held high as if testing the wind, their greatswords drawn. Jonas felt it would be terrible to be up against those mighty weapons and stern faces.

And again they went on into the night.

It must've been hours now since they'd left camp when there awoke in the darkness sharp cries and shrieks, and this time the rangers didn't crouch in whisper. Arrows were strung, swords unsheathed with a ring, axes withdrawn from belts.

"Goblins!" someone cried. "Goblins near!"

Next moment there was a crash of brush and a stamping of hooves: a gordru went by them at a run, the beat of its charge trembling in the earth and with a ring of steel it was making for the head of the column.

"Steady!" Ahkair whisper. "Not until the order is given!"

But then a gordru was there, not the one who'd run past but another with deep silver in its hair and mane. It came silently from the dark. "Hold tight, hold true," it said. "Keep on: the enemy doesn't yet know!"

Word came back to them by whispers that a party of goblins had been lying in the forest and their company had nearly walked right on over them. But by the skill of the gordru all had been slain and the alarm hadn't been raised.

They went on again, and it seemed it would never end, not the dark, not the silent forest, not the endless rustle of leaf or twig. The wood was as eternal as it was black.

When Darkfinger could go on no longer the gordru who kept their company spoke to him. "I will carry thee," it said, "by command of my chieftain and by the honour of my people, for we have far yet to go."

Jonas was ever afterward envious of Darkfinger his good fortune, for no other man alive was ever given the honour.

When the company was halted by command of the gordru chieftain and Anhil it was beneath the roots of a wide-spreading *cicaron* tree. There they were bade to remain quietly, to sleep if they could, and some few of the gordru lingered like silent stone monuments to keep the watch. The chieftain, meanwhile, vanished and they saw him no more for some time.

Jonas slept little, for such was his excitement. It was nearly a day's span of time since they'd fallen in with the gordru company, some of the rangers supposed, and by some reckonings this meant they were very nearly to the western edge of the forest, though of course none could say with any measure of certainty.

When they were called to their feet once more it was by Anhil himself. They went onward by the guidance of those gordru present. Hours more of darkness. Hours of weariness. But Jonas began to realize now that the shadow he was looking at wasn't as complete as it once had been, and by the light of the lantern in the near gordru's hand he could see not the close thickets and trees but low grasses and shrubs. Had they come out at last, he wondered? And in the next moment his question was answered, for beyond the far horizon the sky turned subtly grey: dawn had arrived at last.

The shadows of night further diminished until it was the twilight of very early morning. Then the trees and dense thickets of the forest seemed quite suddenly to vanished. They weren't in the wood any longer, at all, but on a wide, open hill that was covered in deep grass and bordered in treelines in all direction. And now quite presently the company was halting and many were letting themselves down into the grass. The gordru were not to be seen, save the chieftain, and he and Anhil were just now turning away from each other with a nod and a shake. Then with a great shrug of his shoulders the gordru broke into a gallop and didn't falter until he'd reached the forest and was gone. Jonas followed the retreat of the mighty creature, and there his eyes were introduced for truly the first time with the reality of the *Racka Ickari*, for you don't truly understand a thing until you have seen it both from within *and* without. The trunks of the trees were great and towering, their bark was black and broken and scabrous, their canopy dense and uninviting; even the leaves seemed to possess little life, being dull and grim. And beneath the eaves of the forest all things seemed given to despair, like a cloud before the eyes. Its very nature was malice that betrayed the haunts hidden beneath its leaves. It truly was a *dark*wood.

"Two hours march to Jericho," said Anhil wearily, coming in amongst the gathered company. "We'll reach the outer dyke by breakfast time."

Anhil and Carrn now were busy counting their numbers, and Ahkair attended to those few who'd been wounded in the night. Others were set to cleaning soiled weaponry. For a time the entire open meadow of that hilltop was awash with voices in the clear morning air, and Jonas, walking in the grass which was so high it came even above his knees, had never felt more weary in his life – not merely tired for want of sleep but really *weary* as one is who has seen far too much excitement for far too long. But even in all his weariness, in his mind he held as if it were gold the image of the train set a-flicker with sunlight reflecting on the roofs and wheels as it came slowly chugging to climb the valley: its whistle would be loud and clear in the morning air.

Jonas found Darkfinger standing on the northern edge of the hilltop, watching the sun rising in the east. He looked strong, the shadows all but gone from his eyes. Though he winced when he turned to the sound of Jones' footsteps it was nothing more than a grimace that marred his complexion and then it was gone.

"How do you feel?" asked Jonas.

"Well-enough," replied Darkfinger. "We'll be at Jericho soon, won't we?"

"Aye," agreed Jonas.

"And then what?" Darkfinger asked. "Have ye any idea?"

"I've a sort of an idea," Jonas admitted. He didn't have to explain for Darkfinger had the same sort of an idea.

"But what if it all fails?" asked Darkfinger. "What if the walls are breached? Jericho will fall, and the train, too. We can't stop that from happening, Jonas. Not we who are but two men against a vast foe."

"We have to *try*," Jonas answered.

The company was moving again, and they joined the Gallidros rangers on the western edge of the hill. "What roads now are ahead?" Jonas wondered.

"Near and far," Anhil replied absently, "all roads go one way or another. There is only one trouble still to be conquered."

"What is that?" asked Jonas.

"The wall," said Anhil. "The city is besieged and we've no way in, not for as many men as I have in my company."

"Are there no secret ways?" asked Jonas. "Do you not have a back door?"

"A door to *what*?" asked Anhil. "Jericho has withstood the test of time for many ages of men *because* there is no weakness in the wall, not *for* us nor *against* us. Yes, there are secret ways but not by which such a company may sneak through.

"Yet there is a way that we might yet get in by, not through the wall but through the *gate*." This he said ponderously, as if he was still formulating the scheme in his mind. Jonas didn't ask, for what was playing behind the eyes of Anhil Ranger of Gallidros was something that both scared and excited him. Perhaps the captain of the rangers made schemes in his heart to lead those men of his company through the very gate of the city though it was besieged. Such a plan could be nothing short of madness. So few against so many.

The sun came up. It glimmered on the horizon, turning the mountains to gold, then silver. It cast long rays across the sky and it brought the forest to life around them. Those hills surrounding Jericho Valley were like none that Jonas had ever seen before. For perhaps thousands of turns they rolled out to the north and the west, away from the mountains; and to the south they climbed higher and higher to great ridges that sometimes broke timberline.

As the company went forward Jonas soon forgot about his troubles and the torments of the

269

long road. All around him the world was awash with vibrant greens, autumn golds, and shimmering silvers. Wide woods ran away to the farthest mountains; little glens opened up before them, silent and peaceful save for the prongs that leapt gracefully away at their presence. The murmur of brooks through the grass and heather, the crisp scent of the air: these things would've made the oldest man young and the youngest man wild with excitement.

Jonas became so lost in the beauty of the vale that he didn't even notice when Darkfinger stumbled then fell to his knees. It was the cry of one of the rangers that brought him around to see what the trouble was, and then he was running to the Kid's side, taking the *darkirons* from his trembling hands and returning them to their holsters.

"Jonas!" Darkfinger cried in dismay. His eyes were murky and lined in red, and the nail of each of his fingers had turned black. The veins of his hands stood out like the veins in a leaf when you look closely, and his lips were turning blue from a cold that was quickly claiming his body. "Get off me, let me be!" he screamed, clawing for his irons. "I can see home!" he cried. "Home, Jonas! I can see it, the appletrees in autumn, the wheat fields along the road, crisp and ripe for harvest. The windmill is still turning, Jonas, and I can hear my mother calling to me. Oh, what a wonderful thing! Let me be, let me go, I *must* go!"

Ahkair was now at his side and his face was pallid: he looked nearly as ill as Darkfinger himself. He put a hand on the Kid's tired face, then a finger to his neck. "He's nearly gone," he said. "There isn't much time now."

Anhil was there, too, and he gathered a few of his men around. To Carrn he said, "Lead them to the window and shoot the arrow yourself. Don't stop until it is done." To another he said, "and when they are safe you run as quickly as you may to the gatehouse and command the Captain of the Wall to look for our coming at dawn of the day that follows the morrow, and be ready at the portcullis, if nothing else dire has changed in the course of time." To the ranger who still was stooped low over Darkfinger he said, "And Ah-kair, you must find the man from Venicia. You mustn't rest until he is found, if it is the last thing you do see it done!" Then, "Go now, run and do not stop!"

~CHAPTER TWENTY~
JERICHO AT LAST!

"**C**ome," said Ahkair. He gathered Darkfinger's arms about his own neck and hoisted the Kid onto his broad shoulders. And then he, along with the others that Anhil had chosen, and with Jonas bringing up the rear, set out westward across the hillsides of the Gallidros toward Jericho. For a time they ran, and while Jonas felt weary before the tenth part of an hour had passed the rangers seemed never to tire. They went on over rock and grassy meadow, never breaking stride, and even Ahkair, being a large man and bearing Darkfinger on his back, showed no sign of weariness.

Jericho City, that last shining hope in the vale, stood on a spur that went out like the blade of a knife into the valley below. From the west it was sentried by steep crags that divided the city from the mountains at its back. These faced east and north and were spanned by three causeways, each so narrow that both bulwarks could be touched at the same time by outstretched hands. All roads west were guarded by outlying towers and forts high on the crags and turrets on the wall that looked south and west. From the east and the floor of the valley a roadway let right up across a long causeway to the outermost wall of the city, and there the tracks ran up to a portcullis, so that any who sought to force entrance would either have to climb the high crags at the rear of the city or assault the main causeway to the east. In time of war the portcullis could be closed and kept from the walls above. The east bridge itself was so narrow that only six men abreast could climb to the gate, and thus the city was well fortified.

Jonas now saw this all from the southernmost hill in the valley, a short knoll that looked out north on the front gate and the road, and as he stood there on the hill looking on the city the sight that met his eyes sent a knot down into his stomach and made his skin crawl. For as far as he could see all across the valley floor a great multitude of men was marching upon the wall, like a line of insects creeping. Hundreds, perhaps thousands. Already there was a siege line at the wall, only just beyond the range of the guardsmen, and the enemy had shield and helm well down over their heads. They were manning great machines that worked away to bring the wall to the ground. Jonas could hear the roar of the engines like thunder in the ground: *boom! boom!*

The projectiles were flung in volleys to shatter on the buttresses and the curtain wall.

"Not far now," said Ahkair. "Let's hope the dyke is not held against us and the window is open!"

"*What* window?" asked Jonas.

But the rangers pressed on and wouldn't say, down the side of that mound, and then they were in lower hills all covered in scrub brush and thickets. Here at a certain point Carrn called a halt to the company and then he went ahead alone through a stand of trees. A moment later he was returned joyful, for the dyke was not held against them. Indeed, the enemy hadn't seen fit to command the south side of the vale at all and had instead sent all their strength against the gate. All were relieved.

Past the dike which wasn't more than an entrenchment cut into the hill they now ran. Time was coming short. Little paths here and there through heather and underbrush led them higher into the hills again, onto the edge of the crags. West were the watchtowers that guarded the bridges to the highest terrace of the city. When Carrn had stood and looked for some time, squinting his eyes to see, he said, "The bridges *are* held against us. We must look to the window."

Back to the wall of the city they turned. It stood up tall and white opposite them on the spur of the hill, and Jonas at last saw on the highest most terrace, right up on the very top of the wall, there stood a little house with a thatched roof, and though it was so far away it was not more than a black spot on the high expanse of the wall, he could see a window: the shutter was left open.

Now Carrn was stepping forward with his hood and mask thrown back, and he nocked an arrow to the string and drew it back to his ear, and then a little farther. Jonas thought, *He will never make the shot.* And even if he did who would see the arrow land?

The bow sung with a mighty *twang!* that rang in the air for some time, and the rangers all squinted and shielded their eyes from the sun rising in the east to see where the arrow would go. Sharp as his eyes were, Jonas couldn't make it out but he knew from the excitement in their manner it must've made its mark.

"Now quick!" said Ahkair. "Down the path and to the wall!"

"But what good?" cried Jonas.

"The tower!" replied the ranger. "It is our own way into the city. Only we keep it. Far safer than the gates it should be; but *should* and *are* aren't the same thing. The rope is long and the fall is far, and there comes a time when all things must let go."

They were making their way down a narrow path that wound its way into the gorge which ran along the edge of the hill, right down to the very foot of the high wall of the city. And near, far too near to the enemy at the gate. Jonas now understood why Anhil had never supposed to lead his men into the city by this path: on the bare earth before the wall a few might pass swiftly and unseen but never such a host as lingered in the hills. And if they should be caught there in the open the slaughter would be terrible.

Now Jonas looked up at the towering wall of Jericho and his heart caught in his throat. He'd never seen anything so high, so steep. It went right up into the sky, and if he'd not already seen it from the height of the hill he might've thought it didn't stop until it touched the clouds. But when they came to the smooth stone of the wall there was a culvert from which flowed a dark trickle of water. Through this they had to climb and into a cistern. The pipe was narrow and smelled terribly foul, but hanging only just inside, as straight as a rigging line, was a thin, silver cord that went up and up until it vanished into the smooth face of the rock.

"You first," said Carrn to Ahkair. "You're the biggest and the strongest: you take the gunman."

Ahkair didn't object but put one arm around Darkfinger and with the other he fitted a clasp to the cord. "God lend us good will," he whispered, and with that he was whisked away, as effortlessly as if the world had just left him behind instead of the other way around.

After a minute or so Carrn said to Jonas, "Now you. Don't worry, I'll be right behind you. It's not difficult, just hold tight to the gear and it will do the work for you."

Another clasp was fitted to the line, and then the rangers each bid him good-luck. And with that Jonas took the handle and the ground seemed to fall away beneath him, leaving also his stomach with it. Up and up he went, thinking that at any moment he would be dashed against the stone roof of the culvert. But then he realized he was in a shaft that ran vertical through the wall. By arrownock windows he could see the southern hills spread away from him, so big, so wide, and he realized he must already be quite high up inside the wall. It was terrifying to think of all that empty space in the chimney-shaft beneath him. He couldn't look down. He stared at the mortaring flashing by, each stone a blur that lasted into the next and the next and the next. And then he was slowing, and quite suddenly he found he was looking into a house at a narrow window. Ahkair was taking his shoulders in firm hands and helping him in.

"Where's Darkfinger?" Jonas asked anxiously.

But the Kid was there, lying on the floor, his face pale. What delirium had taken him before was an unpleasant dream but this was a nightmare. His eyes were rolled back into his head and he was muttering terrible things beneath his breath like a mad man, like someone who hasn't spoken in years and now has suddenly found his tongue again. And the veins in his skin were black, slowly creeping toward his face, as if they were reaching hands.

"There's no time!" said Ahkair. "When the venom has clouded his eyes there's no force on earth to undo what it's done. You must go at once!"

"Go where?" asked Jonas, confused.

"In the Garden District, on the third terrace, the corner of Hallbor and Tiller there lives a man named Allistair and his daughter, medicians both out of Venicia. Go quickly, bring him here!"

"But—" Jonas stammered.

"Go!" cried Ahkair with a finger to the door.

Jonas didn't stop to ask any more questions. He turned and went out into the city of Jericho.

He was standing at the top of a narrow wall, overlooking climbing streets. It was perhaps the second terrace from the top and there were seven or more below him, each descending by streets and gardens, fields and churches. Houses were back to back, their roofs bright white-washed and blinding to the eyes, shimmering already with the heat of the day. And everywhere Jonas looked he saw crowds of people, soldiers in armour going this way and that on horses or marching in formation, and not hooded as the rangers of the vale but with bright plate and mail and helms on their heads. There were boys, too, and girls, and old women looking out from the windows and doors or standing on balconies or walls. Everywhere was the heat and bustle of the city.

A young boy ran past him, and Jonas caught the lad by the arm. "Who are you?" cried the boy. "I say, get off me, will you! A message for the baron is what's in order, and he won't be taking kindly to you if you delay me!"

"Where is the Gardens District?" asked Jonas in a hurry.

"Are you stupid?" replied the boy. "It's there, of course!" With a skinny finger he pointed down to the terrace below.

Jonas didn't wait any longer. He went to the road and down through the gate. The streets were filled with people going this way and that, people of all sizes and shapes, some with carts, some *in* carts, some on horses. But most were on foot, everyday-sort-of-people like you might find in any city. And they were thick, shoulder to shoulder. He might just as well have been going one way as the other. He probably wouldn't have found his way, at all, but by some happy chance he looked up and there hanging just above his head was a pointing sign that read HALLBOR. He turned down the street and didn't stop until he met another that read TILLER, and then he turned at the corner and knocked on the door. An old man with a snowy-white beard lifted the latch. "Hullo, lad, and who are you?" he asked looking curiously at Jonas in his dirty trousers and ragged shirt all covered in grime and sweat.

"My friend—" Jonas panted "—stabbed by Darkmen. Dying on the wall. Come through dark and forest in night—"

The old man looked at him curiously.

"—Ahkair said to find you, said you could stop the poison."

Now the old man's eyes grew wide, his voice was calm but hurried, and he said, "Ah, yes, of course! Do let me get my things." He vanished for a moment, and through the open door Jonas saw a girl perhaps some years younger than he, and with dark hair and bright eyes, looking up from a chair by the fire where she sat watching him. When she realized he was looking back a shy smile crossed her face and she looked away.

"We can go now," said the old man, returning with a bag under one arm. "Show me the way, good man."

In the house on the wall Carrn and those few others who Anhil had sent were now present, and all were gathered around Darkfinger with anxiety in their faces. When the door opened and Jonas and the old man came in they all looked up but there was no hope in their eyes.

"Do move out of the way, fellows, and let old Allistair work, will you?" said the old man. "I didn't come to stand around and watch a man die. Give me room now. Quickly! Quickly!"

They lifted Darkfinger to a bed that stood in the corner of the room and Allistair opened his bag and didn't relent till his work was finished.

Jonas didn't intend to leave, but when Allistair reopened Darkfinger's festered wound with a burnished knife, and black and putrid blood gushed from the lesion, he could no longer bear the sight. He went from the room to sit on the wall and look out over the city, and for the first time in as long as he could remember he did nothing but sit and think but when he tried to remember what he was thinking about he couldn't. So he relented to taking from his pockets and belts all the shells that remained to him and counting carefully their number. They were too few.

Some long time later the door was opened again and the old man Allistair came out. There was blood on his hands and his shirt, and his face was weary and worn. But there was hope shining in his eyes.

"Your friend is alive," he said. "Just *barely*, but he *is* alive. It will take more than the poison of the enemy to take him from this world, I think."

"He is going to be okay then?" asked Jonas hopefully.

"Okay?" replied the old man with wonderment. "I cannot say. Not the greatest physician in the world could say. It may well be that he will yet take a fever and die and there will be nothing

I can do about it. Or he may live but having already passed that door from which there is no return he would be as a ghost to us. But there is strength within him, a flame that doesn't burn out, and if I were to hazard a guess I would say that no vice of the enemy can hold him. There is some purpose to this world that will not let him leave, I think."

Jonas chanced a narrow smile.

"You have been lucky," said the old man, "very lucky, I think. But what do I know of luck?" He laughed. "You may go see him, if you like."

Jonas pushed open the door and went in. Darkfinger was awake but he was like a man so near to sleep that he will drift away and be gone at any moment.

"Darkfinger?" Jonas called.

"Jonas," Darkfinger replied weakly and with a dim smile. Then his eyes slipped closed and he was asleep.

~CHAPTER TWENTY-ONE~
THE WAR IN THE VALE

That night Jonas stayed in the house on the wall, for it was in fact Anhil's own and the refuge of his company in the city. Through a stairway that let down there were many bunks and also rooms for the storage of their gear. Oftentimes there would be young lads without home or family who would come to live there and train in the ways of the rangers of the Gallidros. Anhil's own wife was a young, beautiful woman, yet the stain of hard work was on her hands and in her brow. She was generous in the keeping of the house, and she fed both Jonas and Darkfinger and made comfortable their stay while they were in the city.

By noon the rest of those who'd entered in at the tower door were gone. They didn't stay in the house on the wall for many of them had dwelled in that house as lads but now had their own homes and families to attend to.

When Jonas awoke the next morning he was aware that a low din and a ruckus was playing in his ears, as if a great machine was turning far away. "What is that sound?" he asked Anhil's wife.

"The sound of war," she replied gravely.

After breakfast, Carrn and Ahkair returned to speak to him.

"The attack was begun during the night," they said. "The enemy has been trying to take the gate for many hours, and while they've not yet succeeded, they are far too many to hold at bay for very long. We've killed thousands of them beneath the walls and still they come. Soon they will breach our walls."

"What of Anhil and the rest of the company?" asked Jonas.

"No word," replied Carrn. "Doubtless they lie in wait and will fight through to the gate if the chance arises; but such a chance isn't likely while the enemy are so many and their siege-lines so strong. A small company has little opportunity to break through, though I doubt that will keep Anhil from trying."

Then Ahkair said, "Those few of us who are present have been stationed to the gatehouse to support the Captain of the Watch, and we would like you to join us."

"I cannot," replied Jonas. "I must be here for Darkfinger."

But the rangers shook their heads. "Nay," they said, "he is well as can be and in good care, and you have still skill in battle. Please join us, Jonas; help us in this time."

Jonas said nothing. He wouldn't have left Darkfinger's side though the Fall themselves commanded it. He could think of no better reason than the suffering of a friend. But at that moment there was a sharp rap on the door and Carrn let it open. Immediately he fell to his knee and bent his head; Ahkair did the same, drawing his sword point-down and resting upon it. "Sire!" he cried.

The man who entered was old, certainly older than Jonas, though not so much that age and wear had made him useless. He was bound in a plain cloak and hood like the rangers but on his greying brow, when he had thrown back the latter, was a circlet of gold and on his finger was an ornate ring. His eyes were quite solemn but Jonas imagined in battle they became fierce, as a man will when he no longer values his own life unto death. In fact he had deep scars on his face and hands, the mark of many stands and sorties.

There was another person, also, who came through the door. He was tall and noble, as was the king, but he wore not band of gold, only a silver ring on his finger for he was the Baron of the Gallidros and a baron is not above the king but adviser to him. "My faithful liegelord, Athais," said the king by way of an introduction.

Now the baron stood forward with a sadness in his eyes, and he said, "We would see and know they who've come from beyond the Teeth. Is this then he?"

"It is, My Lord," replied Carrn; and then, "My lord, Captain Anhil even now is harried in the field and is unable to bring home our company. Please, what is to be done?"

But the baron was still quite intent upon Jonas, and he said, "They've told me you were amongst the company which has avenged the death of my son."

"He is dead then?" asked Jonas in bewilderment.

The baron was heavy-hearted as he said, "Yes, he is dead. The enemy has brought his body before the gate on the morning of yester's day and they've hewn off his head."

"I am sorry for your loss," Jonas said with as much sincerity as he might.

"His death is avenged," returned the baron. "For this you have my undying thanks, for Anhil's men have pledged to your bravery. You *all* have my thanks. And you, stranger, will forever be a friend and an ally in the Gallidros."

"Thank-you," Jonas replied politely.

But the baron took him in an embrace and cried bitterly for his son.

Now the king stood forward. "For the deeds you have done to aid my people you will always be welcome in my city, Friend," he said. "I pray we may be as allies from henceforth, and if one day you should ever have need of assistance such as we can give the men of Jericho and her baronies will most assuredly come to your aid."

"We may be friends," replied Jonas, and he shook the king's hand heartily.

"Then I'm afraid, My Friend, I must call on you now," said the king sternly. "If this city is not held against the armies of Babylon then it will fall and all that once brought life to the Gallidros will be lost."

"I cannot leave my brother's side," replied Jonas, "not so long as he still draws breath."

The king looked hard in his eyes, and he said, "Would you put your own needs above those of my people, Jonas Arthur? Your friend is well tended here. You are no physician but rather you are a man of war and there are other matters that must be seen to. If the walls fall then we are all dead men. He won't escape it lying here, and neither will you. If you would see him safe then come and fight for me. Are you still the same man that once you were? Here you are forgiven your crimes. Are we not all murderers and thieves in these walls? Now we must fight, not as criminals but as free men."

Jonas said nothing, not at first. He bowed his head and then his knee. He thought of his homeland, far now beyond the mountains, of the prairie grass torn in the wind, of the streets of Dodge beneath the heat of the dwindling day, so often riddled with the bodies of the slain. Almost he could've hoped it *were* destroyed. But then he thought of the southlands and how Darkfinger had spoken so fondly of going home, of how he longed for nothing else. He thought of those parts of the vale they'd seen in their flight for Jericho and he felt a sharp pain in his chest. What if it *were* destroyed and gone? No, Babylon wouldn't stop. They never would. Evil didn't ever cease its march, and one day it would reach the southlands. One day everything would be gone, burnt beneath the rising tide of the Lord of the North.

He saw then, as clearly as if he were looking upon it with his waking eye, the coach-train driving its way up the valley toward Jericho, but it was smoking from its windows and its wheels turned ever slower and slower. Goblin and Darkling crowded around it, and he knew it would be taken. And then it wouldn't matter how hard or bitterly they fought for all would be lost: Babylon would devour the mountains and the wastes beyond, and even the prairie grass of his homeland and the far southlands from which came Darkfinger the Kid. "My Lord," he said; he was aware that tears were streaming down his face. "I *will* fight." And he knew that Darkfinger would be alright.

Jonas supposed the king and the baron would then return to their own houses at the very height of the city, as great lords often do to let those of lesser station take to the fight. But they did not. When Carrn and Ahkair went out to join the other rangers at the gate the lords went with them. There they met the Captain of the Watch. "Three times they've come at the gate," said the captain. "Three times we've driven them back. But our defences are waning. I fear if they come again there will be a sortie."

"Then it must be," replied the king.

"I will lead the charge," said the captain. "My knights are already harnessed and brazen."

But the king answered him, "Nay, dear friend, you are needed here on the wall to direct the defence. The baron and I will be in the fore-fight."

"You cannot, My Lord!" replied Carrn at once. "If you were slain—"

But the king smiled. "Then every man in this city would by anger's device alone slay thirty to his name, would he not? Do not be afraid. I'm not afraid of death!"

But the attack didn't come that morning, or even the afternoon that followed. The legion lay in wait and grew restless, and the archers on the wall grew weary of wasting their arrows on marks they couldn't hit. Once or twice perhaps a band of enemies would test the defences, but they always fell away when the arrows flew thick. By evening even the baron and the king were becoming weary of the wait.

As night was falling the battle was struck anew, but the enemy didn't assault the gates; rather the machine of war was rekindled. All through the night the catapults set a barrage of burning projectiles against the wall so that as night beset the city the lowest terraces burned with a bright fire. In the hours of darkness the morale of the garrison fell lower and lower, and just before dawn Jonas found himself sitting with a grim company of rangers in the guardhouse of the gate. They were casting dice and listening to the scream of the missiles.

"If we don't see the enemies' faces soon we'll loose our senses," said Ahkair. "If only I had a row of goblin faces to aim my sword at!"

But at that moment there came down the stairs the cry of the guardsmen: "Every man awake! To your stations! The king rides!"

"The *king*?" cried Jonas.

All the rangers were scrambling to their feet. "The god can damn me if he likes for leaving my post," said Ahkair; "I will *not* be left behind!"

And so they all ran out together into the street and there was the king coming down the road with the knights of the Legion and the Kingsguard at his back and the baron at his side. They were dressed in mail and bore their lances on their saddles, and the full Harvest Moon in its last hours of night shone on their armour and gear. A voice arose, crying, "The time of the Harvest has come, the time of the adjudication is at hand! Let the enemies of Jericho stand and be judged for their transgressions in this place!"

Already Ahkair and the other rangers were bringing horses around from the stable. There was one for Jonas, too. "Quickly, get up!" said Ahkair, and Jonas swung into the saddle. "We'll ride with the company."

They fell in behind the knights who were grave men of honour and seemed neither to notice their presence nor mind it. And then they could hear the watchman crying, "Open the gate! Open the gate, for the King of the City rides to war!" And the much deeper voice of the captain could be heard, saying, "Men of Jericho, your king rides forth to sortie with the enemy! Still your hearts and hold your courage, nock your bows and steer your arrows true, for today you will see such an end as never was heard of before in all of the vale and her baronies!"

Slowly, ever so slowly, the great doors were drawn aside. Beyond was the dark of night before dawn: not a star shone. But the fires of the enemy were strong before them, bonfires burning before the walls. By this light Jonas could see the causeway that went out from the city and the many dead bodies of the foes who had tried to take it, lying with arrows in their throats and their swords useless at their sides. The sound of many hooves upon stone drew his attention to the street at his back, and his surprise was unending for there were men coming from every side! Men in armour, with sword and spear and on great and proud horses. All were smiling and laughing and eager for battle. They took up the cry, "The King of the City rides to war!"

Now they were on the causeway itself. The sky was grey; the horses were trampling the bodies of the fallen in their haste, for the charge was begun, down the ramp and out into the valley where the ground was all gravel and few things grew green. They ran beside the rails, always onward, always toward the enemy ranks. Now captains were coming to the front with their standards and the king was giving orders: "Lamry, to the right flank; Ahmais, bring your company up the left; Ghandris, lead the knights upon the kingsground. Athais with me. And in the name of the god, forward! Forward! For the death that awaits!"

The order was given. The charge was in full. Men were yelling, "For the king! For the king! For Jericho!" Arrows began to fall. In the east the first rays of sun came over the Demon's Teeth. It shone on the mail and spears of the men of Jericho. It glistened in their eyes and in those of their horses. It shone, too, on the weapons of the enemy siege-lines that were assembled before the wall. It caught the white roofs of the city houses and the high-vaulted roofs of the churches and chapels, and then it stretched away beyond the farthest western hills and it turned the autumn leaves of gold and silver to a shimmer like a heat wave on the horizon.

And with a mighty clash that resonated in the earth, the lines were met. Men and horses were reaven on the spears of the enemy. Oh, it was a dreadful thing to see and hear! There were shrieks and cries, blood wetting the earth. Jonas' eyes were bleary and he passed his hand over them to remove the tears, but it *wasn't* tears, it was blood. For a moment it seemed the lines would be met in a deadlock, but the king and his knights thundered through, riding high in the saddle and swinging their swords in great arcs that caught the sun and sent it off in many brilliant arrays. The enemy siege-lines were crumbling both left and right, and then they were shattered. The men of Jericho rode through the forward rank. Swords were swinging; bows were singing; Jonas' guns resounded, even in the roar of the battle. It seemed to him for a fleeting moment that a mighty victory was at hand.

But victory was still so far from reach. They'd only just broken the first wave of the enemy's lines and now there came from behind, rank upon rank, the captains of the goblins and Darklings reforming and bringing their cavalry about for a skirmish. The thunder of the king's men was met with the thunder of the Darkling horsemen. And again the lines met in a clash like a terrible storm, and broke. The king's company *did* come to a standstill this time. The horses shied from the spears, and shield met shield and broke. The lines moved against each other like mighty waves met in the ocean. But the knights and the companies that followed rode on through the center, cleaving the enemy lines like the blade of a knife, and the darklings were sundered and scattered.

"Ride on!" cried Ahkair then, for they were now in the front of the charge with the baron Ghandris and the king's knights, he on Jonas' left and Carrn on his right swinging wide strokes with his sword that hewed the heads of his enemies at each cut.

But again a company of Darklings was amassing with spears to form a defensive line, and the rangers pulled up short. Carrn was yelling, "To the flank! To the flank! Route them out!"

They drew away to the right and the south, along the enemies' lines, toward the hills. But the other companies continued up the center. With the shriek of the horses and the even fiercer cries of the Darklings, many of the ranks of the men of Jericho were broken and destroyed on the spears of the enemy. Their shattered companies withdrew a little, rallying once more behind the banner of the king and his knights for one final, desperate charge – and it would be their last, for the enemy were still far too many and they too few to break through the ranks of longspears.

The rangers were near to the hills now, following Carrn, for he had raised high the standard of the Baron of the Gallidros. A band of the enemy came around to meet them with arrows to the string, meaning to give them a volley before ever they could get behind the spears. But Ahkair and Carrn were in the forefront with their swords raised high, and they wouldn't be stopped. They rode on through and cut down the archers.

The king and his legion were in the midst of the field again, and they rode hard for the enemy lines. They were closing now, perhaps fifty turns; now twenty; now ten. And just when it seemed to Jonas that they would most certainly be broken on the shields of the enemy, a volley of arrows issued forth from the low scrubland hills at their backs. It tore through the goblins and Darklings and opened a breach. The lines met and the enemy broke and were thrown back yet again. The rangers began shouting and cheering, "Anhil! Hurrah for Anhil!" The call was echoed with a mighty roar from the companies riding, and it resounded through the vale and came back until it must have seemed to the hordes of Babylon that a hundred thousand men strong were riding down upon them. But the Darkling captains weren't easily dissuaded: for the judgement of their master would be so much the worse if they turned now and fled. Already they were coming round on foot to charge the hills, but Carrn commanded the ground and all those around him. Whether of his company or not they heeded to his voice. "Stay!" he cried. "Give them no quarter!" From their backs came the shout of battle and a volley of arrows, and then Anhil and the rest of his company and some three-score of men whom Jonas did not know were coming down the slope with swords ringing and their dreadful battle-cry hanging on their lips. It was a fierce fight, hand-to-hand, and any lesser men than those rangers might've been overcome; but not they, not the men of the Gallidros Vale who followed Anhil the Ranger.

From the midst of the charge the king swung round with his knights, never breaking pace. They, too, were riding to meet Anhil and his company. The king of Jericho swung down from the saddle and shook Anhil's hand, and never had Jonas known anyone more glad at the coming of another.

The skirmish was ending; the lines were breaking and the cavalry was coming back around for a relent. "They do not yield!" cried the baron. "There are too many of them!"

"Then we shall meet them again," returned the king, "and perhaps we will make them *less*." He remounted to resume the charge, but to Anhil he said, "Is there word?"

"The king of the corgrief sends this message," returned Anhil: " 'We have not forgotten.' "

The king of Jericho smiled a sweet, mirthful smile, as of someone who has just come back from the brink of despair to find the sun has risen anew. With that smile still reiterating in his eyes, he wheeled his horse around to take the charge once more.

More riders had come out of the city while all this was going on, perhaps five hundred or more. Most were the men of the guard who even against the captain's behest wouldn't remain at the battlements while the battle below was in full tilt. And now they were all joining behind the king on the road. The thunder of the hooves, the war-cries, the singing of the bows: every moment before this now seemed dull and lifeless by comparison. Then swords rang, lances were lowered: the lines were closing once more. Below the rumble of the horse's hooves Jonas was certain he heard also the shrill whistle of a train. And then someone was crying, "Look! Look at the skies!"

"They have not forgotten," cried Anhil, who still was close by Jonas' side.

Jonas looked up. From above the Demon's Teeth they came, perhaps a hundred or more of those majestic birds soaring down the vale. Already their shrill screams were reaching the battle and a fright and a panic was arising within the goblin ranks. They were turning wild, throwing aside their weapons to flee. Those first who did so were slain by their overlords and their bodies ridden down by the Darklings, for the dreadlord now was marshalling his staunchest servants, those he'd held back at the first. Even he who had the very ear of the Lord of Babylon, who drove his armies into battle, now took to the saddle with his blade in hand and led the charge against the king and his knights.

Jonas didn't know what madness had taken him, but when he saw from afar that terrible demon (perhaps the only *true* demon, the dreadlord of Babylon) riding with all his might down on the King of Jericho, he wheeled his horse about and followed the Kingsguard into the fray and the certain death that must be meted. As he rode beside the rails at the rear of the column he reloaded his guns, casting aside the wasted shells and replacing them with the few he still had in his keeping: not even enough for two rounds. *So death it must be then,* he thought. Yet he had no reservations, for this was the end that he had sought. This was an end to be pleased with, not rotting in some cellar but fallen afield of his own choosing. Perhaps this was why so much had stood in his way: he would make an end to be remembered.

The king's line and those of the dreadlord were met with the shriek of steel and horse alike and the gore and wrath of battle. Everywhere around him was death, men fighting by hand, swords once wrought in steel and burnished to a sheen now blood-streaked and dripping, and the bodies and pieces of the fallen littered the earth. It was madness, chaos that no amount of *battle-fire* could cure.

Jonas did not miss his targets, but just the same his shells became fewer, and very soon his guns were empty. There in the midst of the conflict he brought his horse around, intent that he should be well out of the way before he took the time to reload what few shells he still had in his pocket. But a Darkling came upon him with a spear, and the thrust took the horse in the throat.

The ground was hard where Jonas fell, coarse rock and gravel. He was badly shaken but he came up just as quick as he'd gone down. The Darkling who'd slain his horse now drew forth his sword and would've killed him, but the king was there with his own sword in hand, still mounted on his warhorse, and he hewed so deep the shoulder of the Darkling before the kill could be made that his sword stuck fast. He kicked his enemy away and wrenched his blade free, and when he'd also hewn the head from his foe, he cried, "Get out! There is only sword-work here!"

The king turned his horse and rode hard for the rear lines, cutting as he went, opening a path, and Jonas followed afoot, the carnage of that final stand surmounting all around him.

At the edge of the field the king turned again and made once more to join the fight. *No*, thought Jonas. He couldn't be left behind now. He had to finish what he'd come for. Was this not it, the reason he'd crossed mountains and deserts? To protect the coach-train and all that it stood for? Or perhaps to die on a strange land.

Jonas surveyed the field behind. The rangers and those who'd hung back as the king made his charge now were bringing up the right flank beneath the command of Anhil, intent that none of the enemy should win through by that side and to the gates of the city; all others were with the king or the baron.

Jonas turned out his cylinders, dumping the spent casings, and he pushed four of those that remained into his left-hand gun and three into the other. And then, turning again the way the king had gone, he made his charge.

The battle was relenting, even now. Many of the knights who still sat ahorse were drawing away to the north behind the baron, pursuing the enemy who fled. Some few others now remained in the field, though they were on their own feet and fighting viciously as any brave man will when he senses the end is near. And it was amongst these who remained that he found the king, astride his horse and calling to those around him, "Don't give them a pace, even now!" But as Jonas watched the dreadlord drew near with his chieftains, throwing aside any who challenged him, and when he came to the king the demon of Babylon cut down the great warhorse and hurled its master to the ground.

Jonas didn't hesitate even a moment as he saw this happen, but already he was raising his guns. He didn't dare to bring them to bear on the dreadlord, not until he knew with certainty that his shots were sure. All about him time came to that same, aggravating crawl which it often does when the vigour and tumult of war takes hold and the *battlefire* burns bright in the eyes of those who fight. The words rose to his lips, the words of a gunman: "Let my hand—" He shot a Darkling through the eye and counted his shots: *six.* "—be steady and mine eye—" He shot another whose wicked blade was raised to kill a knight: *five.* "—be true—" Another he shot, but the Darkling reeled to the side at the last moment as an arrow took it in the back, and his bullet passed only through its shoulder, not its heart: *four.* It staggered but rose again to its feet, enfuriorated. He shot it again, and this time he did not miss: *three.* "—pull me to—" he said as he pulled the triggers of both his guns and killed in equal measure the last two Darkling foes who surrounded the dreadlord. Without a thought to the matter he returned the empty iron to its holster and brought the other to bear on his enemy who was locked in conflict with the king. The last three words of the rite he yelled, fierce as any war-cry: "—WHEN I STRAY!" and he drove the hammer home, the roar of his gun resounding in the vale. The bullet didn't miss its mark: it tore through the dreadlord's chest, and Jonas could hear the *whine* of it on the wind.

"Fool!" cried the captain of the host of Babylon. "Do you think you can bring me low, to stoop in the dirt and grovel?" He threw the king down as if he were not an equal and he raised in his hand a longsword whose blade was etched in blood and fire and whose hilt was grotesque to look upon, such had it been hammered and twisted to meet the dreadlord's desires. And there the King of Jericho would've met his end, but Jonas took up the sword of a fallen knight and he rushed their enemy to parry the stroke that would've slain the king. His hands with the blade were clumsy and he fumbled and nearly lost it, but his stroke was just as true, for his eyes were keen, and the enemy's own sword glanced harmlessly on the length of his and struck only the earth. The dreadlord howled in rage, for the final kill was his vain hope. He brought his knee into Jonas' chest as the latter was stooped from the stroke. The retaliatory lash was so strong that Jonas fell back, at first unable to breathe, and the sword dropped from his fingers.

"You should've gone home," said the dreadlord. "Did I not give you ample opportunity? Did I not encourage you at every turn, to save your life?" And he rushed at Jonas to kill him. But when he was near now, Jonas rose to his feet in a flourish, clutching the stout sword of the knight in his fist, and he struck: first a parry, then a blow to the knee of his enemy. His hands were not accustomed to grasping the hilt of a sword, it was true, but they were sure and quick, and his eyes didn't miss a thing. Then he brought the blade up and gashed the dreadlord across the face. Though he didn't bleed beneath the burnished flame-scored plate that he wore, not even from an open wound, the captain of the Babylonyan host at once fell away. Jonas did not. Another stroke he dealt, and another, until his foe was on the ground. He struck out the captain's knee and set the blade against his throat. *Death for the one who would destroy this world?* he thought. *For the one who has set his own henchmen against me from here to Perth?* "Aye, death," he said, and he made to hew the captain's head from his body.

"This is but one end to the story," said the dreadlord as the sword fell.

But instead Jonas found he was thrown headlong to the side, for the king had arisen and plowed him over. For a moment Jonas was furious within himself. What new treachery could this be? But a moment later he had the truth of it.

You mustn't think that while Jonas and the dreadlord fought their duel the rest of the vale had looked on in silence: rather the battle had continued in small and in large on most every front. And though the Darkling host was divided and rent, at the very end their chieftains rallied for one last desperate stand with their *taldak* – their chiefguard – about them. And they might've held out for some time, or not been broken at all, ringed in by their fiercest warriors, shield-to-shield. But then the train came up the rails below in the vale, driving fast beneath the cold morning sun of Wintercome, and with a mighty rumble of hooves and a deep roar of a hundred angry voices the gordru rushed down from the hills with their greatswords drawn. They drove against the flanks of the enemy and the Darklings were caught in the midst between the gordru and the baron and his men returning from the north, a cripple in a vice. In a matter of moments the fighting was over, the last of them crushed, though some few turned west and fled up the valley where Jonas and the dreadlord had met for their duel. These, too, were ridden down and killed; but as Jonas watched the knights and the gordru thundering past his only thought was for the dreadlord. Yet when he and the king arose and looked for the body of their enemy they could neither find it amongst the living nor the dead, though they did draw from the ruin of the field the great and twisted sword which he had wielded. Jonas chuckled to himself, and when the king asked, "Do you find it amusing that our enemy lives to brew more hatred?" he answered, "No, but I can't help but laugh. His words have all turned out to be hollow, and his face is that of deceit. Surely, if I hadn't been so blinded myself I would've seen through it when I stood on the edge of the wasteland and all sense of reason urged me to turn back."

In the aftermath of the battle the train drew up and through the field of war, past the bodies of the slain, its wheels turning on the rails in time with the deep *chugga-chugga* of its engines and the puff of smoke from its stacks. It steamed up the valley past the on-looking legions, rangers, and corgrief (the gordru had returned at once to the forest when the Darklings were defeated), and it entered in at the gate of the city. And now everyone knew that it was at last over.

~CHAPTER TWENTY-TWO~
THE END, AND THE BEGINNING

It was perhaps an hour after the battle was over that Anhil and his company of rangers arrived in the city, for they took careful pains to hunt down the last of the Darklings who were scattered – the goblins, they said, could crawl back into their holes and rot for all they cared, and perhaps this wasn't the best course, for while many attended the wounded on the field a great leader of the goblins rallied his shattered troops and tried to take the gate of the city. Only very nearly was his scheme thwarted: Anhil had to bring his company together, and at the last it was a mad rush for the gate where they drove their way right into the ranks of the goblins who even now were rushing up the causeway. As only rangers of the Gallidros can, the men won through and retook the gatehouse. Then the Captain of the Watch himself saw to the countercharge that cleared the bridge, and he hewed the head from the goblin chief.

While all this was happening Jonas stayed on the field of battle with Ahkair and Allistair and also many other men and women of the city who were practiced in the ways of medicine. He noticed the girl, the daughter of Venicia, was not among them, and he wondered that she wouldn't attend her father's healing hands. They tended the wounded and cared for those who were stricken with the waning darkness of *battlefire*, for, though Jonas knew little of herbalism and medicine, the lingering disease that follows battle was something he knew well. He pulled many men back from the brink of madness that day.

There were also still many enemies to be harried in the field, though none now stood in open defiance of the king and his men. It would be many days before the last of their troubles was laid to rest.

When the final battle was over with Anhil himself came to see Darkfinger at once. The Kid was still far from well, though his skin had flushed, the colour returned, and Allistair was hopeful he would be able to get up in the morning. The medicine was working marvellously on all accounts and it wouldn't be long at all before even the memory of that terrible illness would begin to fade. The wound of the knife was beginning to close, too.

Anhil made to Jonas a formal introduction of his wife, as one man to another; Jonas replied with "How do you do, ma'am". Then Anhil welcomed them to his house. "Stay as you will," he said. "You are welcome in this city for what you've done here."

In the cool of the evening Jonas sat before the fire with his tobacco and those spent shells he'd saved from the battlefield. The shells no longer burnished as they once had, and some were useless, it was true; but many still would serve. Yet he had no lead with which to refill them, so he said to Anhil, "Where is the dreadlord's sword? What has the king done with it?"

"He gave it into my keeping and I have shattered it," replied Anhil, "to meld the pieces into spikes with which I will crucify his corpse, if ever I should happen upon it."

"Give me some fragments," replied Jonas, "for I need metal to cast for my shells."

Anhil agreed, so Jonas took a piece of the blade to melt it. The fire he had to stoke and bellow to such a heat that the smelter cracked, but at last the metal softened and he at once cast it into his mould. When it was cool he refilled his shells. Four shots. All that remained to him. He made a note that he must search for more.

Much later in the night, as the candle burned low and the coals on the hearth grew dim, a knock came at the door of the house on the wall. When Anhil drew it open a man of the king's own stood in the shadows of the street, and he said hastily, "Where is the wanderer? He is asked for by name at the home of the Venician."

Jonas still was awake, unable to sleep with the memory of the day still so fresh in his mind: the words of the dreadlord haunted him. But now he came to the door, and he said, "Is it me you are looking for?"

"It is," replied the kingsman. "Come quickly."

Allistair's house was dark: the fire was low and no candle was lit. The king himself waited at the step with some of his men about him, and when he saw Jonas he said, "You are asked for within." What a surprise, for Jonas had been certain it was the king himself who called his name.

When the door was pushed open Jonas remembered the shy girl who'd sat before the fire — only now the chair was empty. But Allistair was there at the hearth, tending a boiling kettle, and when Jonas saw the healer from Venicia he knew at once that something dreadful was happened. "Where is your daughter?" he asked.

"She's ill in bed," replied Allistair. "I'm steaming herbs for their healing properties. But the medicines I have won't avail her."

"Then why have you called *me*?" asked Jonas, for he didn't understand.

"I didn't call for you," replied Allistair. "It was another."

Jonas was led then into a room where a silent form was laid on the bed with a cover over. And now Allistair was more grievous than ever. "Something has claimed her," he said. "She speaks as I've never heard spoken before. It sounds a dark tongue to me, like that of they who come from Babylon. And sometimes she tries to hurt herself." The tears were streaming down his face. "I don't know how to make her well again."

As Jonas looked at the shape of the girl he became aware, like a slowly-arising foul smell, that a certain feeling had come upon him, a feeling he'd felt three times before since his journey began. It was a feeling of panic and fear. But this time he was *not* afraid; something within him had changed.

"I've tried all I know!" Allistair cried. "Sweet herb and weed alike! But nowhere in all the wisdom of men is there a medicine to cure what she has." He faltered now, as if there was more to be said but it wouldn't be said willingly. Then he spoke slowly. "It is a *dascari*, I think, a demon of Babylon."

"I know," Jonas replied, for he could feel it and even smell its stench.

"I don't know what purpose a servant of Babylon would have here," Allistair said, and a certain fear was evident in his eyes, for undoubtedly he guessed as quickly as Jonas did what its purpose was.

"The train," Jonas said only. "It wants the train. And me, though I still don't understand why. This has been their mission from the start. And the dreadlord promised me that there was more yet to come."

"Do you know how to destroy it?" Allistair pleaded. "Is there yet some way we can drive it from the city to be with its fellows in the northern wastelands?"

Jonas didn't know. His guns would kill man and beast and leave their corpses to rot beneath the sun, but truly some of the dreadlord's fell servants were neither, and against these he felt inadequate.

"Who calls to me by name?" he asked boldly then, for he was no longer afraid.

Though the girl didn't stir that which had taken her did, like a dog guarding its bone. It barred its teeth and arose with the hackles on its shoulders bristling. "I've called you and you've come running like a servant," it said, laughing. "Is it not a sweet thing?"

"Who are you?" Jonas demanded. "Why has your master sent you here when the battle is lost before the gates of this city?"

"Lost?" asked it in a dithering voice. Then again more boldly, "Lost?! Nay, the battle is neither just begun nor drawing near to its end. The Lord of Babylon will lay waste to your world as he did to Amoddin; he will see it all burned! Perhaps not today or tomorrow, but the next, or the next, and after that comes a myriad of opportunities and possibilities. And already his most devout servants are amassing, for this has only been the beginning of his campaign. And do you think that all others will hold true, as these have, Jonas? Do you think you can always run before his might and throw back his strong hand?" The demon laughed. "Even now he brings to bear his greatest advance yet, a march that will ruin the world of men, even from the beginning of time unto the end."

"Where is this march? Where will it fall?" asked Jonas. "Speak to me, tell me where!"

But still the demon cackled, and it said instead, "You should've gone home, fool."

Jonas said nothing for a time; he was thoughtful. And suddenly he wondered how he'd been so thick. It wasn't the monster he'd come for but the girl. The world was full of monsters. How then to save the girl? Even a stranger who meant nothing to him. Then these words crossed his mind, and he said them aloud, though he didn't know what they meant: "Oh brethren of the Fall, if I must ride the rails to the Shadowland myself please save this girl's life." But he realized in the moment that the words were only the facade; the *real* prayer was in his heart, and he meant every word: *Keep my hand steady and mine eye true; pull me to when I stray.* "Babylon won't take this city from within *or* without," he also said aloud.

And neither would they take the world; nor indeed his will and resolve, ever again. The venecian healer and his daughter had much to do in righting the wrongs of their foes, and if a stranger from beyond the world could still save them then he must.

That feeling of cold and dread presence didn't falter or leave – in fact if anything it became suddenly much stronger. The demon was standing before him, a grimace on its crooked face, its red eyes piercing his innermost thoughts. It might've even been the very same monster that lingered in the hold of the slave ship, now that it came to it; they all looked so much the same. But he didn't really think it was. "I'm not afraid of you," he said. "Not *anymore*. Go back to your master and tell him what you've seen here this day. Tell him there are men in this world who will see him fall low and grovel in the dust."

"But you can't kill me," it croaked, a wicked laugh. "You can scatter the armies of the dreadlord but you can't kill me!"

Jonas shook his head. "No," he agreed. "I can't. But neither can you stay here. Be gone with you!" And with that he raised one of his big irons and shot it in the chest with the shells re-cast from the fragments of its own captain's sword — twice. With a howl of anger and pain it fell back, though ever after Jonas couldn't be sure if the bullets had even touched its flesh. "Be gone!" he said again. "The Fall doesn't tolerate you and neither do I!"

And it *was* gone, not as the demon in the hold of the ship had been but truly and completely gone so that not even the taint of it lingered for so much as a moment.

The girl didn't awake immediately but seemed to be in a deep sleep. A fever ravaged her body, and for a long while Allistair bathed her head. It was some time before her fever subsided.

The medician offered much gold in repayment but Jonas wouldn't accept it. "I can give you nothing yet you've also saved someone I love," he said. "Consider this my recompense."

Jonas didn't stay in the house of the Venician. When it was done the king called for him and he went at once to the high citadel. It wasn't in the hall he found the lord of the city but in the solar with his liegelords gathered round him. Athais, the baron of the Gallidros was there, and also Lamry, the baron of Ibillis in the west, and Ghandris, the baron of Adris in the south, and Ahmais, the baron of Devaros in the north. Many maps were laid out before them on the table, and when Jonas entered the king said, "So good of you to come."

"What is this about?" asked Jonas wearily, for he was well-ready to be done with the day.

"We've won a battle," said the king, "but the dreadlord is right, Jonas: the war is far from over. He'll strike again and we are quickly losing this small lead that our victory has afforded us."

"You're right," replied Jonas. "There is much more to come, I am certain. But whether or not I have any part in it I am *not* certain."

"I would have your counsel, just the same," said the king. "I must know, if it comes to war in the north at the very gates of Babylon will your own people join us?"

"My people are vain and violent," Jonas answered. "There is little hope to you in the east. Is there no one else who'll fight?"

The king was grim. "Precious few. In the southlands the old stoneborn empire has fallen and those peoples who inhabit that land still are busy fighting amongst themselves. In the far west men care little or nothing for us. And those neighbours we have beyond Ibillis have become consumed in a civil war, content to kill one another when we've a greater foe."

"Perhaps they're not so different from your own kind, Jonas," suggested Lamry.

But the king said, "There *will* come another attack. We must discover where it is before it falls. I know the dreadlord has made you privy to some of his councils, though he may not have realized it himself."

But Jonas shook his head. "I myself tried to wring from his servant the information you seek but he wouldn't give it. And before tonight his words have been only riddles and ruses."

"Then he has divulged nothing at all?" asked the king in some small measure of disappointment. "This is unfortunate."

"Regardless," said Ahmais, "the Gallidros is now closed to him, as we have demonstrated, and this leaves him only a few options. The wall of Danas, for one—"

"A terrible defeat for the Mandaraas, if he were to claim it," agreed Ghandris. "But does he have the strength? The wall has stood for all of living memory."

"By the Wasteland Gap he could also regain his way into the lands of men," said Lamry. "Is it not so that the desert marches stand open to him, that he may pass unimpeded?"

"He could never lead such a host across the wastes," replied Athais. "There is no way."

A terrible truth now occurred to Jonas. "What if this host were not of men or beasts?" he asked.

The king looked hard on him, his eyes cold and ashen. And Jonas knew why: the prospects of what he proposed were terrible.

"Would that I had slain him on the field," muttered Jonas.

The baron of the Gallidros laughed, though it was mirthless, and he said, "We've all our own regrets, gunman. Is it not enough to partake of a mighty victory?"

Jonas supposed that it was. But he thought, *Not if it is taken from our hands at the second advent.*

He left the citadel glum for he'd done little and less to give aide for all his gloomy visions. He couldn't help but feel that somehow the enemy had eluded him. One thing still remained, however, one mystery, and the prospects of it gave him hope.

When he returned to the home of Anhil, ranger of the Gallidros, he found Darkfinger awake and sitting before the hearth. He couldn't recall a time in his life when he'd been happier than that moment. By his face Darkfinger looked well-enough but something dreadful was lurking there still. "What is it that haunts you?" Jonas asked.

For a very long time the Kid would not speak of it, but at last he said, "Jonas, do you remember well the demon that lurked in the hold of the ship?"

Jonas replied: "Aye."

"I've seen its face," Darkfinger said. "It haunted my dreams and led me so far that I thought I'd never find my way back. I recall standing on the edge of a great abyss and it urged me to jump. 'Go home,' it said. 'Go home and be free and without worry.' " There were tears in Darkfinger's eyes when he said, "We ought never to have entered that ship, Jonas, for it was a cursed place. It should've killed us. We shouldn't be here at all. But now, I think, I'm glad we did. I'm freed of that evil one, and now I understand better what it is that's brought me to this place against the will and devices of the enemy. I think I'm ready to face it at last."

"Then tomorrow we will," answered Jonas.

The next day Anhil's wife made Jonas and Darkfinger breakfast in the house on the wall for the last time. Jonas felt some sentiments at this prospect, for he'd grown fond of the company of the ranger and his kin. But as they sat around after the table was cleared, and Jonas got out his pipe and lit up some tobacco, he ventured the

313

question that was weighing heavily on him since the war in the vale had been finished. "Where is the train now?" he asked.

"It's at the station," said Anhil, "beneath the lowest terrace."And he agreed that as soon as Darkfinger was able they all three would go down to the station and there see whatever could be seen.

By that evening Darkfinger got up from his bed, nearly as good as new, if not for the stitch in his side where the wound still remained and a scar would likely always be. So they went down through the streets with Anhil at their side, and there in a wide vault beneath the lowest terrace was a long platform and resting on the rails was the coach that both Jonas and Darkfinger had crossed the world in pursuit of. It stood on the tracks, its wheels still for the first time on the polished rails. Its stacks were empty, its engine silent. The lamp hanging from the caboose was doused, no longer flickering its crimson glow. But though it looked an ordinary thing to see now there was something profoundly *off* about it to Jonas' eyes. Perhaps it was the hue of the carven embossment on the sides of the cars, wrought in all manner of shapes and fancies; or perhaps it was the rusted sheen of the wheels and the couplings. Maybe it was even the deep ochre of the wood that adorned its framed windows. But to Jonas these things mattered little, for nothing would keep him from knowing the truth of what it was. That was all that mattered.

The door of the engine was let open as they three stood there in silence, and down the rungs of the ladder climbed someone Jonas knew by sight, though not by any other means. He was old and his skin wan and stony. There was hoar in his hair but his eyes twinkled merrily, and when he walked it was with a vigour of youth.

"Who are you?" Jonas cried, and Darkfinger too.

"I am the Captain," replied the stranger. "This is my coach, is it not? Have you been searching for me?"

Jonas didn't know how to answer. *I've travelled the world in pursuit of you, you exasperating devil,* he might've said. But instead Darkfinger spoke. "It is *good* to see your face."

The Captain chuckled. "As it is good to see yours again, Darkfinger. When last we met it was in the deep passages beneath the mountains, I do believe. As for yourself, Jonas, I've not made myself known to you since the wasteland beyond the Teeth, though I've been with you at every hardship. Do you know my face?"

"Aye," replied Jonas. "I know it well."

"Do you now know why you are here?" asked the Captain. "Do you know why I've drawn you across the world?"

"I begin to see," said Jonas, "though I don't see *all.* I've many questions that want answers."

The Captain replied, "As do each of us, I'm sure. For now, though, I can give but one, and I know already what you would ask. Yes, you have proved yourself in prowess and honour. The boy is gone, the man is born. Let your demons rest, Jonas, and they will plague you no more."

"*My* demons?" asked Jonas. "Is it not the servants of the dreadlord which have harried me at every turn?"

315

The Captain smiled and his hand was on Jonas' shoulder. "These know only the power we give them," he said, "and you've robbed them of it."

Then to Darkfinger he said, "And your question I know already, as well, and the answer is *Yes*. Your path lies evenso undecided but for you who must walk it, but in the distance I see it climbs a hill and at the height is a city I think you know well, a city that only awaits the day they may welcome home their prince."

Jonas saw well that at these words the Kid's face was glad and peaceful, the look of a man without worries, a man who'll bravely face any danger because he knows at the end is the freedom all men deserve.

"Now I've given you your answers," said the Captain, "and more may come, time allowing. But now I must ask my own questions in turn."

"What would you have?" asked Jonas, feeling as he did so that he would give whatever it was freely. But the answer took him quite at unawares.

"I fear it is no longer my place to stand at the coach and guide its passage," said the Captain. "I've grown old, you see, and a man does yearn in his old age to return to his roots. Just as others have before me."

"What do you mean?" Jonas asked.

"Of course I've not always been the captain of the coach," the stranger said. "There was another who came ahead of me, and another before him. And now it's someone else's turn to ride the rails from this world into the next, to bear hope to the desperate and those in need, to set the captive free and break the shackles of the enslaved. Now it is your turn. Will you, Jonas Arthur, take the helm? Will you follow your heart's desire, to ride the rails and see where the train will take you? You've come all this way in search of me; now will you go on ahead?"

But Jonas shook his head. "I can't run a coach-train," he replied assuredly, for he knew nothing of the workings of a steam engine.

The Captain laughed. "And it is for that reason that it is you that *should!*" he replied. "The mechanics of a coach are a thing for the study of learned men, but the knowledge of men has no place here. I've drawn you across the world for just such as this. The coach was once a thing of evil to you because you were a man alone, a man who sought nothing in friends, who yearned only for his own gain. You were a man without glory or honour or purpose. But a journey has changed all that, and Darkfinger now is your friend where no other has been before. So yes, Jonas Arthur, you *should* be hesitant; indeed, you are quite right to be so. But you should also be bold and take the adventure that is given, because it's been given for *you.*"

"Aye," replied Jonas, feeling a new excitement welling up within him. Perhaps this *was* the reason he'd crossed the wasteland and the mountains. And what could possibly be beyond? The thought was terrifying. But he could go a little bit farther yet. "I will," he said.

"This is good-bye then," said Darkfinger presently and morosely.

"But surely you will come, as well," replied Jonas at once, feeling he couldn't bear to leave the Kid behind now.

But Darkfinger shook his head. "Two questions he answered but only one he's asked. What would you have of me, Sir?"

"Your greatest battle is still before you, Darkfinger," said the Captain.

"What battle?" asked Darkfinger.

"In the north Babylon prepares again to accost the world, for their lord is desperate to be released from his prison. Beneath the walls of this city he was beaten badly. He's learned dearly the kingdoms of the world are not as weak as he'd hoped, but it's only served to nurse his wounds and ascend his anger. Soon he'll march his servants to battle once more, and then who will stand in their way? Who will deny them passage? You've seen for yourselves how the path of the coach-train has fallen to disrepair, become infested with the ilk that call him master. We can imprison him no more as we have for so long. Instead we must fight, and that task must be yours, Darkfinger. As your father and his before him once safeguarded the realms so too must you."

"One last battle," said Darkfinger wistfully. From his holster he drew his *darkiron*-six and looked at it longingly. "Aye, I think I'm strong enough, Captain," he said. "Though I'll need more bullets."

The Captain smiled warmly-enough and said, "This is good."

But Jonas felt heavy, evenso, and he was loathe now to leave when but a moment before he'd be undeniably excited.

He bid farewell to Anhil and Darkfinger then, as he knew he must, without objection.

"If you ever return this way Jericho and my home will always be open to you," said Anhil. "You're more the warrior today than ever you were before, and with that comes both my respect and my many thanks."

"Thanks?" asked he. "For what? It is you who have helped us!"

"Well it may be," replied Anhil, "but your coming has been a reminder and a hope to us all in Jericho that there is more beyond our vale and many who fight for a cause greater than our own. It's time to build new alliances between men of all lands."

Jonas took that as answer enough, and he shook both Anhil's and Darkfinger's hands heartily. Anhil he thanked many times over for what he'd done for them.

Then Darkfinger said, "Farewell then, Jonas, till we meet again." There were tears in his eyes.

"Very well," replied the Captain. "Until the end!" And he stood waving on the platform as Jonas went to the doors of the coach and boarded the engine. Then, and with a groan of the gears and machinery, and with a puff from the stacks, the coach-train began to move steadily forward toward the end of the station. Beyond, the world seemed to come to an end, for there was nowhere to go unless one wanted to run right into the hill beneath the city. But at the last moment a door seemed to open that let out, and then Jonas was rushing down, down, down and out the other side. This sight met his eyes: there before him was undoubtedly the Wasteland Gap, for he recognized at once the leering peak of Mount Tyran, and in the gap was a terrible army stood at arrayment, not men or goblin or Darkling or even gorfalkon or gordru, but demons so wicked and terrible his blood ran cold to look at them, for they were the devout of Babylon. But it seemed to him that the strong, firm hand of the Captain was on his shoulder, and when Jonas looked into his kind, smiling face he forgot his fear. When he looked once more at the army assembled it seemed to him that someone was before them, a lone warrior standing against that horde. He raised a *darkiron* in each hand, the chambers loaded and ready, and then he was running upon that whole vast demonic force, his guns exploding and each bullet finding its marks with such skill that a pathway was cloven right through the middle. Then the train was rushing on through the swath that he made, and as it went by the lone warrior looked up, and behold, it was Darkfinger! His face was grim but he was smiling, and it seemed that he whispered, "Go on: go on to greater things!"

The last sight that Jonas had of Darkfinger the Kid was of him standing amidst that vast wasteland with the hordes of the enemy's host before him. But the boy was no longer alone. At his back now rode the armies of Jericho in their glittering mail and plate and with their spears flashing in the sun of a new year. They raised banners Jonas didn't recognize. And he knew it would be alright. Darkfinger wouldn't surrender to them the deserts and the world beyond, not even so far as the Frontier.

Then it was all gone: the desert gap, the legions of Babylon, the men of Jericho, and Darkfinger the Kid, too. And the coach ran on into a new adventure.

ABOUT THE AUTHOR

AD Bane is an avid enthusiast of science-fiction and fantasy. He's been dreaming and writing both since he first learned the art as a young gunman. He especially enjoys tales that stretch the confines of their genres and imagination. However, this is his first venture into western-fantasy.

AD Bane also enjoys philosophy and is fascinated by the machinery of the human condition. He writes stories such as this one both for pleasure and to present ideas that he believes can be difficult to grasp in reality. He's written many short stories, and while this is his first printed novel, he is working on more, including a direct sequel to *Beyond the Wasteland*.

AFTERWORD
TO THE TEXT

There is a burning hunger in the human soul, a flame that never seems to die, though many of us have doused it with water and earth and built our lives of brickwork made from the resultant mud. We pile our own vain ambitions one upon the other, until we've constructed a veritable wall of stupidity to hide behind. But this longing within is something I doubt that any of us can deny if we are true to ourselves, and neither can we escape from its inexorable pull except by meting its timely fulfillment, overwhich we seem to have no control whatsoever. This hunger is consummate. It's masterful. It makes us feel weak and helpless because we know that no matter how successful we are in life there's still something missing, something vital. No wall of success is high-enough to hide ourselves from it.

It's maddening.

Jonas Arthur felt this pull early in his life.

As a boy living in the little village of Whistletoe he often watched the outlaws – the gunrunners – that passed through. Whistletoe wasn't large enough to host a bank worth robbing, and in all its days the only heist to occur there was the work of a young boy with a dream to be a runner. Neither did the authority in governance care for backwater camps of the sort, so long as they paid their taxes and never complained. And so it became a waystation for the men of the land who'd fallen to disrepute. And in this way Jonas as a boy was well-acquainted with the life.

So when Jonas Arthur was no more than five years old he concluded within himself that a runner was what he was going to be, no matter the cost. He recognized, even as a boy, that inside he was slowly dying for want of something that was missing. Like a leaf in the autumn, he was dried and blowing away, and in his foolish heart he vowed not to let this happen. Like so many others, he hoped to fill the hole with vanity.

Now all this is a tale for another time, and I'm certainly not going to reminisce on the workings of an impetuous youth in these pages; but I want to leave you here with the same understanding that Jonas had as a boy. We are driven by something burning within us, something missing, something we don't understand. It makes us feel empty. It drove Jonas to places he never would've reached elsewise. And this is where this story began, for it was years that Jonas sought after that which he could never quite grasp, years that he vied to sate his need in all manner of ways. But nothing would give him true satisfaction.

Save one thing.

The demon-train.